Horizons

By Judith Blake Schaefer

ISBN: 978-1-945917-04-2

Printed in the United States of America

Cover Designed by: Tracey Capobianco Ranauro
Back Cover Photo: Jodi Schaefer

Also by Judith Schaefer:

Though the Winds Blow

Big Table Publishing Company
Boston, MA

www.bigtablepublishing.com

Acknowledgements

I would like to express my gratitude to several writers who read the earliest version of my novel. Special thanks to Malcolm MacKenzie and Anne Ipsen who read all but the latest changes. I also want to thank Walter Altherr, Ina Jackson, Cass Turner, Grace Taglienti, Phil Dandrea, Mike and Muffy Berlyn, Linda DeStefano, Louise Corman, and Roger Kelley for their reading of parts of the novel. Special thanks also to Tracey Ranauro—cover artist—my last editor, Robin Stratton, and my family—Steve and Jodi, Madi and Max—who were supportive in many ways.

For my grandmother Minnie Barnes Blake
the Dakota pioneer
in Memoriam

and for Jesse, TJ, Geoffrey, Madison, and Max
my grandchildren

Contents

"The day may be approaching when the whole world will recognize woman as the equal of man."
~Susan B. Anthony

PROLOGUE
St. Paul, Minnesota 1879

"Minnie, I cannot believe you would move to that Indian-infested country, or that Peder would even suggest it. You and your children will not be safe there. Settlers abandoned Sioux Falls only a few years ago because the Yankton Sioux were on the warpath."Agnes crossed her arms, expecting a defiant response from her strong-willed daughter.

"Peder says the Indian troubles are over. The Sioux have moved west, beyond the Missouri River. There is land in Dakota for the taking."

"You know you will go to Purgatory if you don't raise your children as Catholics."

"Mother, Peder will allow our children to be raised in the Catholic Church. He is a Christian. He was raised a Lutheran."

"That is the worst kind," Agnes struck back. "Martin Luther started all the trouble."

"Peder will take Catholic instruction." To her it was irrelevant. She loved him. Catholic, Protestant, whatever. But to openly contradict her mother would have been disrespectful.

But Agnes would not give up. "You are a beautiful woman. Educated. Why throw yourself away on an immigrant farmer when you could have any number of wealthy beaus? Or possibly a career as a concert pianist? You are very good. All your teachers say so."

Yes, I spent four years at the Ladies Seminary to improve my chances of marrying into a good family. I read the Bible, Shakespeare, Robert Browning, and more. But the emphasis was on decorum: proper introductions and salutations, how to carry on a conversation and behave at dinner parties, the conduct of ladies toward gentlemen—mostly trivial things. At least, I learned to play the piano and appreciate classical music.

"I love Peder," she had replied.

"Why does he insist on leaving St.Paul? The flour and lumber mills and the new railways provide all kinds of opportunities. Look how successful your father has been working with Mr. James Hill in the Chicago North Western office."

"Peder wants to farm his own land, to be independent. The Homestead Act allows us to claim 320 acres by living there and farming it."

Minnie would never forget the last words her mother had on that subject: "Not many can stand a sod-busting life."

PART 1
Minnie

Dakota 1888-1898

CHAPTER 1
January Thaw
Dakota Territory, January 12, 1888

On this freakish warm winter day, Minnie watched the shifting streaks of orange and pink in the early morning sky as if she were looking for an omen.

"Peder, the Indians believe the sun dogs we saw last night are a sign of stormy weather. The air is so heavy, so murky. I wish you'd put off this trip to town. We're going to have terrible weather. Can't you feel it?"

"This may be the only day in months that I can exercise Ranger by riding him into town. Besides, I want tobacco and you need sugar. I won't be gone long." He mounted Ranger and guided him toward the old wagon trail that defined one boundary of their claim. His destination was Hughitt, a town created in 1880 and named after the Chicago and North Western railroad surveyor who liked the site near the James River. She watched their dark shapes, silhouetted against the pale sky, vanish into the mist. When the sound of hooves faded, she called Sport, their brown and white spaniel puppy, and headed for the four-room frame house that her husband had built to replace the sod hut, their first home on the prairie.

She had long since suppressed any regrets in leaving an easy life in Minnesota to marry a Norwegian immigrant and homestead in Dakota. Peder had convinced her that the Indians were no longer to be feared—despite Custer's death at Little Big Horn and ongoing skirmishes between the Lakota Sioux and the U.S. Army in the Black Hills. So they left St. Paul in 1881, like many other settlers in that decade, to claim land. He had no interest in Black Hills gold; for him, wheat was gold. He wanted to farm the rich prairie land in Eastern Dakota. Minnie understood his wish for his own land and she admired his stubbornness, his refusal to succumb to Mother Nature's obstacles: drought, locusts, hail, and prairie fires. He had succeeded the previous summer by selling steers when hail the size of hen's eggs flattened his wheat crop. She had learned to trust her husband's decisions, but today the strange weather made her anxious, fearful of what was to come.

After one last look at the increasingly ominous sky, she went inside, the puppy at her heels. She hung her shawl on a peg near the door as the calendar clock struck seven. The clock, a peace offering from her parents when her first child was born, was also a reminder of the heated arguments she had with her mother who did not want her to marry Peder.

Agnes was concerned that Peder wasn't Catholic, that he only wanted to farm and that he intended to drag Minnie to Dakota where she and her children would not be safe in "Indian infested country. Finally, Agnes tried to convince her daughter she could do much better in life than marry an immigrant farmer.

But what Minnie remembered most vividly from those arguments was her mother's final comment, "Not many can stand a sod-busting life." After eight years, she had to admit it had not been easy.

Because Agnes refused to accept Peder, the couple finally eloped. They rented a house near the mill on St. Anthony Falls where he worked, but planned to move west when they'd saved enough money to buy a wagon and supplies. Their first child, named Kari after Peder's mother, was born within the year. The baby softened Agnes's heart. She wouldn't help finance their Dakota expedition, but she gave them the seven-day calendar clock in a black walnut case. This belated wedding gift and the old upright piano Peder purchased for her twenty-second birthday were the material possessions Minnie cherished most. When she could take a break from the demanding chores of a settler, she often practiced Mozart sonatas and Bach inventions on the piano.

As the clock struck the half hour, Minnie put a slab of bacon into the iron frying pan and gathered the ingredients for pancakes. Minutes later, as the smell of bacon permeated the house, thirteen-year-old Matthew, the oldest of three boys, lowered the ladder from the loft.

"Wake your brothers, Matthew. Try not to wake Kari. She was feverish last night." Minnie worried about Kari's decision to drop out of school after she graduated this year from the eighth grade. Minnie guessed she expressed disinterest in attending high school, because she disliked being in the same grade as her brother, younger by one year—though she would never admit to that. Both had eagerly attended first grade as soon as a country school had been built nearby and a teacher had been hired.

She moved the sizzling bacon to a platter and saved the grease in a tin can. She set the table and put out butter and Damson plum jam she'd canned the previous summer. As the three boys descended from the loft, she poured batter into the frying pan for the first batch of pancakes.

Matthew and Joe stayed close to the hot pot-bellied stove as they put their school clothes on over the wool long johns they'd slept in. Seven-year old Willie struggled until Matthew could help him. Before the boys had settled at the round oak table in the center of their kitchen-living room, three-year-old Sarah had climbed out of her crib in her parent's bedroom and joined them.

"Where's Pa?" Joe asked as he spread plum jam on a second pancake.

"He went to town. He should be back soon," Minnie said as she tried to settle Sarah in her high chair.

Sarah protested, "No, no, I want big chair."

Minnie tried to entice her with a bite sized piece of pancake. "You're not big enough yet, Sarah." Her youngest child was the most resistant, most demanding. Determined and stubborn like her father.

Kari had descended from her side of the loft to lie on the day bed near the stove; the boys were finishing the pancakes when Peder walked in. "Papa," they said in unison. The dog left his warm spot near the stove to greet him. Their father's presence quieted every one. Even Sarah stopped trying to get out of her high chair.

Peder hung up his jacket and put his boots beneath the winter coats, adjacent to a trunk that held more winter gear. Minnie held out a mug of steaming coffee. He put his free arm around her shoulders, and kissed the top of her head. He whispered, "I have something for you."

In a voice everyone could hear, "I ran into Sam Miller from the veather station as I was leaving the general store. He said the barometric pressure is dropping fast up north. It's already thirty below in Helena and vinds are picking up. Looks like ve could be in for a gale."

"What's a gale, Pa?" William's big blue eyes focused on his father. Although he was sickly, his frequent bouts of bronchitis had not dampened his curiosity.

"A gale is a windstorm," Matthew explained. "We have gales all the time." Big boned and blond, he resembled his father.

"A gale can turn a snow fall into a blizzard," Minnie added. When storms threatened, she imagined how nice it would be to move into Hughitt where weather would interfere less with church socials and visiting neighbors, but she knew Peder would never leave his farm. Her mother had failed to mention the real problem of living on the prairie—the emptiness and desolation, the isolation, the loneliness, the endless work. Few were like her Norseman, fascinated with the tall grass waving on the immense plain, the creatures that inhabited this unique country, or the massive, constantly evolving cloudscapes. For her the fantastic colorful sunrises and sunsets and the meadow with the charming wildflowers and sweet songs of meadowlarks were the riches she would miss in town.

Matthew pushed aside his plate and stood up. "Hurry up, Willie and Joe. We don't want to be late for school."

"Do we have to go to school if there's gonna be a gale?" Joseph, the 10-year-old, was not as serious a student as his brothers. He'd play hooky—ride horseback, fish in Pearl Creek, ice skate on the pond—if he had a chance.

"Yah, you're going to school, Joseph. There's no reason to stay home." Peder's booming voice silenced everyone and frightened Sarah who'd climbed down from her high chair and hid in the folds of her mother's long, dark cotton skirt. "The storm is in Montana. Who knows if it vill get here. Anyway, my boys can deal vith a little vind and snow. Right now, it feels like the beginning of a January thaw."

"Peder, don't discount the sun dogs we saw last night. The Indians know that means bad trouble. And this morning...the balmy, unnatural weather."

"Don't be foolish, Mother," He stood, towering over her. "Ve have January thaws every year. They're natural."

She did not like Peder calling her "mother." "I'm your wife," she'd reminded him more than once. Swallowing her irritation, she persisted, "Peder, it's not worth taking a risk. Kari is sick. She's not going to school. The boys can miss one day. They can help you in the barn with the animals or bring in hay before the snow flies again."

All three boys sat quietly, watching and listening to their parents. Their younger sister hung on her mother's skirt. Kari pretended to sleep.

Matthew suddenly blurted out, "Ma, I *have* to go to school. Mr. Pierce picked me to be a monitor."

"That's nice Matthew, but Mr. Pierce can manage one day without you." She turned toward Peder, "I want my children safe at home today. Kari will be here. Why not the boys?" Minnie stood as tall as she could.

"Don't make sissies out of our boys. They can handle a little snow. They *are* going to school...it's less than a mile away."

The three boys looked at their mother. She knew they couldn't defy their father, yet they couldn't side with her either. That would be worse than choosing between a spanking and having a mouth washed out with soap. Briefly, she wondered if her intuition could be wrong. Is this the first day of a January thaw? *No.* She felt certain in her bones. *A storm is coming.*

"We could do school here, read from "Favorite Poems" or "The Bible," she said, still hoping Peder would relent.

"Get going boys. Your mother vorries over nothing."

Minnie's fear kept expanding as she remembered past storms. Not knowing what to do, she picked up Sarah and held her close. "At least let William stay home," she pleaded. "Please, Peder."

"Villiam is stronger than you think. And Matthew will help him if he needs to. For God's sake, Minnie, stop belly-aching," Peder grumbled as he put down his coffee mug. He started toward the door. "I'm going to turn the animals out and bring in hay we cut last fall."

"Don't worry, Ma," Matthew said as he helped his brothers with their boots. "I'll take care of Willie and Joe."

Minnie wrapped a shawl around her shoulders and went outside. She felt certain the strange copper colored sky, the warm air and heavy atmosphere did not bode well. She looked southwest across the snow covered prairie in the direction of the school, but a fog obscured her vision. Usually she saw the horizon. Today, she couldn't see neighbor Svenson's barn. She could barely see the outline of Peder and the cow he was leading toward an open patch of ground.

She hugged all three boys, reluctant to let go. Delaying, she fumbled buttoning William's coat. Before she'd finished, she said, "Willie, run into the house and stay there."

Matthew's jaw dropped, "Mother! Father said..."

"It's alright, Matthew. I'll talk to your father. *Run*, Willie."

Matthew trudged off. Joseph ran to the nearest snow drift to make snow balls before he disappeared into the fog bank in pursuit of his brother. For several minutes Minnie stared at the spot where they'd vanished like stars obscured by advancing clouds. She closed her eyes and said a few Hail Mary's, trying to convince herself that God would take care of them, would see them through the terrible storm she knew was on the horizon.

CHAPTER 2

To the Rescue

Signal Corps observer Sergeant Sam Miller entered the weather station in the Dakota town of Hughitt at 6:00 AM on January 12, 1888, to find ominous data arriving by Western Union from the station in Saint Paul. A high pressure area was centered over Dakota and temperatures were rising everywhere. In Hughitt the thermometer registered nineteen degrees at 6:00 AM, nearly forty degrees warmer than the previous day. However, the mercury in Helena, Montana had fallen from forty degrees above to nine degrees below zero in four hours, indicating a low pressure area moving rapidly down from Canada.

Around 7:00 AM, Sergeant Miller left his desk to buy coffee at Rosie's Diner. He saw Peder Youngstrom and two other farmers in front of the weather-beaten, square-fronted general store on Main Street. He told them a storm was developing up Montana way and could be headed southeast, toward Dakota. They listened and nodded, unconcerned, enjoying the break in the frigid weather.

"Might as well enjoy the January thaw while we can," one of them said.

When Miller returned to his desk, a telegram from Bismarck in northern Dakota Territory reported falling temperatures and an arctic gale, moving at approximately fifty miles an hour. Miller realized a blizzard was looming. Only the town's people would see his black and white "cold flag." He had no way to alert the families on the prairie, or the country school teachers who boarded with them. He walked to the feed store to tell Robert Groves to warn anyone he encountered. He figured the storm would arrive in the

22

Hughitt area around 11:00 AM. Kids would be in school, possibly at recess. He felt he had to do something to save the children, but what? Time was short.

Convinced they were about to experience the storm of the century, he conferred again with Robert Groves at the feed store. Wasn't there some way to get help to the country school? Groves knew two local families who had bobsleds and horses.

Within an hour the two men had convinced the owners of the bobsleds that a horrendous blizzard was approaching, probably putting the children at the country school in grave danger. Both owners had platforms that they mounted on their bobsleds for hauling purposes. They figured each dray or flatbed could hold six or seven children.

Shortly after 10:00 AM, two drays, each pulled by two horses, left town. Less than an hour later, the storm descended in all its fury.

As Matthew hung his coat in the vestibule of the one room school, he noticed that his brother had no jacket or hat. "Where is your coat, Joe? And your hat and mittens?" Matthew demanded.

"I don't remember," Joseph said as he took off his wet boots.

"Why did you take everything off?" Matthew asked.

"I was hot."

"We'd better find them on the way home or Pa will kill us," Matthew complained. "Do you have any idea where they are?"

"No. Maybe near the Svenson's barn."

Two teachers shared the modest schoolroom. Two rows of ten desks were separated by an aisle with a coal stove in the center of the room. Miss Garber taught first, second, and third grade on one side of the room. Matthew and Joseph sat on the other side, the row where Mr. Pierce taught fourth through eighth grade.

Matthew and Margit Svenson, another eighth grader, distributed the McGuffey Readers, from which the older children recited and chanted a passage in unison. Joseph was cleaning his slate when he looked up and saw a large black cloud through the west window. "Mr. Pierce," he yelled, jumping out of his seat and rushing to the window. "Is this the gale coming?"

"Shush, Joseph," Mr. Pierce said, but he moved quickly to see what had excited the boy. Alerted, all the children looked up to see the cloud, like a huge black boulder, rolling toward the school house. A deafening roar preceded icy pellets bombarding the windows. Frightened by the wind, the ice pellets, the rattling of the door and windows, the terrified children looked toward the teachers. A few plugged their ears or covered their eyes.

The teachers conferred briefly. "I've never seen a storm this violent," Mr. Pierce said as Miss Garber just shook her head, speechless. He continued, "We have two options: stay or go— neither is good. Staying seems the logical choice, but our coal supply is low. I doubt it will last until evening. Even if we don't freeze to death overnight in this unheated structure, the storm could continue for another twenty-four or forty-eight hours. And there's the possibility that the building itself will not survive this mighty wind."

"Then let's go now," Miss Garber had found her voice.

"Before we decide, I want to go outside. Stay calm and try to reassure the children." He opened the door just wide enough for him to slip out. Finely granulated snow saturated the air and pelted him with what felt like frozen sand. Forcing his eyes open, he barely saw his hand in front of him. He sensed that the powerful wind might actually prevent his getting up if he fell. Could the children cope with this? Back inside, he vacillated. Should they stay or leave?

Miss Garber, chilled with the wind and snow filtering in through cracks, was adamant. "We need to head to the nearest farms. They're not far, but we need to leave now before dark or we'll never find our way. We have four hours before dusk." After Mr. Pierce rechecked the coal supply, he agreed to start as soon as possible.

They assigned the children, ranging in age from seven to thirteen, to one of two groups, depending on where they lived. Mr. Pierce's group included two Youngstroms and five others. Six children who lived west of the school comprised Miss Garber's group.

After Matthew helped several children with their coats, boots, and mufflers, he gave his jacket, hat, and mittens to Joseph.

"What'll you wear, Matthew?" Joseph asked.

"What I've got on."

Mr. Pierce offered him his coat when he learned the boy had given his jacket to his brother. But Matthew rejected it, afraid the oversized wrap would hinder his movement. A student gave him a cap, an extra discovered in a jacket pocket. Miss Garber offered her heavy wool shawl, kept in a drawer for those times when the drafty classroom did not warm sufficiently. As she wrapped it around his shoulders and pinned it in place, Matthew said, "I decided to go with your group. Mr. Pierce thought you'd need the strongest boy in the school more than he would."

Joseph's eyes filled when he heard his brother's plans. "I wish you'd be with my group. Anyway, I like getting out of school early. There might even be a chance for a snowball fight."

As they lined up to leave, the teachers told their children to stay close together, hold hands, and keep moving. "We don't have far to go," Mr. Pierce said. "The wind is strong and the snow can sting. But we're tough. We can make it."

Mr. Pierce and his group went first. Although the storm had worsened since his earlier venture outside, he discovered he could open his eyes with the wind behind him. Still, in the dense swirling snow, visibility was near zero. He set off toward the road to Hughitt, wondering if he'd find it, given these conditions. He vowed he would not give up. He had these children to think about. He'd push until he dropped.

When the northwest wind penetrated his coat and gloves, his concern for the children intensified. How long could they all keep

25

going? Should they have stayed at the school, burned the desks? How long could they have provided heat? Looking around, he saw two or three snow-encrusted caps and whirling snow, nothing more. For the first time he felt and understood the effects of bitter cold: the urge to lie down, the desire to sleep.

Was he crazed or did he hear a whinny? And then he saw the horse. After he'd reached out to touch it, to convince himself it wasn't a mirage or a hallucination, he stumbled around the snow-covered animal to find the driver. As the children gathered, the two men began to lift them onto the dray. When the second driver approached, they agreed by body language—their words lost to the wind—to keep all the children on one dray under blankets from both.

When Mr. Pierce counted only six children and realized Matthew was missing, he looked at Joseph. "Did Matthew go with Miss Garber?" he yelled, desperate for Joseph to hear him above the wind. Momentarily, he'd forgotten his request.

"Yes," Joseph whimpered, barely audible. A thin coat of pink ice covered his cheeks. As soon as he'd gone outside, his tears froze. When he couldn't open his eyes, he'd scratched at his face until it bled.

Mr. Pierce had read his lips and turned to the bobsled driver. "Miss Garber is the other teacher," he shouted. "Seven children are with her. If we continue on this trail beyond the school, we may find them."

Slowly, they plodded ahead. Nowhere did they see or hear any signs of life or anything other than blowing snow and howling wind. It was 2:15 PM, according to his pocket watch, when the driver bellowed into Mr. Pierce's ear, "We need to turn back. If we don't get to Hughitt or at least the Youngstrom's before dark, we may all be doomed."

Mr. Pierce nodded. A part of him wanted to continue. Since they'd stumbled upon him, maybe they'd find her too. But it did appear futile. They should save the six children they had. He tried not to think about Miss Garber and the fate of the children with her.

Holding hands with the two youngest in her group, Miss Garber confronted the unrelenting wind, gritty snow, and penetrating cold. She felt optimistic at first. Certain they'd make it to the Fielding's farm which was within sight of the school on a clear day.

But her confidence flagged when she realized how slowly they moved against the powerful northwest wind. She considered turning back, but she'd lost her sense of direction with visibility near zero. Blind in a whirlwind of snow, she could only hope they were moving in the right direction. She worried about all of the children, but especially Matthew Youngstrom with only her shawl to protect him from the elements. She was grateful she could see him behind her, though the mask of snow covering his face frightened her, reminded her how quickly frostbite happens to exposed skin in freezing weather.

Matthew had never felt so cold. He knew enough to suspect his nose and hands were already frostbitten, but he tried to keep moving his fingers and thinking about the hot stove he hoped was awaiting them. If the wind weren't so fierce, they'd be able talk to each other, to help keep up their spirits.

Plodding, barely moving against the wind, Miss Garber suddenly felt the girl on her left become a dead weight. She bent over and lifted the child into her arms, dropping the hand of the child on her right. As she tried to find that hand again, she realized that Matthew stood next to her. She couldn't grasp at first what he was trying to tell her.

She's got to hear me, Matthew said to himself. *The bell is our guide to the farm.*

"I hear a bell," he repeated into her ear. "Let's go that way." He pointed to her left.

For a moment she wondered if he were hallucinating, if the cold had finally altered his mental faculties. Then, she heard it too…faintly. Someone's dinner bell? She turned in the direction of the bell. How far away was it?

Moments before the wind came howling across the Youngstrom's land around 11:00 AM, the sky darkened. William was playing with Sarah while Minnie was twisting hay, fuel for the stove in case they ran out of coal. Kari, still feverish, lay on the daybed. Minnie rushed to look outside, but the icy snow pummeled the windows and obscured her view. Sarah began to cry and tugged at her mother's skirt. Minnie picked her up, tried to soothe her, but she was worrying about the boys getting home from school. Peder must fetch them.

Where is Peder? Minnie's fear intensified as the wind shook and rattled windows and doors. She wanted to open the door, look for him, but she didn't trust her strength. If she unlatched the door, it would blow open and she might not be able to close it. William followed as she checked the windows—all opaque, as if white shades had been drawn.

To calm the children and herself, Minnie sat in the chair she'd used to rock all her babies to sleep. She held Sarah and Willie as she sang lullabies and hymns. When she ran out of songs, she continued to rock, slipping into a reverie: She was a young girl in St. Paul playing a Chopin etude before the girls in her school or skating on a pond with her young brother trying to make perfect figure eights or skating around the pond with Peder. *Peder. Where is he?* Wide awake now, she put the children down in the bedroom and covered them with quilts.

She couldn't rest. She paced. Could Peder have gone to the school to get the boys? Maybe she should have taken her children to Saint Paul, where life was not so harsh, where Peder could not make unreasonable demands on them. But she couldn't leave Peder, deprive the children of their father and he of them. No, her duty was here. And he would never leave this land—she was convinced—not even for his family. She continued pacing until she decided to make a hearty stew that would warm and nourish everyone when they came home. She found antelope meat, potatoes, carrots, and onions in the unheated pantry. Kari and Sarah continued to sleep. When William awakened, she put him to work twisting hay.

As the meat browned, Minnie peeled potatoes. She ignored an unfamiliar scraping sound—as if the wind were blowing something against the door. When the sound persisted, she moved closer to listen. Finally convinced that someone or something was there, she unlatched the door. It blew open almost knocking her over, exposing her to a blast of icy wind and snow.

Encased in snow and clutching a shovel, Peder collapsed on his knees in the doorway. Minnie yelled to William to get quilts from the bed as she helped her husband crawl into the room. Before she could push the big trunk that held winter gear toward the door to shut out the weather, Peder had struggled to his feet and threw his weight against the door. As it closed, he slumped to the floor. Minnie helped him remove his outer clothing and wrapped the quilts William had brought around his shoulders and over his legs. Seconds later, she held a mug of hot coffee up to his lips. She slipped off his gloves and warmed his cold fingers with her hands. "Thank you," he uttered in a raspy voice barely above a whisper.

After his second cup of coffee, Peder stumbled over to the daybed. He sat next to Kari who had gotten up on one elbow when the door blew open. Sarah ran in from the bedroom, climbed up next to her father, and hugged him. "Papa cold," she said as he bent down to kiss the top of her head.

"Why did you have the shovel?" William sat at the table after retrieving the quilts.

"I thought I'd need it ven it started to snow. I used it like a cane and I banged on the door with it." A minute later he asked, "Villie, vy aren't you in school?"

29

"Mother told me to come in the house."

"I see," Peder said as he looked toward his wife.

Minnie lifted the cover of her iron kettle to check the stew and to avoid facing him. She picked up her cooking fork to test the doneness of the meat.

"You did right," he said in a firm voice. "But boys must learn to face life with courage."

As she added the last of the potatoes to the simmering stew, she said, "Willie had a coughing spell." She felt shame and disgust for lying, but the storm proved she'd been right. "Now I wish I'd kept the other boys home too," she continued in a burst of bravado loud enough to be heard above the wind, still howling and blowing snow pellets against the windows.

"They're safe at school," Peder said. "The teachers vill keep them until the storm ends."

She guessed he was right, but remembering her rejected appeal on William's behalf fueled her anger. "Willie would be scared to death," she almost shouted. "And Matthew and Joseph have never seen a blizzard like this. They must be terrified."

Peder did not respond. Surprised at his silence, she asked herself if he was finally having second thoughts.

Later, he got up to check the fuel supply and add coal to the stove. He was stoking the fire when he heard pounding on the door and rushed to open it. Three men and several children burst into the room. Willie jumped up from the table. "Joey," he yelled. Minnie embraced Joseph while she looked for Matthew.

"Where's your brother?" she asked. "Why are you wearing his jacket?" Apprehension replaced the joy she'd felt when she first saw him.

"He went with Miss Garber."

Questions she'd ask later flashed through her head. Why did they leave the school? Why didn't Matthew stay with Joe? What happened to Joe's jacket? Why didn't the teachers stay together?

30

Why go in different directions? She'd ask Mr. Pierce after she cleaned the laceration on Joe's face, checked the children for frostbite, and sent Kari into the bedroom to protect the others from her illness. She showed the oldest girl, Margit Svenson, where the soup bowls were and asked her to serve stew to the children, while she hung the wet clothing and blankets from the sled near the stove to dry.

Eventually, Minnie turned toward Peder, who was conversing with the drivers and Mr.Pierce. "Where is my other son?" Her eyes fixed on the teacher who'd told her once that Matthew was the star of his classroom.

"With Miss Garber," Mr. Pierce answered. "They started toward the Fielding's farm."

Minnie doubted Matthew could survive in this storm without proper clothing. She wanted to cry, but she felt tears would dissolve her thin thread of hope. She looked at Peder, her face contorted with anguish. She wanted to scream at him, to curse him for his stubbornness.

Peder enfolded her in his arms. "I was wrong," he said. "But don't forget, Matthew is a strong boy...and smart. Our son vill make it." Minnie pushed away. She could not be consoled.

After they'd warmed up, the drivers returned to care for their horses. To prevent getting lost in the implacable storm, they used a rope from the house to get the horses into Peder's barn and get themselves back to the house. Their mission completed, they ate Minnie's stew with gusto, emptying the big black iron pot. The children now worked on a jig-saw puzzle near the stove or tried playing the piano.

As Minnie started a second pot of coffee, Margit Svenson collected and stacked the dirty soup bowls near the basin used for washing dishes. "How long do you think this blizzard will last?" she asked Minnie.

"I don't know. But you needn't worry. Your brothers are here, safe from the storm." *If only I knew Matthew was safe!* "Do you think

31

your parents will believe the three of you stayed at school with the teachers?"

"One time we stayed overnight at school," Margit responded. "We slept on the floor. I've wondered where everyone will sleep here."

"The girls will sleep in the bedroom downstairs. The boys in the loft."

By 9:00 PM, Minnie was putting the boys to bed. As she tucked two into Matthew's bed, she hoped her son was sleeping at the Fielding's under a warm quilt. After she checked on Kari, sleeping now on the other side of the partitioned loft, she looked in on the girls downstairs.

Satisfied that the children were comfortable, Minnie joined the men at the oak table. They drank hard cider and smoked as they compared this storm with others. One of the bobsled drivers said, "Sam Miller thought this storm would be violent, one of the worst ever. But he also said it would be short. We should expect thirty degrees below, or colder, before morning. If we're lucky, the wind will stop sometime during the night,"

Minnie knew her worrying was pointless. She'd poured a cup of coffee and sat next to Mr. Pierce. She wanted to ask why they'd left the school. But what was the point? They were here.

Toward midnight the men wrapped themselves in their blankets, now warm and dry from hanging near the stove, and went to sleep on the floor. Peder insisted Minnie rest on the daybed. He intended to stay awake all night to keep a watch on the fire.

She covered herself with a spare quilt from the chest holding surplus winter clothing, turned to face the wall, and tried to remember the time when she loved winter, when she'd met Peder on a skating pond in St. Paul. But she could not blot from her mind the horror stories of the children frozen during the 'snow winters' of '81 and '82 and the images they evoked. Only now, Matthew's face crowded out those images.

CHAPTER 3
The Aftermath

Was the dinner bell louder, or was she imagining it? Miss Garber, carrying a six-year-old, knew she could not stagger on much longer. The weight of the child seemed to increase with each step. Yet the bell, like a beacon, or magnet helped her lift a foot and move forward through the snow.

Matthew, carrying the child whose hand Miss Garber had dropped, whispered again, "We're getting close." Miss Gerber did not seem to hear him as they stumbled forward. And then they fell against something.

"A hay stack." Miss Garber's first impulse was to dig in and rest awhile away from the wind. Maybe not logical—she might be "cold stupid"—but she couldn't go any further. She put the child down and began pulling out arm loads of hay, as she'd done on her parents' farm in Iowa to hollow out a hay stack for playing house with her little sister.

The children joined her. Minutes later they all sat inside the haystack protected from the savage wind. They huddled, shivering as their bodies defended against hypothermia. Miss Garber knew she could not go on. She also realized the danger of falling asleep. "Stay awake, Matthew. Keep them awake."

"I think we should follow the bell," Matthew responded. He preferred to keep going, not to give up.

"No bell. Only hallucination…" She closed her eyes.

"No, No," he stammered as his body shivered violently. "Don't go to sleep, Miss Garber." Two of the children had closed their eyes.

Minnie awoke when the clock struck eight. The sun streamed through the east window and caressed her face. The storm was over. She saw Peder stoking the fire and the sled drivers picking up their blankets from the floor. She heard the boys laughing in the loft. *All will be well when I know Matthew is safe*, she thought, moving toward the stove to start breakfast.

She invited them all to sit while she served coffee, bowls of steaming oatmeal, and a platter of toast. Margit volunteered to spread butter and peach jam on the toast for the children who were emerging from the bedroom or climbing down from the loft. As they ate, the men talked about delivering the children to their homes.

Getting to the sleds required shoveling through the almost roof-high snow drift in front of the door. After the three men cleared a path and dug out the sleds, they fortified themselves with more coffee and waited for Minnie to ensure each child was properly bundled up for the ride home in the frigid weather. She found mittens for and draped mufflers around the necks of two boys who, like Joe, had dropped articles of outer clothing on the way to school. She followed the children to the sleds and covered them with heavy horse blankets. Her thoughts returned to Matthew as the two drays disappeared behind another snow drift on the west side of the house. She desperately wanted to go with Peder to rescue Matthew, but she could not abandon the four children at home.

Peder led Ranger with the sleigh into the barnyard, a white domain that sparkled in the sunlight, a silent setting now without wind or lively children eager for a sled ride. The dominant signs of life were the tracks left by the sleds and the smoke rising from the chimney. The windmill, like a sentinel, towered over the aftermath of the northwest wind. The well pump had disappeared, buried under a white cover.

In the distance Peder could see a bit of the school house, a sliver of brown above the white, but not the Fielding's house beyond the school. He'd follow the hollows of the eastern and southern faces of knolls and fences, skirting the drifted northern and western sides to avoid Ranger's floundering in deep snow. Pale blue gray shadows cast by drifts and fence posts added depth to the luminous white mantle of the broad, flat plain. During the other seasons, dressed in shifting shades of green and yellow, the prairie was more colorful but no more impressive. And above it all— regardless of season—an azure canopy, a dome with a cast of majestic clouds that ranged from wispy to billowy, except on those days when thunderclouds gathered or the raging northwest wind darkened the atmosphere and mixed with snow or topsoil.

He tried to be positive, but he could not suppress images of his cows that froze to death in an '82 blizzard. He tried to pray. Although he'd accompanied Minnie to church occasionally, he was not a religious man, not a praying type. But now he made an appeal to a power he hoped existed. He worried about Minnie almost as much as Matthew. She could be strong, tough. She'd accepted the hardships of the frontier. But she'd never lost a child, though they'd come close once to losing Willie. She told him then that she couldn't bear the thought of it. *Most pioneers lose a child or two. How long can our luck last? And how will I manage if Matthew is not all right? I should have listened to Minnie. Why was I so sure there'd be no storm? She will never blame me, but I will never stop blaming myself for being stupid, for insisting our sons go to school. Thank God, she kept Willie home and the girls were home too.*

Peder parked the sleigh behind the Fielding's house. He noticed the dinner bell before he'd made his way to the door. He'd heard that bell often as one of the team of threshers who worked the farms around here. That's how Mrs. Fielding called them in for their mid-day meal.

Mrs. Fielding opened the door. "Peder Youngstrom, why are you out in this frigid weather? Come in. Come in."

"The children," he stammered. "Isn't Matthew here?" He'd expected to see his son. He sighed deeply when he realized there were no children. His fear for Matthew's well being now expanded, equaling the time Willie had pneumonia and the doctor had given them little hope.

As Peder explained his presence, Ralph Fielding reached for his boots. "We'd better get out there right away," he said. "We'll scour every inch of land between here and the school. If the wind didn't blow them too far off the track, we'll find them." Minutes later they climbed onto the sleigh with blankets Mrs. Fielding had provided. Peder nudged Ranger and they moved ahead. *What should we be looking for?*

As if he'd read his mind, Ralph Fielding said, "We should investigate anything that looks like..." he hesitated.

Peder said, "A body." He remembered that parts of his frozen cows were exposed above the snow. They'd been easy to find.

"There are three hay stacks I never got to last fall." Ralph pointed. "Let's stop over there first." Peder guided Ranger toward three snow covered mounds. When they stopped in front of the nearest one, Ralph hopped off the sleigh and circled the stack. "Nothing here," he said. "You check the one on our left and I'll go to the other."

Peder's hopes rose as he approached the second mound. Bunches of hay, only partly overlaid with snow, were scattered around. Something had attacked this hay stack. He began pulling at a thin barrier of hay covering an opening to the partially hollowed out stack. He saw his son and the others huddled together. They all appeared to be asleep.

"I found them!" he yelled. "Ralph, bring the sleigh."

All day Minnie tried, unsuccessfully, to concentrate on anything other than Matthew. She played the piano, she helped the boys with another jig-saw puzzle, and she baked cookies with Kari while Sarah napped. But her anxiety increased with time. If Matthew had been at the Fielding's, Peder would have him home by now—unless he was taking several children home. Hope flickered briefly. Then her anger flared. Why did Peder insist the boys go to school? Could she forgive him? Thank goodness for the men with the bobsleds, she thought, as she looked over at Joe and Willie working on the jigsaw puzzle. Kari sat on the daybed reading to Sarah, cuddled up to her big sister. *A perfect scene, if Matthew were in it too.*

The two men worked quickly, placing each child and the teacher in the sleigh and covering them with blankets Mrs. Fielding had provided. The teacher and Matthew, the oldest child, came last. Peder couldn't tell if they were all alive or not. He tried to talk to Matthew who mumbled incoherently.

Back at the Fielding's, the men laid the children in a circle around the stove, as Mrs. Fielding directed. They put an unconscious Miss Garber in the bedroom. Mrs. Fielding had prepared hot broth and placed bedding near the stove. After she'd covered everyone with warm blankets and served broth to those awake, she told the men, "A nursing course taught me that cold victims should remain quiet until warmed thoroughly to reduce the stress on their hearts."

Peder said. "I need to inform the parents that their children are safe. What should I tell them, Mrs. Fielding?"

"Tell them they should come for their children tomorrow morning. By then they should be physically recovered from their ordeal."

After he'd delivered the news to grateful parents, Peder returned to see about Matthew. His son sat wrapped in a blanket, sipping broth with school mates. "Hello, Pa," he said. Peder grasped Matthew's shoulder and cleared his throat to mask an emotional surge.

"Peder," Mrs. Fielding guided him away from the boys. "I have terribly sad news. When I went to see about Miss Garber after you left, she struggled to get up. Before I could stop her, she'd collapsed on the floor. Mr. Fielding and I tried to revive her, but she died right there." Mrs. Fielding struggled to keep her composure. "I have more bad news. Matthew may lose two or three fingers…from frostbite." She continued, "I haven't told the children about Miss Garber. I think it's better if they learn that from their parents."

"Mrs. Fielding, I have to take Matthew home now. Minnie will be unhappy if I arrive without him. She might not even believe me if I say he's alright. She didn't want the boys to go to school yesterday. If I hadn't insisted, Matthew would have missed the storm."

When Minnie set a decorated cake before Joseph a few weeks later, Matthew asked if he could light the candles. He was adjusting to the loss of his middle, ring, and little fingers of his left hand, but being right-handed, this task was not so difficult. Before she cut the cake, Minnie played *Happy Birthday* on the piano and everyone joined in song—except Joe, the birthday boy, and Willie, feverish from a new bout of bronchitis. After the verse ended, Minnie reminded Joe to make a wish before he blew out the candles. At the same time she touched her new necklace, the gift Peder bought her on the day of the blizzard, wondering how long it would take for her to forgive him for sending the boys to school on that fateful day.

CHAPTER 4
Minnie's Secret

Minnie's spirit expanded with the longer, warmer days of April and May, the months when green shoots pushed through sod and melting snow, when trees and shrubs surrounding the house burst into pale green foliage that deepened as the days lengthened. But as she walked toward the meadow with four-year-old Sarah to pick pink prairie roses and purple violets, a mourning dove's coah-cooo-cooo-coo struck a different note, tapping into the resentment toward Peder that festered in the deepest recesses of her mind. She could not forgive him for sending the boys to school, despite her pleas, the day the blizzard almost claimed the lives of Matthew and Joe.

And now Peder supported their eldest child's decision to drop out of school after eighth grade. Minnie regretted not going to college, but she *had* graduated from the Ladies Seminary in St. Paul, and she had been introduced to Shakespeare and Tolstoy, Bach and Beethoven. Her mother had urged her to go to college, to pursue a musical career, but she'd met Peder. At eighteen she wanted only to be his loving wife and a good mother.

When Minnie saw thunder clouds piling up in the west, she called to Sarah. "Come, Sweetie. Time to go." After she retrieved the sunbonnet Sarah had discarded when Minnie wasn't looking, they headed toward the house. Minnie tried to dispel her gloomy thoughts by identifying the calls of cardinals, redwing blackbirds, and her favorite, Western meadowlarks, as she and Sarah passed the box elder and the fruit trees nearer the house. But by the time they entered the kitchen, a distressing conversation was replaying in her mind.

"Kari, you don't have to go to high school if you don't vant to," Peder had said at dinner.

Joe popped up from his chair, "I don't want to go either."

"Joe," Minnie protested. "You're eleven. You've lots of time to think about it."

"I want to go," Willie declared.

"Me too," came a forceful comment from Sarah, a recent high chair graduate, which brought guarded smiles around the table.

"You didn't go, Pa." Kari said in defense of herself, knowing her mother did not approve of her decision.

"No. In Norvay not many vent to school after eighth grade. Ven we came to America, my parents needed me to verk on the farm."

"His parents couldn't speak English, Kari. Pa's circumstances were very different from yours," Minnie insisted.

"I just want to get married," she responded. "I don't see how studying geometry or history will do me any good."

Minnie suppressed her anger at Peder. He should want his children to get as much education as possible. Why didn't he support her? In the past they'd seen eye to eye about education. Or had they? When they were courting, they talked mostly about moving to Dakota Territory so Peder could farm his own place. She didn't regret her decision, but she didn't want to limit her children's choices.

She tried to put another slant on it. "School is more than studying. You go to dances and put on plays. You'll be married soon enough, Kari. Enjoy your freedom while you can."

"I don't think I'd enjoy studying algebra."

Later, Minnie took an approach she'd avoided before, sensitive to Peder's limited formal education. "You'll meet boys and girls in town who'll be going to college."

"I've met lots of town boys. At Sunday school. In the feed store. In the livery stable. They aren't special. I want to marry a man like Pa or a rancher." Kari stopped putting dishes on the shelves and stared into the distance. "Riding the range. That's my idea of fun, of a good life."

"I know you're sweet on Carl Svenson..."

Kari blushed as she said passionately, "Carl knows more about horses than anyone. He's special." She turned to face her mother. "How did you meet Pa?"

Minnie took a deep breath as she closed her eyes and evoked an image of the frozen pond where she and her younger brother, Bobby, ice skated. "I was skating, doing something fancy when I caught a blade in a crack in the ice. I went flying and crashed on my tailbone. Before I could get up, this handsome young man helped me to my feet and asked me if I was hurt. Only my pride was hurt. I mumbled 'no' and skated off to the warming hut to take my skates off and go home."

"What happened after that?"

"I looked for him every time I want skating. I guessed he was a Norwegian immigrant, because he had an accent. About two weeks later I finally spotted this tall, blond handsome man on the ice."

"What did you do?"

"I didn't know what to do. I knew girls weren't supposed to be forward, but I was afraid he'd ignore me because I'd been unfriendly. Anyway, I decided to do some fancy figure eights to attract his attention. When I was sure he was watching me, I skated toward him fast on a collision course. He didn't flinch. I threw my weight onto the inside edge of my right skate and turned to execute a dramatic stop in front of him. He smiled at me and said, 'I thought I'd have to pick you up again. Vould you care to skate with me?' I still remember how safe I felt with his right arm around my waist, my left hand resting on his as we sailed around the pond. More than safe. I soared above the ice in a state of bliss. I was in love."

"That's a wonderful story, Ma."

"Yes. And I didn't care that my teachers and the nuns—like my mother—would have disapproved totally, because Peder and I were never formally introduced."

The next morning Minnie confronted Peder as she helped with barn chores. "For Heaven's sakes, Peder, *please* encourage Kari to stay in school."

"She doesn't need more schooling. She already has the basics. The rest comes from living, learning to cook and sew."

"Why deprive her of youthful good times? And options, like teaching, in case she doesn't marry?"

Frustrated by Peder's lack of support, Minnie began dreaming about a trip to Minnesota. She imagined Kari loving the high school in St. Paul while living in the family mansion with her grandmother. She'd take piano or voice lessons and go to the theatre and concerts with her Uncle Bob. Soon her fantasy expanded: she'd take all the children to St. Paul where no one could drop out of school before the age of sixteen—at least she didn't think so. As she worked out details of the trip in her head, what she could not resolve was the length of her stay. She guessed she'd "play that by ear" as well as when to reveal her plans to Peder.

Throughout the summer, working with Kari in the garden or canning vegetables, she raved about St. Paul, the beautiful old houses, the fancy stores, the bridges across the Mississippi. She often talked to Matthew and Joe about the university and told tales to Willie and Sarah about her Minnesota childhood—band concerts in the park, the circus, boat rides on the Mississippi River—to stimulate their desire to visit the city.

Each month she skimmed the household allowance to set aside money for the trip. She even wrote to her widowed mother who sent a contribution and a note saying she looked forward to seeing her grandchildren.

To everyone's surprise, Kari announced in August, "I've decided to go to high school with Matthew." For fear of sabotaging this new-found interest in school—never mind that Carl Svenson was the motivating force—Minnie put her trip on hold.

During the next four years, Matthew and Kari often initiated dinner conversations that originated in a history or civics class. While following the presidential campaign of Benjamin Harrison in 1888, Matthew advised his father, "You should vote. It's your responsibility as well as your right. It doesn't matter that you're a naturalized citizen."

"It doesn't seem fair. I can vote, but your mother can't. She's lived in this country all her life. She knows more about it than I do."

"Our history teacher says that women called Suffragists are trying to change that." Kari looked at Minnie. "What do you think, Ma? Would you vote if you could?"

"I would. And I hope those women succeed. But I don't think it makes much difference to me who is president."

Willie objected, "Yes, it does. What if Lincoln hadn't been elected president?"

Sarah jumped up. "Can I vote?"

"No," Kari said. "We're girls, so we can't vote even when we're twenty-one."

"When you grow up, Sarah, you could be a Suffragist. Fight for women's right to vote." Matthew added, "Then you and Ma and Kari could all vote."

"I *will*," Sarah responded.

Gossip about the division of Dakota into two states and of Hughitt becoming a state capital dominated many conversations and class discussions in the summer and fall of 1889. Kari, quoting her teacher, told the family, "We don't know if South Dakota is the 39th or the 40th state. President Harrison shuffled the documents he signed, making it impossible to determine whether North or South came first."

"Why?" Willie asked.

"He wanted to avoid increased tension between the two sections of the territory. They'd feuded over where the capital should be. Now each could have one." She smiled. "I think it's exciting that Hughitt may be the capital of South Dakota."

"That fight dates to the early '80s," Peder said. "There are other serious contenders."

"Will Hughitt win?" Willie asked.

"Probably not. Pierre is in the center of the state," Matthew answered.

On another night, Joe, the seventh grader who kept the family informed of news from the west, announced that the US Army had "finally got Sitting Bull."

His enthusiasm alarmed Minnie. "I thought fighting in the Black Hills had stopped."

Matthew shook his head. "Ma, the Sioux don't want to be penned in reservations. Or to be driven out of the Black Hills. That's sacred land to the Lakota."

Joe countered, "The Sioux shouldn't have threatened the whites with their Ghost Dances, that stupid ritual. They thought they could bring back the buffalo and drive out the white man. So the army took care of them."

"But the Indians didn't kill anyone. Our army not only killed braves, they massacred Lakota women and children at Wounded Knee."

"Don't be stupid. The Indians have done plenty of scalping and killing," Joe scowled at his brother.

"They would have left us alone if we hadn't taken their land and killed all the buffalo."

Minnie enjoyed the family discussions, even the heated arguments, and wanted to nurture her children's interest in history and politics. She asked Peder about subscribing to *Century Magazine*. "It will be good reading for all of us. The copy I saw in town had articles on the Civil War, Lincoln's White House, the California gold rush. Even a short story by Mark Twain."

"We can't afford it this year, Minnie."

"No, but I bet we can afford another cow."

When the magazine arrived a month later, Peder asked her how she'd paid for it. "Household money," she said, ignoring the look he gave her.

Toward the end of his senior year, Matthew worked for President Harrison's reelection. He sat in the smoke-filled Republican headquarters handing out flyers and listening to the politicians argue about the effects of the Sherman Act on Harrison's campaign. Across Dakota Avenue in a smaller storefront, Kari, encouraged by Minnie, had joined the Democrats who hoped to reelect Grover Cleveland. A Suffragist who was pushing equal rights for women kept Kari interested. Minnie approved of the nightly arguments with the siblings trying to convince Peder to vote for their candidate and also his refusal to reveal his intentions.

When Matthew and Kari graduated from high school in 1892, Joe had completed the eighth grade at the country school; Willie had finished sixth grade; and Sarah, third grade.

Minnie failed to convince Joe to continue in high school. He told Kari who often rode with him that he wanted to join the US Cavalry.

"Leave home? Not go to high school? It's really not so bad," Kari responded.

"Not for you, maybe. I want to do something. Not just sit around."

"Like fighting the Sioux? Joe, you'd better talk this over with Ma and Pa."

"No. I don't want to talk it over. I'm just going to run away some night. If I tell Ma, she'll cry. I can't stand that. Promise me, Kari, you won't say anything until I'm gone."

"I don't know. Ma will be very upset."

"She'll get over it. Promise me, Kari."

"All right. But I think you're making a big mistake."

Two nights later Joe was missing at dinner. "Where's Joe?" Minnie asked. "He might be late for school, but never for dinner." After she'd finished setting the table, she said. "Let's wait a few minutes before we start."

"Ma," Kari mumbled with downcast eyes. "I don't think he's coming. Joe wants to join the cavalry and I think he's on his way."

"Cavalry? I've never heard such nonsense. He's only fourteen."

"He loves horses and riding and he's big and strong for his age. He'll lie about his age and get by."

"I worried about Joe leaving once he finished school," Peder said. "He's never been interested in farming—only in the horses."

"Why didn't he talk to us?" Tears loomed in Minnie's voice.

"Because he couldn't stand to see you and Willie cry."

"Maybe the army won't take him. They'll find out how old he is."

"They'll take him if he lies about his age. He's tall and sturdy and knows how to handle horses. Minnie, think about this. He'll be happy in the cavalry doing vat he loves."

Later, Minnie told Peder she felt she had failed Joe. Not only had he dropped out of school, he couldn't even talk to her about what he wanted to do.

"No, no, Minnie. Some boys need to leave home, strike out on their own. Don't feel bad. You're a good mother. I knew long ago our sons vill not take over the farm. Matthew vill go to college, become a lawyer…maybe a politician. Joe, a soldier. He'll learn discipline in the cavalry. These boys have never been interested in farming. And Villie is sickly. He should train for a job that does not have physical demands."

In that moment Minnie felt Peder's pain. She remembered their idealistic dreams of a homestead, a farm that one of the sons would take over eventually. "What will happen to the farm, Peder?" For an instant she wondered if he might relinquish the farm, move to Hughitt, or even St. Paul. She'd love to be in the city again, to be free of the unforgiving stresses of the prairie—though she knew she would miss the tapestry of variegated yellow and green fields, the delicate wild flowers, the magnitude of the blue or star-lit sky, the orange-pink-purple sunsets, the sweet song of a meadowlark.

"I don't know, Minnie. Maybe one of the girls vill marry a farmer."

"Peder, I've been thinking about taking the children to St. Paul. Matthew should visit the University of Minnesota before he makes a final decision. And all of them should meet their grandmother and uncles."

"Not a good time, Minnie. I need Matthew and Kari to help plant. And all of you for chores. I can't do everything myself."

"There's never a good time." Minnie tried to remain calm.

"Farm verk is never done," Peder acknowledged.

"*Well, I'm sick of it.*" Minnie hissed. Surprised at her own outburst, she covered her mouth.

"Get a hold of yourself, Mother. Don't be irresponsible." Peder walked out.

Minnie sat down to control her shaking. She was furious. How could Peder call her "irresponsible?" Suddenly, she was determined. Maybe this wasn't the best time to revive her plan to visit St. Paul, but she wasn't waiting a day after the harvest.

June dragged on for Minnie who knew she was trapped until September. Joe's departure, Willie's bouts of bronchitis, Peder's unrelenting drive, and Kari's withdrawal—initiated by Carl Svenson's decision to go west—added to her desperation. Only Sarah could cut through her gloom with her lively, frequently mischievous, behavior.

But Kari's listlessness and Willie's cough finally drove her to approach Dr. Buchanan, their doctor from their first days in Dakota. He shook his head.

"There's not much you can do for Willie's poor lungs…or Kari's broken heart. Only time will help her. But you could be a big help to your husband if you could find a strong, young man to work on the farm. Peder's heart is going to give out one of these days if he doesn't slow down. Why don't you talk to Tom Crawford at the Land Office?"

The doctor's comment struck a chord. Minnie knew she nagged, always asking Peder to slow down, stop sod busting more acres, and buying more livestock. A farm hand would be good for him, if he'd be willing to pay for one. With a splinter of hope, she walked toward the Land Office, enjoying the activity on the street and appreciating the new brick buildings that were replacing the square-fronted frame structures on Dakota Avenue, the main street of Hughitt.

She knew Mr. Crawford as a member of her church. Appointed to the Government Land Office by President Cleveland and reappointed by Benjamin Harrison, Mr. Crawford hung the signed documents with their presidential seals on the wall opposite the door for everyone to see. Minnie studied them as she waited to ask Mr. Crawford if he could find a hired man for the farm.

"Settlers still coming through, Mrs. Youngstrom. Not like in the '80s before the drought. I'll keep my eyes and ears open. Peder's a good man. A new settler could learn a lot from him."

She left the office, a burden lifted from her shoulders. She'd tell Peder what she'd done, guessing he wouldn't object because he'd doubt anything would come of it. She assumed a farm hand would show up, and she'd be relieved of guilt over leaving Peder overworked. But she still had his opposition to deal with. How could she get herself, the children, and the baggage out of the house and to the train station without Peder being any the wiser? She felt certain he would block her if he had any inkling of her plans. She needed to conceal her intent from Sarah and Willie, both too young to keep a secret. At least she didn't have to worry about Joe. Matthew would be leaving anyway to establish a residency in Minnesota before he matriculated. He could be a major help in getting them to the train station—*if* he were willing to collude with her.

And Kari? She'd expressed little interest in St. Paul. Minnie also doubted she'd approve of the trip if her father did not. One night as they cleaned up after dinner, she decided to sound her out. "Would you like a trip to St. Paul? See the university with Matthew?" She tried to sound casual.

"No, not really. I liked high school, but that's enough schooling for me."

"I understand, but you'd see your grandmother and uncles...and the city."

"Remember, Ma, I'm a country girl."

Disappointed, Minnie retreated. How should she approach her daughter? And if she failed? She couldn't insist Kari make the trip. Leave her here? Peder might be hard to live with.

When she finally mustered the courage to approach Matthew, she crossed her fingers. How childish, she thought. I haven't done that since I was ten years old.

Matthew pulled back. "And not tell Pa? I don't know. Why not tell him?"

"He doesn't want us to go. Leaves too much work for him."

"He's right, Ma. Anyway, why do you want *all* of us to go?"

"I want all of you to meet my mother. She's getting old. And my brothers. I know *you're* going to meet them, but I want everyone to meet them."

"I'd prefer to arrive in St. Paul on my own. I'm too old to be traveling with my mother."

"Please, Matthew."

"I don't know."

CHAPTER 5
A Disastrous Journey

Edward Bishop arrived on a late June morning looking for the job Mr. Crawford had recommended. Clean shaven and ruddy-complexioned, Edward extended a calloused hand to Minnie who immediately tabbed him a hard worker. He was not as tall as Peder, but his broad shoulders, stocky build, firm grip, and youth were all in his favor. Minnie judged him to be no older than thirty.

"Mr. Youngstrom will be in soon for the noon meal. Please stay and eat with us. In the meantime, I'll show you around."

Peder arrived around noon with Kari and Matthew. He quickly suppressed his surprise and sized up the young man before he said, "Have a seat at the table, Mr. Bishop."

"Call me Ed, Mr. Youngstrom."

When Peder asked for his farming history, Ed described his grandparent's 300 acre farm in Wisconsin where he'd worked from the time he was a child. After his grandfather's death, Ed took charge, but his mother, in need of money, sold the farm. Ed decided to go west. Peder asked why he came to Dakota.

"I came for cheap land. To farm. It's all I know. Mr. Crawford told me I should wait until bottom land comes up to stake a claim. While I waited, I could learn a lot from you."

As the men talked, Minnie and Kari set the table with baked ham, oven roasted potatoes, sautéed greens, and a loaf of bread. Minnie hoped it was not just her imagination, but Kari seemed to have more energy and enthusiasm than she'd displayed in months.

After they'd all finished eating, Peder extended a hand to Edward. "Let's give it a try. You verk with me for a few days. Ve'll see how it goes."

50

"Sounds good to me."

In less than a week Peder told Minnie that Edward was a kindred soul, a hard worker who lived to grow things and appreciated his natural surroundings. Minnie's twinge of jealousy evaporated with the gratitude she felt for Edward's potential as a surrogate son. Within a few days Minnie and Peder had cleared out the storeroom so Ed could have his own space in the house.

Besides helping Peder, Ed weeded Minnie's garden, fed and groomed horses with Kari. He helped Willie and Sarah with chores in the hen house and took them for rides in the buckboard.

As Edward settled in, Minnie adjusted her travel plans. She'd leave Kari, who'd never shown interest in St. Paul, in charge of the house. She even fancied a romance might develop between Kari and Ed. She'd catch him staring at Kari and she knew her daughter liked him too, though Carl Svenson's name still popped up in conversations.

But uneasy about possible entanglements in Wisconsin, Minnie waited only a few weeks to approach Ed. "Please don't be offended, but I've wondered why you've never married."

"It's a fair question," he said. "The truth is I've never had enough income to support a family." He added, "Another truth is that I've never met a woman I wanted to marry…not yet."

The *not yet* sounded good to Minnie. "That makes sense," she said, remembering that Peder wouldn't marry her until he had a decent saw mill job in St. Paul.

Believing that Edward's physical and moral support had lightened Peder's load significantly during July and August, Minnie finalized her travel plans. Better to leave before Edward claims bottom land and moves on. She made mental lists of what to take, alerted Matthew to be prepared, and visualized their escape in the morning when Peder and Ed would be engaged in field work. Getting the horse and carriage, the children and the luggage all assembled without an inquisition would not be simple. To avoid

Peder's getting suspicious if he heard references to St. Paul, Minnie reminded him that Matthew should leave soon to begin Minnesota residency requirements. Only Matthew was privy to her plans.

While Matthew packed a bag in the area of the loft he shared with Willie, Minnie worked on another for Sarah, Willie, and herself. She had told Willie she was packing a second bag for Matthew and was surprised when Willie questioned her at dinner.

"Ma, why are my clothes in Matthew's bag?"

"What?" Minnie glanced at Peder. "Oh, I'm sorry, Willie. Your shirts look so much alike." Not wanting to linger on that untruth, she said, "Peder, Matthew is leaving tomorrow. Does it matter which horses he hitches to the carriage?"

"Any of the draft horses. It doesn't matter." Peder looked at Matthew. "I'll miss you, Son. You've always been a big help even though you don't much care for farm verk. I vish you the best of luck in St. Paul."

Minnie closed her eyes and took a deep breath. Would Matthew melt under the warmth of his father's words? Would he reveal her secret?

Silence. She didn't exhale until Matthew said, "I'll miss all of you."

"Take the buckboard, Matthew…no need for the carriage." Peder added, "And take someone along to bring it back."

"I'll go," Kari volunteered.

"No, I'll go." Unnerved, Minnie didn't know how to respond. Without the carriage her plan failed. The buckboard was too small.

"YOU! You hate to drive the buckboard," Peder chuckled.

"I know. But I want to go. And I want to take Willie and Sarah. Why can't we take the carriage? I don't like to drive the buckboard *or* the carriage. You know that. At least the carriage will hold all of us."

Matthew got up and started clearing the table. Minnie guessed he wanted to avoid continuing this charade.

"Let Kari drive the buckboard and everyone say their goodbyes here," Peder advised.

"But I want Willie and Sarah to go along to see the train." Why hadn't she thought of that sooner? Going to see the train got them out of the house without raising suspicions. "The buckboard can't accommodate all of us."

Ed shook his head. "Sorry, Minnie, you can't take the carriage."

"Why?" She glared at Ed. How dare *he* mess up her plans?

"A back wheel is broken,"

Minnie groaned internally. Must everything go wrong? "Ed, you're handy. Can't you fix the wheel tonight or first thing tomorrow?"

"I'll work on it tonight…but I don't think I can fix it."

After dinner, the men retreated to the barn to see about the wheel. Minnie made no attempt to conceal her bad mood as Kari helped with the dishes. "Ma, take the buckboard. Matthew can drive to the station. You'll only have to bring it back."

"It's not just the buckboard or the carriage or the sleigh…or anything else for that matter. I've never had the experience you've had with horses. I'm not comfortable with them, and they sense my insecurity. I want the carriage because I want Willie and Sarah to see the train and the buckboard isn't big enough for all of us."

"Ma, Willie and Sarah have seen trains before. And they'll have more chances."

For a second Minnie verged on telling Kari all.

She joined the men after the kitchen work was done. Ed was bent over the right rear wheel. "It's almost done," Peder told her. "It'll need a replacement soon, but it's good for you and the children tomorrow."

Later that evening Minnie wrote a note to Kari, putting her in charge of the kitchen and advising her to remind Peder—if he were angry—that his wife had not seen her mother or brothers in years. She tucked the note in a pocket and stepped outside for a last look at the boundless sky. Would she ever see this many stars again?

53

Never in the city. As she retraced her steps from the meadow, she heard a coyote in the direction of the Wessington Hills. She'd never hear that plaintive cry either, unless she came back. Would she? Could she really leave Peder?

While Matthew hitched the horses and secured the luggage on top of the carriage, Kari fed Sarah and Willie. Minnie checked her mental lists. When she put a bottle of cough medicine in her bag, and Kari asked why, she answered, "Willie's caught a cold."

"I know, but he'll be back here after the train leaves."

Flustered, Minnie finally muttered, "The train could be late."

Kari stayed on the platform with Minnie and the children while Matthew purchased tickets in the station. He emerged as the train pulled in. Minnie gave the note to Kari, hugged her, and said, "I know I've been acting strange. You'll understand when you read the note. Forgive me."

Seconds later Kari stepped back, jaw dropping, as Minnie and Matthew scooted Willie and Sarah onto the train and followed them into an empty car. Minnie chose a window seat and directed the children to sit opposite her. When Kari saw her mother through the window, she shrugged and raised her arms as if to say, "What's happening?" Minnie mouthed, "Read the note." Already she regretted not confiding in Kari. But what could she tell her. She didn't know how long she'd stay away, only that she'd have to come back someday.

Thrilled at being on a train for the first time, Sarah and Willie waved to Kari as they examined the cushiony, upholstered seats, and gawked at the light fixtures. When the conductor, in his navy blue uniform and cap, entered the car, they settled down to watch him collect tickets. Willie's flushed cheeks caused Minnie to reach over and touch a feverish forehead. She dismissed any thought that his cold had worsened. They'd look for a lung specialist in St. Paul. Or go to the Mayo Clinic in Rochester.

Later, Willie's coughing brought the conductor. Minnie requested a pillow and asked Matthew to switch places, so Willie could stretch out, his head on her lap. Soon he napped, while Matthew entertained Sarah with card tricks and games. Minnie could look out on a panorama of fields and farms bordered with giant sunflowers, but the view was lost on her as she imagined scenarios of Peder's response to her disappearance. During brief stops in Iroquois, De Smet, and Brookings, she read a Century Magazine until the train chugged ahead. When they approached Sleepy Eye in Minnesota, she asked the conductor if her son had time to send a telegram. He advised waiting for the longer stop in Mankato.

Minnie's brother, Robert, met them at the Chicago & North Western station. With everyone settled in his carriage, he ordered his driver to take the scenic route to the family mansion. Along the way, he pointed to landmarks Minnie remembered—the pond where they skated, the mill where Peder worked. As they approached the Mississippi River, Willie perked up and recited facts about the river. He was telling them how Mark Twain got his name when a coughing spell wiped him out. He laid back, quiet for the rest of the trip.

Minnie's childhood home, an 1860's Victorian set back on a large lot in a fashionable area not far from the river, looked the same, only now mature rhododendron and blue spruce hid more of the façade. Sarah and Willie, subdued as they approached the double front door, windows with beveled and etched glass, waited for an adult to lift the brass knocker.

Agnes, Minnie's mother, still vigorous at 74, awaited them in the parlor. After embracing her daughter, she greeted her grandchildren and engaged them in conversation about their first train ride. Soon a maid announced that dinner was ready. Minnie realized her own motherhood had softened her feelings toward Agnes, feelings reinforced when she said grace, rather than requesting it of one of the children, something she'd always done during Minnie's childhood.

As the children began to eat, Minnie made it obvious which piece of silverware they should use. She noticed that Willie only picked at the potatoes on his plate. She chalked it up to excitement, until he asked to be excused.

Alarmed, she followed him out of the dining room. He staggered and fell before she reached him. "Robert," she screamed as she knelt and straightened out Willie's legs. In seconds her brother swooped down and picked up the boy.

"Put him in the blue room," Agnes said in a firm voice. "I'm calling Dr. Stewart." Everyone stood in the hallway, uncertain about what to do. Sarah grabbed Matthew's hand and the pair followed their mother up the stairway.

Sarah cried softly, "I want to go home."

As Robert laid the boy on the bed, Willie opened his eyes and looked up at his mother. "I don't know what happened. I got a pain in my chest and I couldn't breathe. Then I fell."

"Hush, just rest, Willie." His rapid breathing, his flushed cheeks and hot forehead frightened her. She pulled up a chair and sat holding his hand as he drifted out of consciousness.

Agnes entered and put a hand on Minnie's shoulder. "Dr. Stewart will be here soon. I think everyone but you should leave. Let the boy rest."

"He slept most of the way here, Grandma," Sarah said.

"I know. But he needs rest. He's very sick. Come with me Sarah, we'll find something down stair to keep us busy."

They'd barely left the room when Willie's teeth began to chatter and he began to shake. Minnie tucked a quilt around him trying to control his chill. When he began to cough, she put her arm behind his neck to support him while he brought up rust-colored mucous.

An hour later, Dr. Stewart bent over the boy, moving his stethoscope around Willie's chest and then his back. Silently,

Minnie waited, watching him take Willie's pulse and temperature. Abruptly the doctor straightened up and stepped out of the room. He returned with Matthew and Sarah. "I asked them to stay with their brother while I talk to you in the other room."

"I'm sorry," Dr. Stewart said as soon as they were alone. "I'm sure you know he's a very sick boy or you wouldn't have sent for me. There's no question. He has lobar pneumonia."

Shocked, Minnie sat on the arm of the nearest chair. "What can I do, Doctor?"

"Good nursing care, my dear. There's nothing much else to do. Lots of liquids and bed rest. And prayer."

"Should I send for his father?"

"Yes."

Minnie couldn't catch her breath. Between deep sighs, she said, "I had an uncle who died of pneumonia when I was ten. I remember my parents waiting for the 'crisis.' They thought the fever would break that night and he would get well. But he didn't make it. He died that night. What about Willie?"

"I don't know, Mrs. Youngstrom. I don't know how soon there will be a crisis. Willie's young. That's good."

"But he's always had weak lungs."

"That makes him more vulnerable, but you must not give up hope."

Minnie stayed by Willie's side all night. She kept a cool cloth on his forehead and raised his head to help him bring up blood-streaked sputum during paroxysms of coughing.

At sunup Matthew entered the sick room. "How is he? Did you get some sleep, Ma? Grandma and I took turns trying to calm Sarah. She finally fell asleep."

"Willie is the same. I slept a little," she lied.

"Grandma's ordered a nurse."

"Matthew, Willie wants to go home. Last night he sat up. Delirious. 'I want to go home,' he said twice." Anxious, agitated, Minnie's thoughts spilled from her mouth. "We've got to let your father and Kari know how sick he is. Joe, too. Maybe, they'll come here. Do you think we should take him home? That's what he really wants, I know. We'd better ask the doctor if he can make it."

"Slow down, Ma. Uncle Robert has already sent a telegram to father."

Seconds later Robert entered with a plate of food for Minnie. "A nurse will be here soon, but I thought you might like some sustenance now." Robert put the plate on the night stand. "No word yet from Peder."

"Robert, Willie wants to go home. If it's his last wish, I'd like to do it…"

"I don't know, Minnie. Ask Dr. Stewart. He'll be back this afternoon." He added, "I'm sure I can arrange for you to have a parlor car to make the trip easier. Father was an important Chicago &North Western official."

Peder and Kari arrived the next afternoon by train. Robert recognized Peder, a gray haired and slightly stooped version of his younger self. Kari, like Matthew, resembled her tall, once blond, father—not at all like dark-haired, petite Sarah who took after Minnie. "Be prepared to see a very sick boy," Robert said as he led them to his carriage.

"Poor Villie," Peder said, "He vas never healthy. But he never complained. Not ven he couldn't play ball with his brothers…or do anything that required much exertion. I sent Joe a telegram…told him to let you know if he could get here.

"We haven't heard from him yet," Robert said.

"How is Minnie doing?" Peder asked. "I always thought Villie was her favorite."

"Oh," Robert expressed surprise. "Well, given his poor health, he probably required the most attention. Minnie is holding up. She's a strong woman. Stoic. She hasn't left Willie's side for two days now."

"Yes. She *is* long suffering. She's had a hard life with me, a stubborn Norvegian. She's been a good vife and mother. Sometimes I'm surprised she's stayed on the farm all these years."

"Minnie's loyal. One of her qualities." Robert added, "She also has an affinity for the land and nature. She's always loved the outdoors—family trips to the north woods in the summer, ice skating in the winter…"

"Ve met skating on a pond near your house," Peder said. "And ve skated together for years. I made a rink every November near our barn so the children could learn to skate. The girls were good but never as good as their mother."

"Ma also loves the prairie, picking wild flowers in the meadow," Kari interjected. "And watching the big sky and the beautiful red, orange, purple sunsets and sunrises. We used to tell each other stories based on the shape of the clouds. Uncle Robert, you should visit sometime."

"Thank you, Kari. Well, here we are."

"The place hasn't changed much." Peder said as the carriage moved into the circular driveway. "Not that I expected it to."

Sarah was the first to greet her father. She grabbed him around the waist and began to cry. "Willie is sick and I'm afraid he's going to die," she said between sobs.

"Sarah, hush," Kari put her index finger to her mouth. "You don't want Willie to hear you. Can you take us to his room?"

Willie was sleeping. Minnie threw her arms around Peder as he reached for her. Momentarily, she felt safe, secure, a child comforted by a parent. "He has lucid moments," she said. "Usually I can't make out what he's mumbling, but I know he asked for you and Kari … Joe, too."

"You look so tired, Ma. Why don't you rest? I'll sit here," Kari offered.

"I can't rest. I have to be in here. Kari. We'll have a talk later. Go see your grandmother now and comfort Sarah. Peder, please stay."

He pulled up a chair and took the hand that wasn't holding Willie's. "Minnie, how could you leave like that? I don't understand."

"Forgive me. I should have told you. I was afraid you'd stop me." She couldn't look directly at him. "Oh, Willie's awake." She slipped another pillow behind his head.

Willie smiled as his father bent over him. "I'm glad you're here," he said.

"You've got to get better, Son, so I can take you to the State Fair."

"Did Ma tell you I saw the Mississippi River...before I got sick? We read about it in school." He closed his eyes as his words trailed off.

"We'd better let him rest," Minnie said. "I'm so grateful you're here, Peder." Before she let go of him, she said, "Go greet my mother now." She turned away, to conceal her tears.

When Peder saw Robert in the library, he asked, "Vat does the doctor say?"

"Not much. And there's not much we can do. We're all just waiting. Only Sarah says what's on her mind. You heard her earlier."

They turned toward Matthew who'd answered a knock at the door. "A telegram," he said. "Joe is coming."

"Maybe he'll get here in time," Minnie said, when Peder told her the news. "But I know Willie is going to die. He's never been sick like this. I should have stayed home with him."

Sarah had tiptoed into the bedroom. "Ma, come eat with us. Kari or Matthew will sit until you get back."

Minnie reached for her daughter's hand. "Sarah, sweetie, I can't leave. Ask Kari to make a plate for me."

Minutes later, Peder entered with food. Minnie put up her hand to stop him. "Listen," she said. "His breathing has changed."

"Yes," Peder said as he put down the plate and slipped an arm around her shoulders. "It's very shallow and fast."

"Oh, Peder, Is he turning blue or is it just the bad light in here? Go get Dr. Stewart. Hurry." In her need to do something, Minnie began to recite Hail Marys and Our Fathers. She knew she could not atone for her sins, but this ritual—a regression to her childhood religion—gave her comfort, calmed her anxiety. When Matthew opened the door, she waved him away.

Desperate as she watched Willie become cyanotic, she raised his head and slipped another pillow behind him. "I love you Willie. We all love you. Please don't leave us." She kissed his forehead and sat again, stroking his hand. Minutes later he stopped breathing.

She stood when Dr. Stewart entered an hour later. "He's gone," she said. She left to join the others in the main room. Peder took her in his arms. She felt nothing. The switch that turned off Willie's breathing had shut off a crucial part of her brain.

"Is Willie an angel now?" Sarah asked no one in particular.

Kari turned away and began to sob. Matthew, eyes-filled, reached for Kari and Sarah.

The family returned to Hughitt in a Chicago & North Western parlor car. A red plush settee had been removed to make room for Willie's closed casket. Minnie sat in an overstuffed arm chair staring out a window at fields of hay stacks, farmhouses, silos, barns, and train depots—but images of Willie in her mind's eye blotted out most of the physical world.

Although Peder and Kari's attempts to engage her were futile, Minnie couldn't ignore Sarah who threw herself, sobbing, on her mother's lap. "Why did Willie have to die?" she gasped. Minnie held her and rocked gently. Sarah's pain added to her already aching heart *The truly sad thing, is how short Willie's life was, and I may have shortened it by taking him to St. Paul. How selfish I have been.*

When Sarah's breathing returned to normal, Minnie wiped the tears from her face and covered her with kisses. "Everything will be alright, Sweetie. Willie will always live in our hearts and minds. And he isn't suffering anymore."

Joe arrived in time for Willie's burial in the Hughitt Cemetery. Surrounded by Joe and the others, Minnie was temporarily busy and distracted. When her sons were preparing to leave, she wondered if they'd return to Dakota again before Peder died, a thought she quickly dismissed. Everyone said that losing a child was the hardest, but she wasn't sure. Could anything be worse than losing Peder, her partner, the man who'd held her every night since Willie's death until she cried herself to sleep? Yet she had left him, not certain she would return.

Minnie's morbid thoughts began to ease when she saw Kari and Ed holding hands, exchanging glances, or simply looking at each other in the caring way she and Peder had in years past. Kari finally approached her mother. "Ma, Ed and I want to be engaged. Would that be all right with you? We've talked about getting married and living in a cottage Ed could build on land beyond the meadow down near the creek. Do you think Pa would approve?"

"Of course, Kari. Tell Ed to talk to your father. I'm so happy for you...both of you." But a gray cloud momentarily passed over her. She'd be "losing" another child. In this case though, grandchildren will probably be compensation. In the meantime, she still had Sarah.

PART 2
Sarah
DAKOTA 1899-1909

CHAPTER 6
Living with the Halls

Fifteen months after he became engaged to Kari, Edward put the final touches on the cottage he'd built near the creek and the small stand of cottonwood trees on the southeast quarter of Peder's section of land. While Kari and Peder helped him, Minnie and twelve-year-old Sarah filled Kari's hope chest. Under her mother's supervision, Sarah sewed, crocheted, and appliquéd. As she finished trimming a sheet, she declared, "I'll never do this again…even if my hope chest is empty and no one will marry me."

Minnie shook her head and smiled. "My friends and I had filled our hope chests before we were your age."

"All they wanted in life was to get married. I want more." Sarah hoped her mother wouldn't ask what. She didn't know. She looked forward to high school in Hughitt after she finished the country school, but she hadn't thought much beyond that. She only knew for certain that she did not want to live on a farm. As much as she liked her father and Ed, the last thing she'd do was marry a farmer.

Kari and Edward said their vows before family and friends on a sunny spring day in the Presbyterian Church in Hughitt with a reception in the farmhouse. Missing in the small group were Kari's brothers. Joe was in the Philippines with a U.S. cavalry unit and Matthew was taking year end exams at the University of Minnesota. Little Willie, the brother Sarah had been closest to and missed most of all, had been dead for two years.

As she helped her mother put things back in order after the guests had left, Sarah saw tears in her mother's eyes. "What's wrong, Ma?"

"You're my only child still at home."

Impulsively, Sarah jumped up and hugged her mother. "Don't worry, Mama. I'll stay with you and Pa until I get married…if I do."

As the twentieth century dawned, Sarah started high school in Hughitt. At fourteen she was petite like Minnie and had her mother's dark hair and fair skin, but her deep-set, blue-gray eyes; and thin, determined lips were her own. Initially quiet and self-contained in her new school environment, she retained her boundless curiosity, if not her outspokenness. When a teacher told her that she resembled the young Sarah Bernhardt, she rushed to the library to find a picture of the actress. Sarah failed to see a likeness in the photos she found, but she cut off her braids that night.

Getting to and from school was not an issue in the late summer and fall, but Minnie felt it prudent to make arrangements for Sarah to live in town with the Hall family during the winter months. Sarah objected as strongly as she could, arguing her brother and sister had managed while living at home. Minnie pointed out that there were two of them and both more skilled with horses and buckboards than she.

Sarah finally complained that she'd "die" living in the same house as Robert Hall who'd picked on her in Sunday School. He pulled her braids, and even made faces when she recited Bible verses, so distracting that she forgot the twenty-third Psalm during a special event.

"He's older now, a student in high school," her mother responded. But Sarah would never forget how he tormented her. *A snake may shed its skin, but it is still a snake.*

Sarah continued to fuss about moving to town, convinced that living under the same roof as Robert Hall would be an ongoing nightmare. She also wanted to stay close to Charles Edward, born exactly one year to the day Kari and Ed married. This brown-eyed dumpling's gurgling smile and waving arms signaled his delight whenever she approached him. She missed her dead brother less now, believing that Willie's soul inhabited Charlie.

But she not only failed to convince her mother that she could manage the trip to school—by horseback or buckboard through winter wind and snow—Peder, Kari, and Edward also met her pleas with unyielding resistance. She stormed around the farm for weeks, dismissing Kari's horror tales of horses spooked by trains and tracks. She relented only when the first heavy snowfall in late October made her late for school.

Minnie arranged for her daughter to live with the Hall family from November through March. Margaret Hall was a friend through the women's auxiliary of her church. Her husband had been a prominent lawyer and politician working to establish a college in this town of 8,000 when he died at forty-two, leaving his wife with three small children and few resources except a big handsome house that also carried a big mortgage. Mrs. Hall told Minnie she'd appreciate the rent money and she'd also keep a maternal eye on Sarah.

Sarah had seen the Queen Anne style Victorian as it was being built in 1895. Impressed by the wraparound porch, stained glass windows, gingerbread trim, and wrought iron fence gracing the perimeter of the property, she imagined a glorious interior. If only Robert didn't live there.

Mrs. Hall's greetings to Minnie, Sarah, and Edward quickly focused on Sarah. "I'm delighted you're going to live with us," she said as she ushered them into the foyer. Sarah was dazzled by glimpses of grained oak woodwork, dark flowered wallpaper, and a stained glass window over the stairway. She tried to focus on the cameo at the center of Mrs. Hall's high necked brown dress as a way to restrain her impulse to gawk.

"Let's go to your room first," Mrs. Hall said. "Edward can drop your bags. We'll come back to the parlor for tea."

"Ohhh," Sarah eyes widened as she took in the flowered chintz curtains, the rose design of the wallpaper, and a multicolored hooked rug with another flower design. "I'll love it here," she gushed, momentarily forgetting Robert. "I'll feel like a princess in that bed." The five foot Eastlake style headboard was like nothing she'd seen before.

Mrs. Hall's daughters—Elizabeth, twelve-years-old, and Eleanor, ten—shared an adjacent room, and sixteen-year-old Robert had the room across the hall. The door at the end of the corridor opened to a bathroom with a footed bathtub, marble sink, and toilet. *What luxury! I'll never want to go back to the farm and the outhouse.*

More luxury, Sarah mused, as she sat at the mahogany dining table that evening beneath a multi-colored lamp shade (Tiffany style she'd learn later) while the two daughters served dinner on china plates. The silver, with an elaborate rose pattern, was heavier than the coin silver at the farm. Robert entered the room last. She watched him with trepidation. When Mrs. Hall introduced them, Sarah imagined the snake coiling, preparing to strike. He welcomed her with a nod and a smile. No fangs, but Sarah was convinced his intent was evil.

"Really, Mrs. Hall, I should be helping," Sarah said as Elizabeth set a steaming bowl of split pea soup before her. Anything to get away from Robert.

"Not tonight, Sarah, you're our guest. Beginning tomorrow, you'll just be one of the family. We all have to pitch in."

Sarah soon learned that Mrs. Hall expected her daughters to do light housework and to master sewing so they could make their own clothing. Robert cut the grass, shoveled snow and coal, and stoked the furnace. Sarah helped in the kitchen and cleaned upstairs until Mrs. Hall asked her if she could type.

"I'm learning in school," she said. "My accuracy is good but I'm slow."

"Would you type letters for me? I'm on the board of trustees of the college...the only woman. That's why I'm expected to take care of correspondence. I never learned to type. Mr. Hall bought the typewriter...hoping I'd learn, I'm sure."

"I'll do my best," Sarah said, thrilled to have a job that was more mental than physical.

Initially awestruck by this family's life style, she strove to be what she thought Mrs. Hall wanted. But she did not feel at home for several weeks. Walking to school with Robert began as torture. Since Mrs. Hall had suggested it, Sarah could not refuse. Robert reminded her of the rattle snake Joe had trapped near their barn. Except the snake gave warning before it struck. Robert pulled questions out of nowhere just to aggravate her. When he wasn't a snake, he was a hawk swooping down on its prey. "Sarah, who is the President of the United States...and vice president?"

"McKinley is president," she snapped back.

"And Teddy Roosevelt is vice president," Robert added.

"I would have said TR. You didn't give me time. How could I *not* know him. My brother is in the cavalry and fought in the Spanish-American War."

"Your brother is a Rough Rider?"

For once he's impressed, Sarah thought. "I'm not certain." She backed down, fearful of getting caught in an untruth. Joe had written about the Philippines, not Cuba.

Gradually, she began to take pride in knowing Robert, reputed to be the smartest student in the school, admired for oratory and debating. Although she thought him arrogant, she suspected a few girls were jealous of her walking to school and living in the same house with him.

When the threat of snow was past, Sarah moved back to the farm where boredom soon engulfed her. She hated the hen house and helping Kari with the large animals. With Matthew and Joe gone, the girls had to do more. Little Charlie was the only saving grace.

She eagerly returned to Hughitt the following November, two months after President McKinley had been killed by an anarchist and Teddy Roosevelt had become president. Unlike her parents, Robert and his mother thrived on political talk.

"I'm not sure I approve of Mr. Roosevelt," Mrs. Hall said at dinner shortly after Sarah's return. "And I can't even vote to express my opinion."

"He *is* a Republican, mother," Robert said.

"Too progressive. What do you think, Sarah?" Mrs. Hall asked.

Sarah hadn't given any thought to Roosevelt's politics, but luckily remembered an article she'd read in *Century Magazine*. "He has a ranch in North Dakota. Maybe he'll be sympathetic to all Dakotans."

"We'll see. Don't forget he's also a rich New Yorker," Mrs. Hall countered.

As she gave Sarah letters to type one day, Mrs. Hall told her that the South Dakota legislature had rejected women's suffrage five or six times, but the state constitution allowed women to vote in school elections.

"Why do they reject suffrage?" Sarah asked.

"Why, indeed? I've given that question a lot of thought. Come, let's make a pot of tea and I'll tell you more." They went into the kitchen and she continued, "My interest in women's rights began when I was teaching in a rural school. But after I married, I worked with Mr. Hall to establish Hughitt College, and soon had three babies and little time left for anything else."

"Your life has been so different from my mother's," Sarah said. "Ma graduated from a women's seminary in St. Paul. I think she regrets not going to college. She met Pa and wanted to get married instead."

"Few women of our generation went to college. I attended a normal school to prepare for teaching. Your mother chose to help your father establish a productive farm. I grew up on a farm, so I know how hard they've worked." Mrs. Hall put the tea kettle on the stove, opened a bread box and pulled out a plate of cookies. "I was hoping Robert hadn't found these."

Sarah laughed. "Will Robert go to Hughitt College next fall?' She knew the answer, but the question provided an excuse to talk about this fascinating and intimidating boy. "Will he live here?"

She smiled to herself when Mrs. Hall said they were only building a dormitory for girls. Since Sarah would be returning here for two more winters, she liked knowing Robert would be around. He was a pain, but he made life interesting and kept her on her toes.

After she poured tea, Mrs. Hall continued, "Once my work at Hughitt College is done, I'll focus on women's suffrage. Not long ago, I saw a local politician bringing a group of illiterate railroad section hands to vote on a bond issue. I'm sure they knew nothing about it. They barely spoke English. I was incensed. They could vote and I couldn't."

"It is unfair. But what can you do?" Sarah asked. Before Mrs. Hall could respond, Elizabeth and Eleanor bounced into the room with questions about their homework. Sarah volunteered to help them. Mrs. Hall said she'd start dinner which would be late that night to accommodate Robert who was at school preparing for a debate competition.

When they were out of ear shot of her mother, Elizabeth asked, "Don't you like Robert? You hardly ever talk to him."

"What? Yes, I do." Sarah frowned at Elizabeth. But she knew she lost her voice when he was around. *Why can't I talk to him? Why do I get flustered?* She followed the girls into the library where their school books lay open on the large, oak table in the center of the room. *My problem is that I can't think fast enough. I want to be clever, put him down in a way he can't twist around to make me look bad.* She sat next to Elizabeth, still thinking about how to overcome her uneasiness with him.

"*Sarah*," Elizabeth bumped her elbow. "I need help with this."

"Oh, sorry," Sarah stammered. "Which problem?" When she'd helped Elizabeth solve the equation, she returned to her own thoughts. *I want to conquer my fear of Robert. He can't really hurt me. Sticks and stones.* She decided to confront him. Well, not confront, exactly. Start a discussion around a topic she knew well. But what could that be? Robert always seemed to know more about anything than anybody else, except maybe his mother. Mrs. Hall had been a school teacher, so she knew a lot. That must be the answer. She'd study up on something and then bring it up at dinner.

She saw an opportunity one night after Robert returned from a debate tournament in Sioux Falls, She swallowed hard and blurted out her fool proof point of view. "It must be easier to debate *for* prohibition than *against* it, since alcohol is an evil substance."

"That may be *your* opinion. It's not everyone's. And you're not an authority. Only *their* opinions count. To win the debate you need *proof* or *convincing evidence* that alcohol is evil."

Sarah's confidence disintegrated into confusion. The snake had struck. As his venom took effect, blood rushed to her face. His piercing blue eyes seemed to penetrate her paralyzed brain before he looked away, dismissing her as irrelevant. Mrs. Hall interjected, "Just a minute, Robert." But Sarah, devastated, heard only a buzz as Mrs. Hall defended her position.

With the advent of spring, Sarah looked forward to going home. She liked the Halls, but her feelings about Robert vacillated. She hated him when he treated her like a stupid little sister, but she wanted to impress him, convince him she was intelligent. Shortly before her departure, she decided to engage him in discussing American writers. He praised Mark Twain for *Huckleberry Finn* and *Tom Sawyer*. When she mentioned Louisa May Alcott, he brushed

Alcott off as a writer of children's stories. She pointed out that Huck and Tom were young boys, after all.

Robert shook his head and accused her of being ridiculous. "Twain deals with the race issue, writes about the Civil War."

She knew she was on shaky ground. But his put down wasn't as devastating as it might have been.

Back home, she resumed her boring responsibility for the hen house and the garden. She spent as much time as possible with the adored Charlie, now a toddler, trying to suppress her eagerness to return to Hughitt. The harvest was barely completed when Peder had a heart attack. The doctor told him he was lucky this time but warned him to slow down—the next could be fatal. They all knew Peder could slow down about as easily as the north wind could stop blowing across Dakota. Sarah offered to stay home, not return to Hughitt for her junior year, but she was grateful that Minnie would not allow her to drop out even temporarily.

When Ed drove her into Hughitt, she tearfully asked him to talk to Peder.

"Your pa wants to work until he drops," Ed said. "He needs to be in the thick of things. He's always striving for a better harvest, the healthiest livestock. I'm doing all he'll let me do to lighten his load. The next months are the easiest. We'll be working on machinery and planning for next spring." Ed reined in the horse in front of the house, jumped out of the wagon to tie up at the hitching post, and helped Sarah with her bags.

Within a week, Sarah's concerns shifted from her father's health to her courses and the articles she was writing for the *Hughtonian*, the school newspaper. Compliments from students and teachers and a growing friendship with John Anderson, her editor, armored her with new-found confidence, and a desire and determination to be editor herself when John graduated. She also felt bold enough to ask Robert, now a college student, if he thought she should join the debate team.

"No, you're not cut out for it," Robert responded when she raised the issue at dinner.

"Why?" She envisioned the snake coiling, and felt her anger rising.

"You're too emotional. Like most girls. You're not logical or analytical."

Mrs. Hall gasped. "Robert, what are you saying? You need to apologize to Sarah and me. Women may express their feelings more freely than men. That doesn't mean we can't think intelligently. That attitude is one obstacle in women getting the vote. I'm shocked that *my* son said that."

Sarah covered her mouth with a napkin to conceal a smile. She relished Mrs. Hall's taking Robert down a notch.

"Mother, I didn't mean you."

After she turned out the bed lamp and pulled the patchwork quilt up under her chin, Sarah reviewed the scene at dinner. What is it about Robert that attracts me? His sharp tongue? His endless knowledge? The impossibility of winning an argument with him? The challenge? He is smart, good looking if you don't mind the red hair. John, my new friend, appreciates me more. And he isn't arrogant like Robert. I can't see Robert working in a field. He probably looks down on farmers. Maybe that isn't fair. He's never said anything to denigrate them. But tonight—his contempuous attitude toward women. I'll show him I can be analytical and logical. I'll investigate the history of women's suffrage and write an outstanding essay. As she was falling asleep, Sarah asked herself: *Is it possible to love someone you don't like very much?*

That winter Sarah saw less of Robert, whose college activities kept him long hours on campus. Late in the evening she might find him in the kitchen searching for leftovers in the ice box. She'd reheat food for him and sit while he ate and told her about his college life. She was grateful Mrs. Hall went to bed early and she had Robert all to herself. She hoped to tell him about the suffrage movement paper that both her civics teacher and his mother had praised. But Robert was full of himself—more a puffed-up adder than a rattle snake.

When she met him in the kitchen a week before her departure for the farm, she told him John Anderson had asked her to the prom. He seemed not to hear or notice. Instead, he began lecturing her on the differences between Hobbes and Locke, Bentham and Mill, philosophers he'd been reading for his political science course. She tried to understand the essentials and to feel good about the possibility that he believed she comprehended what he was saying. Later, after he'd eaten a sandwich, he looked at her, his head cocked, "John Anderson. Isn't he the editor of the school paper?"

As always, Sarah was eager to see her parents after the long winter, but her pleasure faded when her father came in from the barn for dinner. She tried to conceal her surprise at the new streaks of white in his hair, his haggard look, his shrunken frame. She guessed her mother's agitation reflected her awareness of Peder's declining health.

She resumed her daily playtime with Charlie, and looked forward to the nights when Kari, Ed, and Charlie ate dinner at the homestead. Ed was more chatty than Peder, and curious about Sarah's life in Hughitt. She described her courses, class papers, and articles she'd written for the school paper, and her dream of becoming editor. She talked enthusiastically about the Halls, except Robert. She'd partitioned off those confused feelings in her private mental lair, not to be revealed or exposed to anyone.

One night Kari asked her to talk about the paper she'd written on the Suffragettes.

"Suffra*gists* in this country. Suffra*gettes* in England." Sarah looked at her father and brother-in-law. "What do you men think about women having the right to vote?"

"It's unfair that I can vote and your mother can't," Peder answered. "I wasn't born here, so I can never be president. Can a woman be president if she vas born here, though she can't vote? Vat do you think, Ed?"

"Sarah should look that up in the constitution. I think the idea is too farfetched to even be considered. I haven't given much thought to women voting, but I know many men oppose it. A mill worker back in Wisconsin put it bluntly. He said women would vote for prohibition."

Sarah took a deep breath, "Mrs. Hall told me that liquor interests have spent lots of money to defeat equal suffrage amendments in Wisconsin. Other states too. Do you believe women should be deprived of the vote because they might disagree with men on an issue?"

"Maybe not, but if they don't get the vote, we won't have to worry about prohibition. I'd be very annoyed if I couldn't legally have a bottle of beer occasionally. And Peder would certainly miss his hard cider."

"What do you think, Kari?" Sarah asked before she turned to her mother, "Ma, you've said before that you don't think it's so important."

Kari was looking at Ed, annoyance registered on her face. He looked sheepish. "I didn't say I wouldn't support women's suffrage, but I'd like reassurance I won't be deprived of a minor pleasure. Sarah, you must have heard about the WCTU, the Women's Christian Temperance Union? Or Carrie Nation? She's been going around with a hatchet chopping up bars in Kansas."

"I heard that she read from the Bible and sang hymns. I guess she did get out of hand in Wichita…throwing rocks at liquor and beer bottles in saloons."

"Now it's 'hatchitation.' You don't want to be associated with that battleaxe."

Sarah dropped the discussion. She didn't want to fight with Ed. For one thing, she didn't know where she stood. She remembered

Robert's comment about needing evidence that alcohol caused bad behavior. She'd never seen her father or Ed drunk or even tipsy. On the other hand, she'd heard Mrs. Hall talk about women who suffered because their husbands drank up their weekly paycheck. She guessed there was a lot she didn't know.

But she wouldn't forget Ed's comments. She'd expected him to be supportive of equal rights for women. If good men like Ed were indifferent or negative, she understood why women had not yet achieved suffrage. At that moment she decided she'd have to join the fight someday.

Toward the end of the school year, she focused on helping John put the final edition of the *Hughtonian* to bed. "I have bad news, Sarah," he said. "I tried to convince Mr. Martin that you should be editor next year. But he's picked Richard Olson. I'm sorry…and angry because you deserve it."

Sarah was shocked. She'd been so sure she'd win that prize. A surge of anger and determination not to cry forged her response. "Forget it, John. A male faculty advisor will never pick a girl to be editor of the paper."

"You're probably right."

She needed to change the subject before her real feelings came pouring out. "My brother-in-law has got me thinking about prohibition and maybe writing a paper about it. What do you know about Carrie Nation?"

"A crazy, wild lady. I guess she believes she's saving souls. The WCTU is more reasonable. They don't go around with hatchets. You should write an article on prohibition for next year's paper. But don't start yet," he said with a grin. "Help me decorate the gym for the prom. In a moment of weakness, I volunteered my services."

"I'd love to." She looked forward to the dance and decorating the gym sounded like fun. "I should warn you. I don't really know how to dance."

"That makes two of us. We can take turns stepping on each other's feet," he said. "Only you'll get the worst of it. I must weigh half again as much as you do."

When prom night came, she danced with several boys, including two who gave her instruction. With her enthusiasm and a natural sense of rhythm, she caught on quickly and guided John through waltzes and two-steps. Although she later described the evening glowingly, the main event for Sarah was John's good night kiss. Her first. She would have floated into the house in a bubble if he hadn't broken the spell.

"I've been wondering when I'll see you again. I graduate next Friday and start working at the James River Daily the next day. I'd like to show you around the press room before the summer is over…if you're interested."

"Congratulations. I know you wanted a job there. I'd love that tour."

"I'm only a copy boy, but it's a start. Journalism may not be as profitable as some professions, but I think it'll be more interesting than most."

"You're lucky. I don't know what I want to do. Except I don't think I want to get married. Or be a teacher or a nurse. Those seem to be the only choices for girls."

During the summer, Sarah and John picnicked four times on the banks of the Jim River. She'd bring the lunch and he'd bring a book of Robert Browning's poetry. On Wednesday nights, they listened to band concerts in Winter Park. As soon as he got acquainted with the staff and got their permission, he gave her a tour of the newspaper quarters. He warned her about catcalls and whistles in the city room. Forewarned, she kept her composure.

Early in the fall, he got permission for her to sit in his American History class at Hughitt College. After class, she enthused about the professor. "He knows so much about Jefferson and the

Louisiana Purchase. I knew we bought it from France, but I didn't know farmers had problems exporting from New Orleans and that the Spanish started the trouble by withdrawing the right of deposit. I hope I can come here next year and take history from him."

As they approached the central corridor, she asked, "Do you ever see Robert Hall?"

"Of course. He's everywhere, doing everything. Robert is our famous debater, our state champion extemporaneous speaker. Are you infatuated with him? Most girls seem to be. Personally, I think Robert is an arrogant ass."

"*John,* what language! What a question! Robert *is* interesting, but I'm not infatuated." *At least I don't think so.* Nevertheless, she could hardly wait to move back to town for her senior year. That, she told herself, is because farm life is boring.

But her restlessness persisted after she returned to town. She tried to conceal her discontent and focus on her writing. But she resented working with Richard Olson, her new editor, who had the position she thought she deserved. Remembering John's advice, she researched and wrote an essay about prohibition, focusing on the WCTU—an organization also supportive of women's rights—and Carrie Nation's outrageous behavior. Richard showed little interest, but John praised her efforts and convinced his city editor to publish her essay in the *James River Daily.*

When Sarah saw her name in print in a real newspaper, she felt transformed; thrilled at this recognition. Her bitter disappointment at not being the editor of the *Hughitonian* almost evaporated and her interest in a career in journalism intensified. Were there any women journalists? She hadn't seen any in the city press room. Maybe she'd be the first. Curious about the reactions of Mrs. Hall and Robert, Sarah hoped one of them would mention her achievement at dinner. She couldn't bring it up herself. Mrs. Hall did eventually acknowledge Sarah's writing and thorough research, but Sarah caught an implied criticism of her neutrality, her failure to support prohibition totally. Robert was not home that night, so Sarah could only suppose that he would have approved her effort to present both positions.

On nights when Robert was home for dinner, the conversation inevitably focused on his future. Where should *he* study law? Minnesota, Wisconsin, Michigan? Or Harvard, Yale, Columbia? Financial support was critical, but everyone assumed Robert would be admitted to whichever school he chose. Sarah's verbal contributions were limited to what her brother said about Minnesota. Otherwise she sat quietly, wishing the day would never come for Robert to leave Hughitt. She also began anticipating how much she would miss living in this house next winter.

Sarah's graduation from high school carried less significance for her than the scholarship she received for Hughitt College. She suspected, but never knew if Mrs. Hall had played a role in her receiving that coveted award. She hoped the summer would pass quickly. As much as she loved her family, she'd increasingly wished to escape the labors and limitations of farm life. She felt no remorse in moving into the dormitory long before the harvest was over. Peder's health had stabilized and Minnie had accepted Sarah's departure and moved on to being a grandmother to little Charlie and his new baby sister.

The more time Sarah spent with John, between and after classes, the more her interest in journalism grew. As her knowledge of history, politics, and economics increased, she began to dream of being an effective voice for women's suffrage and equal rights. Her enthusiasm escalated when John told her that he'd been promised a job as a reporter. Maybe, with his help, she could get a job at the paper. Secretary or typist? Copy boy? Could there be a copy girl?

"It's worth a try," John responded. "But I don't know that I can help. I haven't been there long, so my recommendation won't mean much. And there's the gender problem. All the reporters are men, and they do their own typing. There are no girls anywhere at the newspaper."

Why are men referred to as men and women as girls? Sarah asked herself. "Time for a change," she declared. "I'm going to make it somehow."

CHAPTER 7
Back and Forth

Sarah's spirits soared when she received a dinner invitation from Mrs. Hall. The occasion was Robert's visit during Christmas vacation. He'd only been home once since he'd left for Yale Law School, a visit Sarah had missed. Her eagerness to see him trumped an underlying fear that she would make a poor showing, that he'd expose her deficiency in whatever they discussed.

She wanted her enthusiasm to quash her family's growing belief—especially Kari's—that she was serious about John Anderson. She *had* spent many hours with him and his recent talk about moving to Chicago to work for a newspaper had alarmed her. How would she manage without the person who understood her best of all, her best friend? She believed her brain would shrivel, undernourished, without John or Robert around.

Everyone liked John, even Peder who said with deep feeling, "He knows an awful lot about farming for a town boy."

Sarah's response was, "He spent many summers working on his grandparents' farm in Iowa." She wanted her family to approve of John, but she didn't like Kari making more of the friendship than it was. She felt too young for a serious relationship.

On invitation day, Sarah pleaded with Ed to drive her to the Hall's in his new 1904 Model-A Ford, purchased after an unusually good harvest and livestock sale. But it had been snowing all day, so Ed, unsure of the reliability of his new contraption, apologized but insisted on taking the sleigh. "I'm sorry, Sarah, your wish to impress Robert by arriving in a new-fangled, horseless carriage has been buried in two feet of snow."

After hugging Elizabeth, Eleanor, and Mrs. Hall, she stood facing Robert. He gave her a peck on the cheek and helped her remove her coat. Before she could thank him, Elizabeth had grabbed her elbow and ushered her into the parlor to sit between the hearth, ablaze with a crackling fire, and a Christmas tree decorated with colorful bulbs, popcorn, and candles. Robert offered her mulled cider and Eleanor passed a plate of cheese and crackers. As Sarah nibbled on a piece of cheddar, she watched Robert poke at the fire and add a small log. The shifting flames cast shadows that highlighted his classical features and red hair. His looks haven't changed, she decided. Has his personality?

Uncomfortable with the silence, Sarah stammered, "You've built a wonderful fire." She awaited a sarcastic retort.

"How do you like Hughitt College? Did any of my recommendations work out?"

Had he missed an opportunity? His gaze, focused on her now, seemed to penetrate her skull, expose her thoughts, and create disorder. "Professor Carpenter's history courses are wonderful. Literature is next. Not the professors as much as the Shakespeare plays we're reading." She felt prepared to discuss Hamlet or Othello, but she appreciated Mrs. Hall announcing dinner before "wonderful" slipped out of her mouth again.

"Tell me about Yale, living in the East," she said after she'd taken her old place at the table across from Robert.

"Law school is tough, but I'm doing well—thanks to classmates who only do enough work to earn Cs. No worry for them about a job after they graduate. They'll be going into their father's law firms in New York and Boston. With a little more work, I look good."

Has Robert lost some of his arrogance? "Will you stay in the east or will you return when you graduate? She wasn't sure she wanted to know, but she had to ask.

"I've made important contacts at Yale. I could make more money in the east. But I haven't decided. Tell me about you. Mother says you've had essays published in the *James River Daily*. Congratulations. Are you thinking about journalism as a career?"

"Yes, thinking about it. Mr. Layton, the editor at the *Daily*, won't hire women. I'm not sure why. He definitely doesn't want females in the city room. He says he'll buy my essays if he likes them. He might even hire me to do the Society page, if I do my writing at home."

"He's protecting you from the reporters—their crude language and behavior—and saving himself from a revolt. Women are not accepted in a city room culture. If you're really serious about being a journalist, you may have to leave Hughitt. Big city newspapers like *The New York World* or *The Sun* have hired women. I'm sure you've heard of Nellie Bly, the 'stunt' reporter, famous over night by committing herself to a mental asylum to expose how inhumane those institutions are. Then she traveled around the world in less time than Phineas Fogg."

"I'm not as clever as Nellie Bly, nor as brave." What could she say? Should she be flattered Robert thought of Nellie Bly while discussing her interest in journalism?

"Or as self-promoting," he added. "Bly is a phenomenon. But you're a good writer. Take the Society page job and keep writing intelligent essays about equal rights, women's suffrage, and whatever fires your imagination. Who knows? Layton may change his mind, or you might decide to tackle a big city paper."

Robert's comments drove Sarah to the college library the next day where she was reading articles by and about Nellie Bly. When John joined her, he suggested she read next about Margaret Fuller, "A brilliant New England Transcendentalist. She was made editor of *The Dial*, a literary magazine, by Ralph Waldo Everson. Later Horace Greeley, *The New York Tribune* editor, hired her. She not only reviewed art and literature, he eventually appointed her a foreign correspondent and sent her travelling all over Europe. And all this happened before 1850."

"She sounds more impressive than Bly. How did you know about her?"

"Professor Roberts wrote his doctoral dissertation on Transcendentalism. You should take his philosophy course. Hey, let's go outside. I'm tired of libraries and classrooms. Besides, spring has sprung."

They left Davis Hall and walked toward the main drag. The sun, high in a cloudless azure sky, had begun its descent as they strolled north beneath the bare American elms that lined Dakota Avenue. The distinctive call of a cardinal jarred Sarah out of her lingering thoughts of women reporters. She looked for the red bird, as she and Minnie had done when they listened for meadowlarks while picking wild flowers in the meadow. His bright color made him easy to spot on a high branch of a leafless tree.

John broke their silence. "I'm going to Chicago in June."

"June!" Instinctively, Sarah hooked her arm in his, as if to hold him back. "Why now? Why not wait until you have your bachelor's degree?"

"Experience is more important to me. I wish I were in San Francisco right now reporting on that earthquake and fire that killed more than 500 people. I've got to get to a big city newspaper." He hesitated. "Will you walk with me to the station? I need a train schedule."

Sarah didn't know what to say. She'd been warned, but she hadn't expected him to leave Hughitt this year. "My family will be terribly sad to see you leave." *Kari, especially. She's been hoping for wedding bells.*

"How about you? Won't you miss me?"

"Of course. Life without you will be bleak. Who will I talk to?" She stopped, suddenly inspired. "John, take me with you."

"Sarah, I'd marry you in a second if I had any money…that is, if you'd marry me."

Sarah looked down, trying to identify her feelings. "Why get married? I'm not ready to make that commitment."

"I know that you don't know what you want to be or do and I don't have the money to get married. But it wouldn't look right for us to go to Chicago together unmarried."

"I *do* know I don't want to be a farm wife, not like my mother...or Kari. At least Kari didn't have to start from scratch like Ma and Pa. And she has her horses, her first love."

"I admire your mother for not wavering from her commitment to Peder. I doubt she had any idea how tough farm life would be in Dakota when she married him."

Images of the trip to St. Paul, Willie's death, and the sad trip back to Dakota on the train flashed through Sarah's head. *Someday I'll tell John that my mother was fed up with farm life once, that she defied Peder. But not now.* Choking back tears, she said, "I love and respect my mother, but I don't want her life."

John put his arms around her. "Sarah, I love you too much to take you to Chicago with me now. I don't know what I'll find when I get there. It's certainly too risky for you. Once I get settled and get the lay of the land, we'll try to figure something out."

That night Sarah's sleep was punctuated with a recurring dream of arriving at a train station just as her train was pulling away. She didn't know where it was going, but she knew she had to be on it. In the morning she concluded she couldn't catch the train because she was a girl. Alone. Even spunky, unconventional Nellie Bly took her mother to New York with her. Sarah could not, would not ask Minnie to accompany her, to be separated from Kari and her grandchildren. But why couldn't she, Sarah, live in her own room in the same rooming house as John? Because single men and woman lived in different boarding houses, she guessed. Stupid mores! Ridiculous. What if they claimed to be cousins or brother and sister? Would that make a difference?

Later she sat in class, unable to concentrate. College had lost its flavor. More than anything, she wanted to go with John. Age was not the issue. John was only twenty-two, but being a man he could come and go as he wanted. Being a woman, she could not. Ever!

Four weeks later she stood on the Chicago North Western platform with jagged feelings, determined not to cry. It would be easier if John's parents were present, if he had not insisted they say goodbye at home.

"This is it, Sarah. I'll let you know how things go. Write to me every day."

She threw her arms around his neck and pulled him toward her for a kiss that was more bitter than sweet. She stepped back when the conductor called "All aboard!" and John reached for two suitcases that held most of his belongings. After she waved, she waited, searching for his face in a window. When he appeared, she waved again and he threw her a kiss. As the train began to move, gaining speed, John was lost from sight and she began to cry. She stumbled back to the dormitory, oblivious of the people staring at her.

Sarah began to pack as soon as she got back to her dorm room. Ed wouldn't arrive for two days to take her home, but she had to keep busy. Thinking about another summer cleaning up after the noisy, smelly chickens almost brought her to tears again. Abruptly, she slammed shut her suitcase, examined her ankle length blue dress with the white collar, decided her clothing was appropriate, and rushed out of the room. She stopped in the lavatory to splash cold water on her face, and tidy up her hair. She wanted to look fresh, neat, and bright-eyed as she searched for a summer job in the town center. If she were offered a position, she'd see about boarding with Mrs. Hall.

She passed a livery stable and a saloon before she came to the Miller Block, a row of adjoining brick buildings with shops on the ground level and offices on the second floor. The first stop, a music store, spurred her imagination. If she worked there, she could probably buy sheet music for Minnie at a discount. The owner apologized; he employed only his family.

Next, Sarah climbed the enclosed stairway, an ascending dark tunnel, to George Miner's law office on the second floor. Lawyers needed secretaries, Sarah told herself. The fact she had known Mr. Miner's son in high school might count for something. Hope evaporated when the elderly woman who greeted her in the outer office returned to her typewriter after notifying Mr. Miner about the young woman who wished to see him.

Mr. Miner—tall, gaunt, balding, and middle-aged—brushed aside Sarah's reference to his son and pointed out that he already had a good secretary. But he appreciated her college background. "Would you be interested in legal research, searching for cases in these dusty old tomes?" He gestured toward two walls of floor to ceiling bookcases.

She hadn't expected anything like this. "I'm interested, but can I do it?"

"Basically, all you'd have to do is locate relevant cases for me. I'd give you lots of guidance at first. You've done library research for papers, right?"

"Yes. Oh, if that's all, I think I'd love the job." She wasn't certain she'd love it, but she desperately wanted work. Apparently, he thought she could handle it.

After they discussed how much she'd need to live in town and support herself, they agreed on ten dollars a week, her employment to begin in two weeks. She didn't tell him she wanted the time to visit her family and convince them she could manage on her own.

Before returning to the dormitory, Sarah visited Mrs. Hall, to be certain she could board there.

"The girls and I will love having you here again," Mrs. Hall enthused when Sarah told her the news. "You can have your old room, or Robert's. Eleanor has taken over your room, but she'd move out in no time to please you."

The thought of living, sleeping in Robert's room rattled Sarah. She knew she wouldn't be able to resist looking through his books, papers, whatever he'd left behind. It'd be interesting, she thought, and creepy. I'll feel like a Peeping Tom. "Mrs. Hall, I'll stay wherever you wish." Seconds later, she added, "Really, I don't think Eleanor should have to move on my account. I'll move into Robert's room two weeks from now."

With arrangements settled, they had tea in the parlor. Sarah learned that Mrs. Hall was about to begin work on women's suffrage and that Robert was still undecided about what kind of law he wanted to practice. Mrs. Hall also mentioned she was reading *History of Standard Oil*, a book he had recommended. Ida Tarbell, author and reporter, had acquired the title of muckraker because she collected data from public records and exposed questionable practices of John D. Rockefeller and the oil company.

"Robert read the book because one of his interests is antitrust law. If this interest overrides others, he'll stay in the east where the big corporations are. When he recommended the book to me, he said you might be interested in this woman reporter whose approach is unique."

Sarah only listened, but she knew she'd ask her new boss about antitrust law.

Edward arrived at the college to take Sarah home in the red Ford. Though Ed's was not the only car in town, they were rare and attracted the curious like gawkers at an accident scene. Sarah thanked him for this unexpected treat before she told him about her plan to work in town over the summer and to board with Mrs. Hall. She expected his approval.

"Don't you think you should have discussed this with us before you made plans?" The question and the tone of Ed's voice made it clear he disapproved. "Your mother needs you. Peder is not well and Minnie does many of his old chores. Kari is going to be very angry with you."

"I will be making money. I'll be able to pay for college myself. I think everyone should be happy about that." She was miserable and confused—one minute feeling angry at Ed and Kari for expecting her to come home every summer, and the next minute feeling guilty and sad for Peder and Minnie. Her worst nightmare was giving up all her dreams, becoming a spinster, living in the country and caring for an aging mother.

To Sarah, nothing seemed to have changed on the farm, except Peder's aging. The early struggle, the years Mother Nature conspired against him, had taken their toll and at fifty-nine he was an old man. By contrast, Minnie, also in her fifties, seemed healthy and vital. With only a few streaks of gray in her hair, she had hardly aged. When Sarah told them of her plan to return to Hughitt, she ignored the immediate silence and the quizzical look that crossed her mother's face. Minnie recovered quickly. "We'll miss you terribly, but I'm happy for you if that's what you want."

Peder's response surprised Sarah more, since he usually agreed with Minnie. "You don't have to verk. We've had good harvests for two years. I hate to think my baby girl has to verk."

"Pa, I want to work. You should understand. You're a workhorse if there ever was one."

Peder shrugged. "There's always verk on the farm. Minnie and I can keep you busy."

Sarah let that go. She hadn't expected any argument, but having her mother's blessing was all she needed.

On her second night home Kari, Ed, and their three children arrived for dinner. Sarah, sensitive to Kari's icy greeting, offered to help her and Minnie as they finished dinner preparation. "Never mind," Kari said. "Just keep an eye on baby Marion." After dinner Kari pulled Sarah aside. "I want to talk to you. Let's go outside." The sisters walked in silence toward the meadow. The vast star-studded sky lit up the meadow, making a lantern unnecessary. Sarah regretted not knowing more about the treasures overhead. They stopped to listen to a coyote in the direction of the Wessington Hills. Then Kari spoke.

"I don't understand you. How can you be so uncaring? You can see Pa is in terrible health. Don't you understand how much Ma needs you? I spend as much time here as I can, but I have my hands full with three children. I think you should be ashamed of yourself."

"I thought I'd be helping the family by making money to pay for my college."

"I don't believe you. You just want to get away from the farm. I'd say 'fine' if Pa was healthy and Ma wasn't under so much strain. You're selfish, Sarah, and impulsive. That's the truth. You don't really care about us. You only think of yourself."

"Not true." Sarah fought back tears. "How can you say such horrible things? I love all of you." But she knew Kari was partly right. Maybe that's why it hurt so much. "I'm committed to the job now."

"Well, you can uncommit."

"Kari, you don't understand. You don't know what it's like to be on your own."

"You don't have to be. Come home. I'm totally unsympathetic with your being alone, unmarried. You let John Anderson get away. I guess you thought you were too good for him."

"Stop it, Kari. You don't know anything about my relationship with John."

"I know you're not married and he's gone to Chicago."

"I hope to join him after he gets a good job and can afford a wife." What was she saying? Why was Kari doing this to her?

"You're engaged!" Kari's voice echoed across the prairie.

"Shhush, Kari. No," She was afraid to say more, to get trapped in a morass of her own making. "Kari, you're like a bull terrier that's got hold of something and won't let go. I feel bad for Ma and Pa, but I'm not going to give up the job. Ma wants me to do what's best for me."

"You always were Ma's pet. And a stubborn brat, always headstrong, had to have your own way. You'll be sorry someday. Wait and see. I have to go back to the house now. It's long past Marion's bedtime. I should have known talking to you wouldn't make a difference."

For two weeks Sarah struggled to be the perfect daughter. She responded to Minnie's and Peder's requests without complaint. She helped with the barn animals and kept the henhouse as clean as possible. She felt no regret when Peder wrung the necks of two old hens and then chopped off their heads. As she stepped back from the spurting blood, she wondered if Minnie would ask her to clean and pluck them. She'd seen her mother do it many times, but she had always been spared. *Maybe I have been Ma's favorite.* She didn't mind looking at the entrails—in fact, they fascinated her—but she cringed at the thought of touching them.

She survived two weeks by dreaming about her return to Hughitt. Minnie's questions about the job at the lawyers left her feeling less guilty, convinced her mother was living vicariously through her. What troubled her most was not hearing from John. She ran to the mailbox every day, only to return empty-handed. He must be settled somewhere by now, she thought. I hope he's busy at work and he hasn't found a new girlfriend.

Once the idea of a girlfriend entered her head, she couldn't shake her mushrooming fears. Why wouldn't John fall for a sophisticated Chicagoan? He must meet many women more intelligent and more beautiful than she. Was that his reason for not writing? Or did John's love of reporting surpass all other interests?

When Ed arrived in the Ford to take her to town, she asked if Kari had told him about their fight.

"I told you she'd be upset. She's afraid that Peder will have another heart attack, maybe die, and Minnie will be alone, unable to get help. You could be moral and physical support. I've looked into getting telephones, but the phone companies are barely beginning to service towns like Hughitt. They won't be out in the country for quite a while."

Sarah felt bad, but she said nothing. Both were silent for the rest of the trip.

While Ed was removing Sarah's bags from the car, Mrs. Hall walked out to inspect the red Model-A. "There are more horseless carriages in town every day," she said. "We're truly entering a new era."

CHAPTER 8
Another Goodbye

Sarah's "new era" began with a paying job, a return to Mrs. Hall's, and anxiety over John's failure to write. After two days of climbing ladders to reach upper shelves, her sore legs told her she'd been hired as much for her youth as her college background. She wondered how Mr. Miner or Miss Bailey, both middle-aged or more, had ever managed without her.

Nevertheless, Sarah liked her job. Mr. Miner responded with patience and good humor when she bombarded him with questions or failed to find the cases he needed.

One day she said, "A friend of mine may specialize in antitrust law. Can you tell me something about it?"

"The 1890 Sherman Act is an effort to eliminate abuses of big corporations. Doesn't affect me directly. I only work for individuals and small businesses, not monopolies like Standard Oil. Can't tell you much else."

Sarah's move into the Hall's presented no challenges with Robert away at school. Immediately, she eyed the poetry, novels, history, and text books that filled his bookcase and couldn't resist looking through them. His marginal comments were gems that often determined what she read at bedtime. She doubted that Robert with his professorial tendencies would mind. Didn't impressing others always give him great satisfaction? She eventually immersed herself in *War and Peace*, in a Russian world she could not have imagined. The character, Pierre, reminded her of Robert, and she identified with the young spirited Natasha, though they had little in common except youth.

During her second week on the job, Ed made an unexpected visit to Mr. Miner's office. Sarah, high up on a ladder when he walked in, descended quickly, afraid he was bringing bad news. She didn't relax until he smiled. She introduced him to Miss Bailey and learned that Mr. Miner was in conference with a client.

"I'll meet him some other time," Ed said. "I was in town to buy grain and brought these for you." He handed Sarah two letters, bearing a Chicago return address. "Minnie gave them to me this morning when I stopped by to see what she needed from town."

As soon as Ed left, Sarah confirmed the handwriting was John's and buried the letters in her bag. She knew the day would drag on forever now. She returned Miss Bailey's questioning smile with her own, but without an explanation.

That evening Sarah excused herself as soon after dinner as she could. Alone in her room, she ripped open the letter with the earliest postmark. In this short first letter John told her he'd found a boarding house close to the Loop, the business district defined by the elevated railroad, an area that included several newspapers. He'd start his search for a job the next day. He missed her, wished all was well at the farm, and hoped to hear from her soon.

The second letter was dated two days after the first.

Dear Sarah,   June 2, 1906

I spent yesterday morning at the library reading newspapers. By lunch time I knew I would try the Chicago Tribune and the Chicago Daily News first. The Tribune is the oldest and is probably the most prestigious.

The Daily News appeals because it recently established a foreign news service. If I fail to get a job at either of these, there are seven more newspapers in this city, including two Hearst publications.

Wish me luck. I have no idea what my chances are.

My boarding house is close enough to the elevated for convenience, but far enough away so the house doesn't shake every time a train goes by. I experienced that twice before I found this place.

Four other men live here. Two of them work on the Union elevated railroad. The five of us meet at 5:30 when Mrs. Caine, the proprietor, serves supper. The food is not the greatest, but she is a nice woman who keeps a clean house and tries hard to please. Although none of the boarders talk much, they've all asked me about Dakota. I've told them the Homestead Act is still in effect and cheap land is still to be had. Then I emphasize that sod busting is no picnic.

When will I ever hear from you? I hope the chickens haven't done you in. Please write soon and tell me how much you miss me. I miss you too much.

I Love You,

John

She started a letter to John as soon as she'd reread his to tell him where she was. Having his first two letters arrive at the farm was good, because they informed Kari that she and John were in touch. But from now on, she wanted her mail to come to Hughitt. She wrote about her job and staying with Mrs. Hall. She did not mention Robert Hall's room or his books. Undecided at first, she wrote about her argument with Kari. Half aware she was looking for support, she ended by asking John if he thought she was selfish.

His response surprised her. "Most people are selfish. Maybe you're more selfish or self-centered than the majority of women who put their children's and husband's needs above their own. After all you are pretty determined to have a career. I think men typically act in their own best interest, yet they can and often behave heroically, like rushing into a burning building to save someone. Women can be heroic too, especially when it comes to children."

Sarah was annoyed initially, but dismissed his seeing her as less than perfect, and rejoiced at the news that he had been hired by the *Chicago Daily News*. He couldn't tell her much yet, only that his first assignments would be local. He deemed this a test period when he would be evaluated for his reporting skills. He wanted to hear more about her situation, and questioned her about Robert's visits home and where he intended to practice law. Was she still committed to journalism? Had she written any more articles for the *James River Daily*? Had the job in the law office affected her interests? She wasn't thinking about law school, was she?

Ed's second visit to Sarah's workplace came toward the end of summer. This time he had a request from Minnie that Sarah return to the farm for a few days before she moved back into the college dormitory. Sarah couldn't deny her mother this simple request and agreed with Ed on a date when he would come to take her home. She hated to leave Robert's room with all the books she wanted to read, but she'd be leaving soon for the dormitory anyway. She had managed to finish *War and Peace,* loving it once she mastered the complicated Russian names. She struggled through the ending, less interested in Tolstoy's philosophy of war and history than his specific descriptions of Russian life and the Napoleonic war. She would never tell Robert that she'd only skimmed the two epilogues.

Before her departure, Mr. Miner asked her to work for him during the school year on a schedule she could dictate. Sarah accepted reluctantly, not wanting to sacrifice valuable writing time. If Mr. Layton had offered her anything more than a once-a-week Society section, she might have rejected Mr. Miner's offer.

On the way to the farm, Ed warned, "You know your father is not doing well."

"How are Ma and Kari and the children?" Sarah longed for positive news.

"My family is thriving. Charlie is a great kid, and the girls are sweet. Minnie is worn out. Kari wanted me to ask you how John is doing. Will he stay in Chicago?"

"John is a reporter on one of Chicago's best newspapers. He'll stay there, unless he becomes a foreign correspondent. If he achieves that, I guess he could be located anywhere in the world. Right now, his reporting is mostly in Chicago. He did go to Springfield when the state legislature was in session."

Minnie's appearance shocked Sarah more than Peder's anticipated decline. Always petite, Minnie had never looked haggard or frail before. Both women were on the verge of tears when they embraced. Later, Sarah would learn that Minnie not only worried about Peder's physical condition, she also suffered from nagging guilt for her defiance of him, for sneaking off to St. Paul with the children against his wishes. Worst of all, she blamed herself for Willie's death, for taking him on a long train ride away from his home when he was ill.

"Pa forgave you long ago for leaving him like that." Sarah struggled to understand why her mother was obsessing over these past events. "Willie would have died of pneumonia wherever he was." Mentioning Willie, remembering his last days, brought tears to Sarah's eyes. *Does one ever get over a loss so devastating?* She'd thought about death a lot because she still missed Willie. *And now poor Ma faces another loss she feels partly responsible for.*

Although Sarah had planned to stay a week at the farm, she realized that leaving so soon would burden her with guilt. By rescheduling her classes, she'd be on campus only three days a week and home before the evening meal. Mr. Miner regretfully accepted her apology for canceling plans to work for him.

She gradually got into the rhythm of the daily chores, the monotonous and distasteful routine. As before, the disgusting smells in the hen house and barn revolted her, but she loved to stroll across the prairie with her mother, listen to the melodic song of meadowlarks, and help Minnie pick small delicate blossoms or large yellow sunflowers for the seeds to be roasted in the evening. She saw a rosy pink glow return to Minnie's cheeks and a smile when they startled a gopher or rabbit. As they skirted the corn field, they'd often scare up a ring-necked pheasant with his colorful iridescent plumage and red wattles. She hated it when her father shot one of these beautiful birds, but she had to admit they were tasty.

Kari came almost daily with her children to visit and help out. Charlie fascinated Sarah. She imagined that she was to Charlie what Robert Hall had been to her. Only she, unlike Robert, would never put down this curious, eager-to-learn boy. He asked her endless questions about high school, even college, and living in town.

"Should I take Latin in high school? Physics and chemistry? I'm more interested in history and politics. Should I go to Hughitt College? I think I'd like to go out of state, like Uncle Matthew."

He shared his interest in the American Civil War, stimulated by reading articles in the Century Magazines Minnie had collected over a decade. Sarah asked him if he might be taking after his Uncle Joe, who'd made the cavalry his career. Charlie shook his head at the suggestion. "Aunt Sarah, did you ever read *The Red Badge of Courage?* If you did, you'd understand why I never want to be in a war."

"No. But I have friends who've read it. And I've read *War and Peace* about Russia and the war with Napoleon. You should read that when you get older. It's too long and philosophical for you right now."

The three women were preparing the large midday meal for the threshing team when Ed appeared, followed by two men carrying Peder. "He collapsed in the field. Kari, help Minnie and the men get him to bed. I'm going for the doctor."

Two hours later, the doctor told them what they already knew. Peder had suffered another heart attack. "Keep him in bed. His heart is failing. Frankly, I'm surprised he's survived this long. There's nothing I can do. There's no medicine for this."

"How do we keep him in bed?" Minnie asked. "He won't listen to us. Maybe he'll listen to you."

"He's a stubborn old cuss. I've warned him more than once, but I'll try again."

Peder did not return to the field. After one week, when he felt strong enough to get out of bed, Minnie and Sarah helped him walk to the table. As Minnie prepared his favorites, beef stew and apple pie, the fragrance of apple and cinnamon filled the house. But Peder only picked at his food. Efforts to lift his mood by reminding him of the abundant harvest had failed.

Suddenly, Charlie spoke up. "Grandpa, come outside with me. You need sunshine and fresh air." Peder smiled for the first time in days and accepted the offer. With Ed's support he went out to sit on a porch chair and absorb the late October sun. Charlie and Ed sat with him.

"Ma, go sit with him too. Kari and I will take care of the cleanup." When they were alone, Sarah said, "I was afraid he'd given up. Life isn't worth living if you can't work. That's been his philosophy. He should have stopped working long ago, but he would have been miserable. We've always known he'd work until he dropped. Ed has been wonderful, making it possible for him to be out there, doing what he could. I guess that's over now."

"How long are you planning to stay, Sarah?"

"Depends on Peder's health…and Minnie. I decided not to register for courses next semester, so I can be here full time. I've a good start on the courses this semester, so I'm hoping I can finish them. We'll see."

Peder's strength did not significantly improve, though Minnie and Sarah, at his insistence, helped him to a porch chair almost every day. The November sun lacked warmth, so they tucked blankets around him and brought him steaming hot coffee. Ed would join him toward noon and converse about the proceeds from the harvest, the current price of hogs, the machinery needing repair, and what they should be planning for spring planting.

Ed frequently stayed for the midday meal, leaving after Peder returned to bed for a nap that often lasted until supper time. As the sun was setting late one afternoon, Minnie went to check on him. He hadn't called her as he usually did when he awoke. Sarah was setting the table, expecting Ed and Kari and the children to arrive any moment, when Minnie, pale and trembling, came out of the bedroom.

As she reached for Sarah, Minnie let out an anguished cry, "He's gone." Sarah held her, trying to comprehend "gone." She knew his body was still there. *Where had his spirit gone?* Peder's heaven would be a wheat field or a sea of grass. *Why can I almost feel Minnie's pain, but not my own? Why are my feelings cut off, buried?*

Mother and daughter were standing in a frozen embrace when Ed and Kari arrived. Ed headed toward the bedroom as Minnie turned to Kari whose open arms encircled her. Sarah put her hand on Charlie's shoulder, not certain what he understood until she saw the tears welling up in his eyes.

"Grandpa's dead, isn't he?"

Sarah sighed and nodded. Did he feel as sad and lost as she felt when Willie died? Again, Ed left for the doctor. And not knowing what propelled her, she moved to the head of the table and removed the place setting. Kari was guiding Minnie to the piano when Sarah picked up baby Marion who had begun to cry in sympathy with her big sister. She tried to hush the baby who only stopped when Minnie began to play Bach's Prelude in C. Minnie's fingers stumbled at first but not at the second playing. The sweet music calmed everyone in the room, quiet now except for the soothing melody.

For five days after Peder's death, local farmers and their wives, Mr. Miner and Miss Bailey, Mrs. Hall and the two girls, and other acquaintances from town came to pay respects, to bring food and flowers. On the first day, Sarah asked a visitor to mail a letter to John, telling him about Peder's death and her dropping out of school.

On the day of the funeral, Sarah had little appetite, the knot in her stomach still unresolved, but she forced herself to eat to show appreciation for the church women who had prepared and served the meal. She worried mostly about Minnie, wondering how long before she'd recover from her benumbed, lost state. Meadow walks in springtime would help. And the piano. She'd convince Minnie to start playing Bach's Inventions and Mozart's sonatas again. *But will she ever stop missing Pa? They've been together over thirty years, had five children, and created this amazing homestead.*

Sarah watched the lowering of Peder's casket into the earth adjacent to Willie's resting place. She cried for both of them. Trying to gain control, she began to count the people standing on the far side of the graves. When she saw John partially hidden in the group, her heart began to pound. She hadn't expected him to receive her letter in time for this. She was happy to see him—if only it were under different circumstances. He approached her as she walked back to the carriage with Minnie and Matthew.

"I'm so sorry, Sarah." He paused. "May I come to your house tonight? I'm going home now. I haven't seen my parents yet."

"Of course. I'll be waiting." They embraced, a brief perfunctory hug, before he departed.

That evening Sarah waited patiently while John talked to the adults in the main room and presented each child with a book he'd purchased at Marshall Field's, "a very special store." Once alone on the porch, they kissed and held hands. He had a present for her too, but he didn't want her to open it until after he'd left.

"I'm waiting for you to tell me about your job," she said.

"It's cold out here. Aren't you cold?" He wrapped his arms around her. "The job is exciting. Chicago is a lively, unbelievable city. But my boss is sending me to Panama to interview the man in charge of clearing land and establishing quarantine facilities. This is in preparation to building a canal. The question is how successful he's been in eradicating mosquitoes, carriers of yellow fever and malaria."

"What if *you* catch yellow fever? Shouldn't he send someone older, more experienced? What do you know about Panama?"

"I think a couple of married reporters have begged off. Anyway, I'll never be a foreign correspondent if I'm afraid to go where it's dangerous. Now tell me about you?"

"I'm stuck here. If you mean when can I break free, I can't leave my mother now. Maybe in the spring. Will you be back in Chicago by then?"

"I assume so. If I'm not dead from yellow fever," he added with a chuckle.

"Don't joke about things like that."

"You're right, that was tasteless. Sarah, do you still want to be a reporter?"

"Yes, definitely. And talking to you makes me restless, eager to be out of here."

"As soon as I get back from Panama, I'll look for housing for you. We'll find you a job next spring. If not at a newspaper, in an office or library. Anyway, work that uses your brain."

"I don't know. I think Kari and Ed, Minnie too, would disown me if I lived alone in a big city."

"Then would you consider marrying me?"

"You think you can afford me now?" Her tone was light, teasing.

"Probably not in the grand style you'd like, but if I put you to work, I could swing it, maybe. I'm not sure it's a great idea. You should marry someone with a more predictable and profitable future." Again, he smiled. "By the way, I showed your essay on women's suffrage to my boss. He was impressed, even said they should have a woman on staff since women's issues keep popping up. But he claims finding a cool-headed female is next to impossible."

"John, what if we tell our families we're married, that we eloped?"

"Lie? I don't think either of us could do that."

She sighed, "I guess you're right. Anyway, fact or fiction would raise a new set of questions, like 'When are you going to have a baby?'" She blushed. "Maybe I can change their minds by next spring. Convince them you'd sort of watch over me even if we weren't married."

"Why not just get married? I love you, Sarah. I have since high school."

"I think I love you too, John. But I don't think I'm ready for marriage. I want to finish college and I want to do something important before I settle down."

CHAPTER 9
Commitment to Suffrage

Ed set up a large balsam fir in the main room one week before Christmas. The tree failed to engender much holiday spirit in the adults, but no one had wanted the children to be deprived. As Sarah helped Charlie and Margaret hang the colored bulbs and strings of popcorn, she inhaled the balsam scent permeating the room and wondered if the fragrance evoked memories for Minnie of Christmases past with Peder and even earlier family vacations in the North Woods of Minnesota. Now that Peder was gone, would Minnie return to St. Paul? Would the memory of Willie's death negate that?

Every day Sarah slogged through drifts of snow to the mailbox, hoping to find a letter from John and an invitation from Mrs. Hall. Her craving for contact beyond her narrow, constricted world intensified as the days passed and neither a letter nor an invitation arrived. Her interest in the invitation faded when she learned that Robert was not coming home this Christmas.

John's first note, an apology for not writing sooner, arrived after New Years with a promise to send articles he'd written about Panama. His second letter came a month later.

Dear Sarah,   February 15, 1908
    My sympathy goes out to Minnie and the rest of the family. I'm sure it's a sad time. I'll miss Peder too.
    I wish you could be here. Chicago is alive and exciting with lots of fabulous writers (some reporters) and Suffragists. By the way, have you heard about the Mad

March in London? Three thousand women, representing all social classes, trudged through muddy streets from Hyde Park to Exeter Hall advocating for women's suffrage—earning deep respect because they persisted despite miserable weather. A few days later Suffragettes stormed Parliament with some ending up in jail.

Must go now and talk to my boss about a London assignment. I love you.

More love,
John

She wondered why he was so eager for her to come to Chicago, since he was eager to go to England. Why would he want her there if he were somewhere else?

Nevertheless, after reading John's letter, Sarah felt like a hibernating bear awakening in the spring. Aroused, excited, she was ready to fight for voting rights. When she told Mrs. Hall at church the following Sunday about the scrappy British Suffragettes, she was invited to tea. There, perched on the edge of a maroon tapestry covered parlor chair, she listened as Mrs. Hall described her strategy.

"I'm confident we can get a suffrage bill introduced in the state legislature next January. Between now and then, we'll ask legislators and candidates on the November ballot for support."

"This is a presidential election year. Will that make a difference?" Sarah asked.

"I don't know if that will help or hinder us. Anyway, I'll start speaking around the state to any organization that will listen. I'd like you to write speeches that emphasize equal rights and point to progressive Western states where women already have the vote. Success would mean we could vote in the 1912 presidential election." She added, smiling, "Thank goodness. Mr. Roosevelt will not be a contender, unless he has the gall to run for a third term."

"Let's do it!" Sarah radiated excitement. "Can we do it alone?"

106

"I know women who'll join us and politicians who'll support us. Money will be a problem, but I've raised money for the college. Still, I'm sure we'll have to go out of state to find wealthy women who are interested in suffrage."

When Mrs. Hall took a breath, Sarah interjected, "Maybe you shouldn't count on me. I'd planned to go to Chicago…before my father died. I haven't given up the idea. It's just that I can't leave my mother alone so soon after his death."

"Chicago? Why would you go there?"

"I have a friend, a reporter for the *Daily News*, who will help me find a job on a newspaper." Suddenly, she felt ridiculous, embarrassed. *Young women don't travel without a chaperone or live alone in a big city.*

"You are brave to travel by yourself. But you may not be wise. Living alone in a big city can be dangerous." Mrs. Hall poured each of them another cup of tea. "Are you telling me that you can't work with me because you already have a commitment, a plan to be elsewhere?"

"No. Not for a few months. I don't know for how long I can commit. I'd prefer to work on suffrage with you in my home state, but Chicago offers the possibility of working on a major newspaper. And I *could* join a suffrage group there."

Thinking about it later, Sarah realized that staying in Hughitt was the sensible option. Mr. Minor would rehire her and Mr. Layton would probably offer her the Society page again. She could handle those jobs and have time to help Mrs. Hall with speeches. Living in Chicago would be more expensive, and even with John's help, she might not get employment. But she couldn't relinquish her dreams: Chicago, the unknown, the fantastic, excited her more than anything in Dakota—except the suffrage fight. And she knew that existed in Illinois as well. Her interest in the city began—more than ten years ago—when she first read about the World's Fair in Chicago, the 1893 Columbian Exposition, in a *Century Magazine*.

Although the idea of abandoning her mother haunted her, she couldn't conceive of spending the rest of her life on the farm. Her staying in Hughitt and living with Mrs. Hall would make visiting the farm relatively easy, though Minnie would still be alone much of the time. After much agonizing, Sarah thought up a solution that might work for all of them: Kari and Ed would move into the homestead with Minnie. The farm house would give them more space, and Ed would be closer to the center of the farming operation. They could rent their cottage to a farm hand who'd work for them. While Ed added a new bedroom/sitting room for her, Minnie, could be visiting her family in St. Paul.

She approached her mother first. "What do you think, Ma? After all, it is your house."

"I like it, but Kari may have reservations."

Sarah silently agreed, but on a warm spring evening she described her options—Chicago or Hughitt—to the family. Kari's hostility flared in her first question.

"If John has proposed, why would you consider anything but Chicago?"

"We're not engaged, Kari. But John will find me a place to live near his boarding house and help me find a job, ideally with a newspaper."

"You told me he wanted to be a foreign correspondent. Has he given that up?" Ed asked. "If he goes overseas, how can he help you? Chicago is not a good place for a young woman to be on her own. Peder would definitely put his foot down."

Sarah tried to counter Ed's negativity. "I'll meet people at the boarding house and at work." She expressed more confidence than she felt. "John thinks I'll find a good job." *That's only a slight exaggeration.*

"And what about Ma? You'd leave her here alone?" Kari's anger was scorching, but her question gave Sarah the opening she needed. She resisted the temptation to point out Kari's inconsistency, her acceptance of Sarah's leaving Minnie if she were going to Chicago to marry. "I thought you and Ed and the children might move in here with Minnie. You'd have more space. I was hoping Ed could expand the small room into a nice sitting/bedroom for Minnie. The children would be closer to school and Ed closer to the barns."

"You have it all figured out, don't you? So you can escape the farm and family responsibility. You don't care about anyone else." Kari, her cheeks flushed, glared at her sister. "I'm settled in my home. As for Ed, he's managed all these years. The walk to the country school from the two houses is six of one… Besides the walk is good for them."

Charlie, who'd been sitting quietly, stood up. "Ma, I'd *like* to live here."

Sarah waited for Kari to say something about children being seen but not heard, but she ignored him and took a different tack. "Minnie shouldn't have to share her home with the five of us. If we lived here, there'd be no room for you to visit or for Joe and Matthew."

Minnie cleared her throat, "Kari, I'd love to share this house with all of you. We'd find space for Sarah. And Matthew and Joe. Anyway, I doubt they'll be back in my lifetime."

"Don't be morbid, Ma." Kari looked at Ed. "You've been awfully quiet about Sarah's plans for us. What do you have to say?"

Sarah held her breath. She'd expected Kari to find fault. Would Ed accept her ideas?

"Taking your chances here or in Chicago reminds me of an old adage: A bird in hand is worth two in the bush. You don't know what Chicago holds. In Hughitt you can count on a job with Mr. Miner and experience at the Daily that should help you land a job at a bigger paper later. And you could pursue your suffrage goal…and finish college."

"But Chicago has such great newspapers, and I could join an Illinois suffrage group." She deliberately avoided mentioning John or her desire for a more exciting life.

"If you are not going to marry John, going to Chicago is outrageous. A single woman living alone is not respectable." Kari looked at her mother. "Ma, *you* tell her."

Ed interceded. "Kari, don't be so hard on Sarah. Isn't it her turn to find what she wants? You and your brothers have pursued your dreams. So have I. It's her turn." He looked at Sarah, "I think you're making a mistake if you go to Chicago, but I heartily approve your suggestion that we move in here. I'll convince Kari and start working on a new room for Minnie."

During the next few weeks, Sarah often felt like the tiger she had seen at the St. Paul zoo, pacing back and forth behind a fence. Reading articles and studying pictures of Chicago she'd found in the college library and Minnie's old Century magazines increased her restlessness and her desire to move on. Trips to Hughitt—starting lists of names and addresses with Mrs. Hall, talking to Mr. Miner and Mr. Layton—provided temporary distractions and relief from boredom.

By late May, Ed had expanded the small bedroom at the farm, the room he'd originally occupied, into a sitting/bedroom with one large window looking out toward the meadow, another with a view of Minnie's herb garden. Kari and Ed and the children planned to move into the homestead as soon as Minnie had settled into her new space.

Sarah returned to Hughitt without regret, yet she knew she'd miss the daily conversations with Charlie and walks in the meadow with Minnie. She resumed the legal work for Mr. Miner during the day, consulting with Mr. Layton about writing essays during her lunch hour. Most evenings she helped Mrs. Hall work on lists and drafts of letters—this was after they had visited the local Republican headquarters on Dakota Avenue. Mrs. Hall was adamant about checking in daily between June 16 and 19 to find out the latest at the Republican national convention in Chicago. From the start, Mrs. Hall had rooted for William Howard Taft and expected him to win the nomination.

"Why are you so sure Taft will win?" Sarah asked. "My reporter friend, John, likes Robert La Follette from Wisconsin."

"Well, I hope he isn't expecting La Follette to win. Taft is by far the best choice. With Roosevelt backing him, I don't think he can lose. La Follette is too progressive. The sad thing is none of them is strong for women's suffrage."

After Taft won the nomination, Sarah and Mrs. Hall continued to frequent the headquarters trying to drum up interest in women's suffrage. With the Democratic convention less than a month away, most everyone was focused on whether the Democrats would nominate. William Jennings Bryan for a third time? "We'll come back here later, Sarah. We need to spend time at the Democrat headquarters too, but I doubt they'll pay any attention to us. They know I've never been in their camp."

Letters from John about his time on the convention hall floors in Chicago intensified Sarah's eagerness to go there. But she'd gradually come to a new reality. Even if John did not have a foreign assignment, he could be anywhere in the U.S. She had moments of anxiety, wondering how she'd fare alone in the city. Recently John had been sent to West Virginia and Pennsylvania to report on coal mine explosions and to write human interest stories about the survivors and the families of the victims.

Doubtful she'd ever get assignments like those helped Sarah commit to Mrs. Hall and their efforts. But giving up her Chicago dreams—except temporarily—was impossible. She told herself that she was only putting her dreams on hold. At times she needed Mrs. Hall's enthusiasm to buoy her up, to remind her that they hadn't yet convinced all the legislators to vote for suffrage. After all her work, Sarah couldn't imagine failure. Occasionally, a harsh, surly comment of a politician—"I'll *never* vote for your bill"—shocked her, and she'd wonder, briefly, how many legislators felt that way. But her confidence, partly influenced by her determination to go to

Chicago the following spring, quashed any doubts about the outcome of the vote. Anyway, in the unlikely possibility they'd lose, she could continue suffrage work in Illinois.

She wrote John in July that she'd stay in Dakota to push for women's suffrage until the legislature voted in February. She'd move to Chicago next spring as soon as she graduated from college.

Mr. Miner, Mr. Layton, and Mrs. Hall kept Sarah busy, but she squeezed out time to take college courses during the summer and fall. She fully intended to garner enough credits to ensure spring graduation. She chose one course on *Julius Caesar* because Robert had underlined and written marginal comments on his copy of the play. By late October she'd finished a paper, had written many speeches, and had convinced organizations like the Masons and the Knights of Columbus to invite Mrs. Hall to talk to their members. If she met resistance, she'd remind the leader that he could hardly refuse a woman of Mrs. Hall's stature.

Hearing her speeches thrilled Sarah initially, but after awhile she began to resent Mrs. Hall getting all the credit. Being treated like her secretary and maid—not her co-author or speech writer—and constantly hearing, "Sarah, could you find this or that for me" irritated her. Adding to her discomfort, she disagreed with Mrs. Hall about President Roosevelt. At first she said nothing, but eventually she voiced her opinion.

"He's done so much for conservation and regulating monopolies," she argued. Under her breath she added, "I like his progressive ideas."

"Well, thank goodness he's done some good. But he's a braggart, a bully in the bully pulpit, an imperialist, a war monger. I'm so glad he'll be gone in a few months." Mrs. Hall added a few seconds later, "And I still think he's responsible for the panic of '07."

Sarah had no comeback. She didn't like to think her brother Joe was an officer in the Cavalry of an imperialist nation, but what could she say in light of the war with Cuba and the Philippines?

On election day, Sarah and Mrs. Hall haunted the Republican headquarters. Returns were mostly in Taft's favor, but William Jennings Bryan pulled in votes from unexpected areas. By midnight, Sarah was ready to go home to bed, but Mrs. Hall would not leave until convinced Taft had won. Sarah could not conjure up much enthusiasm for Taft, and she'd begun to feel sorry for three-time loser Bryan.

Sarah left for the farm two days before Robert's arrival for a short Christmas vacation. Before she left, she made certain she had a dinner invitation one evening while Robert was home. She looked forward to hearing his opinion of their suffrage work and also to conversing about literature—maybe *Julius Caesar*. We've never discussed *War and Peace* either she reminded herself. Once and for all she wanted to convince Robert that she was not stupid.

On her first day back at the farm, Ed handed her a letter from John. She retreated to the loft for privacy. She was thrilled, her heart racing, as she anticipated his coming home for Christmas, until she realized her invitation to the Halls was on the day he'd arrive. Waiting to see John was bad enough, but how would he feel about her having dinner with Robert the night of his arrival? What should she do? Canceling dinner didn't feel right. Besides this was probably her only chance to see Robert for a long time. John would be around for a week, so she'd have lots of time to be with him. Nevertheless, she worried about John, about hurting him.

Kari did not hesitate to state her opinion, "You should invite John for dinner the day he arrives."

"You know I accepted a dinner invitation for that night before I knew John's plans. Anyway, he should spend the first night with his parents." She could not think of a better excuse, one that family-focused Kari should appreciate.

113

"He's staying with his parents. He'll see them every day. Sarah, you can't treat John that way. Besides, you see Mrs. Hall every day."

"I know, but I haven't seen Robert in ages. John will understand. I'll see him every day after the first night. I'll invite him for dinner the second night."

"I don't understand you. Robert was your nemesis not so long ago. And John wants to marry you."

Don't be too sure. He says he loves me, but I think he might gladly trade me for a foreign assignment.

Mrs. Hall had waited for Robert to set up the Christmas tree. When Sarah arrived, he and his two sisters were decorating it. Sarah joined in, mildly discombobulated by Robert's mustache—brown, not reddish—an addition that would take some getting used to. She liked seeing a side of Robert she'd never seen before. To her surprise, she felt comfortable and relaxed, stringing popcorn with the three of them, but soon Elizabeth's babble about her first year in college put a damper on other conversation. Sarah's impatience was ballooning when Mrs. Hall called her daughters to come help serve dinner.

"Elizabeth's a talker," Robert said. "Not much of a thinker."

"I like her enthusiasm," Sarah replied, concealing her feelings about Elizabeth as she recalled a comment he made years ago. In fact, she remembered exactly what he had said when he told her she was not fit for the debate team in high school. "You're too emotional. Like most girls. You're not really logical or analytical."

As soon as they sat down to eat, Mrs. Hall bombarded Robert with questions about legal issues, anything possibly relevant to passing a suffrage bill. He said he had picked up literature for them in New York and Washington. "I'll read and comment on your arguments if you like, but right now, Mother, just let me enjoy your cooking."

Sarah was delighted that Robert offered to critique the speeches and letters she'd written, but disappointed that they'd discussed only suffrage and politics at dinner. No *War and Peace* or *Julius Caesar.* She also appreciated Robert's approval, despite Mrs. Hall's criticism, of TR and his efforts toward breaking up the big monopolies. But he shook his head when she asked, "Will you be specializing in antitrust law?"

By the time the girls had cleared the table and the women were washing dishes, Sarah heard the doorknocker and knew Ed had arrived to take her home. As Robert admired her new bear-fur trimmed cape with the satin lining, she told him Minnie had ordered it for her from the Sears, Roebuck catalogue. "Very nice. What would we do out here without Sears Roebuck?"

Sarah cocked her head and smiled. "Well, we also have Montgomery Ward."

"Oh yeah, I almost forgot about Monkey Wards."

She was putting on her gloves when he asked, "Would you like to go to the Christmas pageant at the college tomorrow night?"

"I'd love it," she answered. But sitting next to Ed in the carriage, she remembered telling Kari that she would invite John to dinner the next day. *Oh goodness. Now what have I done?*

Kari was waiting up, working at the kitchen counter when Sarah walked in. "Well, you missed John. He stayed late hoping to see you."

Not wanting to quarrel, Sarah said nothing, hoping Ed would show up momentarily. She needed a buffer, an ally to support her during the imminent storm. "What are you doing?" she finally asked, an attempt to delay the inevitable. An inane question with the flour flying around and the smell of apples in the air, but she had to say something.

"I invited him to dinner."

"You're baking a pie for John?" Still no sign of Ed, so she took a deep breath, preparing for lightning and thunder. "I hope you invited him for the midday meal, because I'm going to a Christmas program at the college tomorrow evening."

"What are you talking about?" Kari banged her rolling pin on the cutting board. "Are you saying you're going to stand him up again?"

"Be sure to wake up everyone in the house while you're screaming at me."

"I invited John for dinner at six. I expect you to be here. If you accepted a date with Robert Hall, you'd better cancel it."

"If we lived in a civilized place, I could. We'd have a phone, like the Halls and John's parents."

"You think a phone would solve all your problems? If you treated John better, he might marry you and then you could live in Chicago and have a telephone."

Ed entered in time to hear the last comment. "We'll have a telephone one of these days. What's the problem here?"

"Sisters being spiteful." *That's exactly what Kari is.* "Kari, I'll invite John to go to the pageant with Robert and me."

"I'm sure that's what John had in mind for his first evening with you in over a year." Kari turned back to her pie and finished rolling out the top crust. Ed shook his head and left the room.

Sarah sat at the old oak table listening to the scraping sound of the pie tin being turned as Kari crimped the edges of the pie dough, a sound soon drowned out by the screaming in her head. *What is wrong with me? How could I accept an invitation from Robert with John in town? Why does Robert hold this...what? Am I in love with him? John has always been a good friend, supportive when Robert scoffed at me.*

Minutes later she stood up. "I'll sleep on it."

CHAPTER 10
Bitter Disappointment

Sarah tossed and turned well into the night trying to understand why she'd accepted a date with Robert with no thought of John. He'd always occupied more of her thoughts than Robert...or had he? Her feelings about Robert had always been more intense, both attraction and repulsion. What was it about him? His cleverness? He always knew so much about everything. But so did John, and he even knew about farming, which, admittedly, she cared less about. Both were good looking, if not really handsome. John was tall, big boned, blond, Swedish. Robert was tall and slight, not as broad-shouldered as John. She disliked his red hair originally. Now it was the handlebar mustache that bothered her. She definitely liked them both, but Robert seemed to hold a spell over her. *Is that love? Is it possible to love more than one? I've loved two parents, three brothers...and. oh yes, one sister.*

John arrived mid afternoon in his parent's carriage. Sarah grabbed a shawl and went out to greet him. "Can we be alone for awhile?" he asked.

"I'm sure Kari will see to it." She expected him to take her in his arms and kiss her. Instead he was angry and started toward the house ahead of her.

Kari had seen John arrive and quickly corralled Margaret into Minnie's new sitting room for a piano lesson. Sarah had convinced her mother to give lessons to her granddaughters, hoping this activity would be therapeutic for Minnie. With Marion napping and Charlie helping Ed in the barn, Sarah and John had the main room to themselves. She'd brought him a glass of mulled cider and confronted the problem head on.

"John, I did something stupid last night and there's no way to fix it." She sat down next to him. "Please forgive me."

"Kari told me you hadn't seen Robert Hall in two years. I can understand your wanting to have dinner with him."

"It's more than that. I agreed to go to a Christmas pageant at the college with him tonight. There's no way to cancel." She hesitated, started to chew a finger nail. "Please come with us." She sat quietly, trying to interpret his long silence, the expression on his face.

"I'll pass, Sarah."

"Oh, please come."

"I'm sure Robert would appreciate my presence. If the tables were turned, I'd *love* to have him come with us. Is he as arrogant as ever? I was hoping they take him down a notch or two at Yale?"

"I'm really sorry. I had too much Christmas punch, I guess."

John stood up. "Will you give my apologies to Kari? I won't be staying for dinner."

Sarah was less surprised than annoyed with herself. "You have a right to be angry with me, John, but *please* stay for dinner." She tried to make light of it. "Save me from my sister."

"Save you? Kari seems harmless." He chuckled before he frowned. "I can't imagine a more awkward moment than Robert's arrival while I'm sitting at your dining table. Awkward for everybody. But I do want to talk to you. How serious are you about Chicago. Do you really want to come or are you just playing a game?"

"I'm *serious*," she almost screamed. She didn't care how desperate she sounded. "Please, John. Just because I stupidly made a date with Robert doesn't mean I don't want to be a reporter or writer in the city." She began to cry.

"Stop it, Sarah." He put his empty glass next to the sink. He softened his tone. "Forget it. I have no right to tell you who you can associate with or when. I've already written you the most important stuff about Chicago. We can review it the next time we get together…if you want."

As he retrieved his coat, she grabbed his arm. "Promise you'll come by tomorrow." She understood the phrase, "beside herself" as she saw her dreams, her Chicago fantasies fading, receding into a nonexistent future.

"I'll come by if my parents don't need the carriage."

She felt brushed off, discarded; but she knew she deserved it. A new fear gripped her.—the fear that she'd lost her best friend, that John would never trust her again.

When Sarah impulsively accepted Robert's invitation, she hadn't considered how she'd feel when he saw the farmstead for the first time. Compared to the elaborate Victorian he called home, the farmhouse was modest, plain—words that Sarah decided characterized the families as well. Robert's father had been a lawyer and an important figure in state politics; Peder had been a simple, uneducated farmer. Robert's mother had been a teacher, educated in a normal school; Minnie, a humble farm wife. Sarah knew her mother's education had been excellent for her era, but she lacked the intense drive that Mrs. Hall brought to the campaign for women's suffrage. Minnie accepted her situation in life, never complaining or asking for more. Her one rebellion ended badly. Yet she supported her daughters, encouraging Sarah, especially, to pursue her dreams, however unconventional.

Robert declined Kari's invitation to join them for dinner. "Thanks, I had a bite before I left home. But Sarah, take your time. The pageant doesn't start until 8:00. And this is no Broadway production."

Sarah had no desire to linger, though being alone with Robert in the carriage made her even more uncomfortable than his presence in the house. She wanted to ask if he'd had a chance to

119

read her speeches, but she didn't want to seem forward. He broke the silence. "I've read your letters and speeches. They're really good. I'd vote for your amendment." He laughed. "Best of all, I liked your question, 'Mr. Legislator, how can you deny suffrage for South Dakota women when Wyoming, just west of here, gave women voting rights at its inception several years ago?'"

Sarah wasn't sure how to take his response. Maybe he was laughing at her and his mother, mocking them. "Robert, haven't you always been on our side?"

"Don't be too sure. There are reasonable arguments against women's suffrage."

"What? Women supporting Prohibition? Any other *reasonable* argument? You don't think women are smart enough to vote intelligently?"

"I didn't say that. But women will vote as their husbands do, so what's the point? Just more votes to count, more people to register…"

Was he serious? Sarah hadn't expected an argument from Robert. Maybe he was teasing her. "Not all women will vote with their husbands. And what if they did?" Provoked, she added, "What about unmarried women? Who will they copy? Their fathers, their brothers? How someone votes is not the issue. All citizens should have the *right* to vote." She took a deep breath. "You don't think we'll succeed, do you?"

"Sarah, I was teasing you. Just don't be so naïve as to count on the next legislature. You're making progress. You shouldn't expect your efforts to pay off so quickly."

"Quickly? Women have been fighting for equal rights forever. In England since the eighteenth century." She hesitated, and then asked, "Robert, why is your mother so anti-Roosevelt?"

"She liked McKinley, a true conservative in her eyes, and she believes Roosevelt, who was McKinley's Secretary of the Navy, led him into the war against Spain. And if my mother is anything, she's anti-war. But she does believe in the 'white man's burden,' educating and Christianizing the Filipinos. Most of all, I think she hates TR's style—his bluster, his arrogance. Still, she'd probably support him against any Democrat. In fact, she did vote for him in '04."

After the show, a medley of local talent, they walked out of the auditorium into a white glistening world. Large fluffy snowflakes danced around them as they approached the carriage. Snow squeaked under their shoes. Sarah couldn't resist an urge to stick out her tongue to capture a few flakes. Robert stopped walking, opened his arms, and said, "On a beautiful night like this, I wish I were a poet instead of a law student."

"Can't you be both?" Sarah asked. "I couldn't. I don't have a poetic bone in my body."

"Truth is, I don't think I do either." With that, he looked directly at her, "If one non-poet kisses another non-poet, could they make poetry that way?"

Sarah smiled, "Maybe. Why not?" As she watched the feathery flakes settle on his reddish hair and dark brows and mustache, his arms encircled her waist. She closed her eyes as he bent down and his soft, full lips touched hers. Momentarily, she felt light, buoyant, transported. Her one-time nemesis had cast his spell on her again. She liked it, but at the same time, she felt guilty. She was John's girl, wasn't she? Now he'd have more reason to distrust her.

A giddy feeling persisted until Robert broke the spell. "Sarah, will you write to me?"

She wanted to say yes but thoughts of John interfered. "I don't think it's a good idea. We're both so busy with school." She paused. "You'd have to write first…I don't have your address."

He chortled, "You're so practical. Don't worry I'll write first. I don't have *your* address either, but I'm sure my mother does. And, you should know, she has *my* address too."

"Did you like the show last night?" John, who'd arrived in his father's sleigh, stomped the snow off his boots as he stood in the doorway. Without waiting for Sarah's answer, he said, "I thought you might like a sleigh ride."

She'd been awake half the night trying to understand why she'd let Robert kiss her. By the time she went to sleep, she was only absolutely positive about one thing. She wanted to go to Chicago. "The snow looks perfect, but I thought we were going to have a serious discussion. After the legislators vote on suffrage next month, my work with Mrs. Hall will be done." She grabbed his arm and pulled him into the house.

"What if the women's suffrage bill doesn't pass?" he asked.

"Mrs. Hall is optimistic. So I'm optimistic." Sarah helped John with his coat.

"But what if it doesn't?" They moved into the main room.

Neither Robert nor John thinks our bill will pass. It's got to pass. I don't want to do this anymore. Not now anyway. "I'm going to Chicago," she blurted out. "Whether the bill passes or not. I'll be too disappointed and angry to spend more time trying to convince bull-headed legislator. Please sit. Would you like beer or cider?"

"Seriously. You'll come to Chicago after the vote? Regardless?" He sat on a straight back chair at the oak table with a glass of cider in his hand. "You've reneged once."

"Not again. I've been dreaming about Chicago. If we win, I'll feel deserving after all the work I've done. If we don't win, I'll be even more eager to move out of here. But I do intend to graduate from college. I'll have enough credits by the end of next semester."

"I do worry about your being disappointed. Finding a good job will be the biggest challenge. It is risky. Housing won't be a problem, though. I talked to a Mrs. Barkley who rents to young single women. Two teach at Hull House. She says she'll have space in April when one of those teachers leaves to get married. Should I tell her you'll take it?"

"Yes. Will I be close to you?" Unhappy about exposing her dependency, she also felt energized and elated, confident that everything was turning out the way she wanted. She'd ask later about Hull House. "Let's go for that sleigh ride now."

As she snuggled next to him in the sleigh, half buried under blankets, she closed her eyes, took deep breaths of the cold, crisp air, and listened to the sleigh bells over the clip-clop of the horse's feet. Everything seemed perfect. Almost perfect. She didn't like being so dependent on John. But she didn't see any way around it, at least until she was settled in Chicago. And what about Robert? The memory of that kiss was fading. She doubted she'd ever see him again or that he would write.

Mrs. Hall arranged for their transportation to Pierre, the state capital, and booked two nights in the St. Charles Hotel. Mr. Layton asked Sarah to gather material for human interest stories relevant to the legislative sessions while she was there. He expressed interest in the suffrage legislation, but he also wanted her to write about the Capitol building itself and, possibly, Fort Pierre—the settlement established on the south side of the Missouri River not long after the Lewis and Clark expedition.

Sarah was surprised to find Pierre smaller and quieter than Hughitt, except for the noisy construction work on the Capitol. She walked up the front steps with Mrs. Hall toward the columned portico of the State House, a classical building still under construction. They could not enter, but Sarah admired what she could see. She'd read that it would have many features of the Montana State Capitol, including an impressive dome. Gazing at the superstructure before her, she imagined a large, beautiful dome which she hoped to see some day. She felt a twinge of sadness that they were too soon to enter what promised to be a magnificent structure.

Inside the frame building that still served as the State Capitol, they found seats in the balcony overlooking the House floor and watched the legislators milling around. When the Speaker finally gaveled the House to order, Sarah came to attention also. After listening to the introduction of their suffrage bill and the pro and con arguments, a legislator called for a vote. Sarah looked anxiously at Mrs. Hall as seventy representatives began to cast their votes. At first the votes were in their favor, but soon the *nays* dominated and the bill was defeated.

Sarah, close to tears as they walked to the hotel, admired Mrs. Hall's quiet acceptance of defeat. "We'll get there eventually. Don't despair. We did our best. More men will accept the inevitable in two years when we'll try again. Don't feel all your hard work was for naught."

But I do. And I want no part of this heartbreak again. But she wasn't ready to tell Mrs. Hall that she'd be leaving for Chicago in a few months.

Those few months dragged on. Sarah's excitement ran high with occasional moments of anxiety. *What if I can't find a job or I get homesick?* She kept busy writing stories about the legislature and the defeat of the suffrage bill. She also arranged to finish her college work early so she could graduate *in absentia.*

When John wrote in early March that he'd paid a month's rent to hold the room for her, she told the family that she'd be leaving in April. Kari's response was no surprise.

"I'm glad he didn't give up on you. I hope you'll finally get married."

"Well, don't get your hopes up too high. We are not engaged." Although Sarah surmised that Minnie would be sad to see her leave, her mother supported her.

"I hope this will compensate for your suffrage bill not passing. I admire your courage, but I will worry about you in that big city. I'll expect you to write often."

"I think you're crazy," Ed said. "But I hope you find the job you want."

Charlie expressed the greatest enthusiasm. He told her she had to see Lake Michigan, the Museum of Science and Industry—a retooled building left over from the 1893 World's Fair—and visit the stock yards. He slyly asked her how old he'd have to be before he could visit. "I want to see the site where Mrs. O'Leary's cow caused the great fire. I read about it in the *Century Magazine*."

Mrs. Hall shook her head. "I don't think you'll like it, but I wish the best for you. Write me when you can. I'll be especially interested in what the Illinois Suffragists are doing. I'll keep you informed about what is happening here." Neither of them mentioned Robert. Sarah had not heard from him.

When departure day arrived, Sarah was prepared. She had one bag of clothing and items she'd need immediately. A steamer trunk with clothes and two cartons of books were ready to be sent. Minnie had prepared her favorite breakfast, an omelet with bacon and fried potatoes. Though the sizzle and smell of the bacon would have enticed her in the past, Sarah could barely swallow a small glass of orange juice.

"You need to eat, Sarah, to keep up your strength. You're facing a long, tiring train ride. I'm packing you a nice lunch, but you should eat something now."

"I know, Ma. I'm trying. Where is Ed? I think we should be leaving."

"Calm down, Sweetie. Ed. will drive you to the train and John will meet you in Chicago."

Sarah nodded. She hadn't heard from John in three days, or was it more? She wouldn't even think about the possibility of his not being there.

Though eager to begin her new adventure, Sarah had moments of wistfulness. As they crossed over the Jim River on the railroad trestle just east of town, she said goodbye to Hughitt. She knew she'd be back, but it would not be the same. She stared at the flat, broad, prairie—characterized by some as empty—that she knew from her meadow experience was teeming with life, amazing flora and fauna. But not the life she was looking for. Grazing Holstein and Guernsey reminded her of a rare argument between her father and Ed about which breed to purchase. But mostly, she thought about her mother, mindful of reversing the journey that Minnie had made over thirty years ago.

After stops in DeSmet and Brookings, Sarah opened the lunch bag and bit into a sandwich, savoring Minnie's meatloaf and wheat bread. She smiled to herself when they crossed the border into Minnesota and it started to rain. She remembered how Peder and Minnie would jest about the perpetual rain in Minnesota vs. the perpetual drought in Dakota.

Several passengers exited the train at Rochester. Sarah wondered if they were all sick and heading for the Mayo Clinic. She remembered when Willie was ill and they considered taking him there. She had been too young to be part of that discussion. When they crossed the Mississippi, she was reminded of a dinner table argument with Robert about Mark Twain and Louise May Alcott. Soon after, the rhythmic, repetitive motion of the train rocked her to sleep. She had a frightening dream. She was in a dark cavernous space looking for John. She kept running after men who disappeared as she approached them. She awoke as they pulled into Madison, Wisconsin.

"Best place to get off the train for fresh air and exercise, Miss. We'll be here for about twenty minutes." Sarah was eager to stretch her legs, wander about the station for a few minutes.

Next was Janesville, where she ate her second meatloaf sandwich, then Beloit and Rockford. As they approached Chicago, Sarah's excitement intensified until she felt supercharged, ready for anything. Although John hadn't written in a few days, she was confident he would meet her. He knew the train she was arriving on.

The conductor took her bag and then her hand to help her step from the train to the platform. "Isn't someone meeting you young lady?"

"Yes, but I don't see him yet." She'd never been in a setting this scary before—dark, cavernous, noisy with belching engines—about as different from the prairie and Hughitt's train station as one could imagine. When John didn't appear, she scurried with the crowd toward the part of the station away from the trains and tracks, scanning faces as she went. Where was he?

By the time she'd reached the waiting area, she was getting panicky, losing hope they'd find each other. She looked for an information booth as soon as she realized there was no obvious place to meet. Maybe he left a message.

"Sorry, miss, no messages for you."

Believing that John would meet her if at all possible, she began to imagine a variety of scary scenarios, horrible accidents that prevented him from getting to the station.

She paced for several minutes before sitting on a bench close to the information booth, hoping to feel safe there. But as time passed, her fear intensified. She could not quiet Kari's voice repeating in her head, "You stood him up twice, now it's his turn." Could he have abandoned her? If he didn't show up, what would she do? She had never been so frightened.

PART 3
Sarah
CHICAGO 1909-1919

CHAPTER 11
Chicago at Last

To get control of her feelings, Sarah focused on the never ending parade of women and their elaborate hats—especially those sprouting flower gardens, harboring fruit baskets, or growing pheasant feathers. She had detested hats since her sunbonnet days. She realized a man accompanied every woman except one—a girl, really, though not much younger than Sarah—shabbily dressed, who lurked in the shadows near a side entrance. This scene made Sarah feel more vulnerable, self-conscious, and exposed, another fear she had never experienced before, almost as frightening as being abandoned or losing John some other way.

She had checked twice with the man in the booth. No messages. By the end of an hour, whatever the cause of John's absence, she felt like a lost child, scared to face the city on her own. With no other option, she summoned up her courage to hand the man in the booth a slip of paper with an address which John had given her. "How can I get to this place?"

"You'll find a cab outside, Miss. Any of them will take you to Wabash Avenue."

Uneasy, she headed out into the balmy April night and surveyed the carriages on the boulevard. As she slowly descended to the street, a young man, short and dark, came bounding up the steps and reached for her bag. "Would you like a taxi, Miss?"

She pulled back, keeping a firm grip on her suitcase. "Yes, but..." In this unexplored territory Sarah wasn't sure what she should say or do. This man was so unlike the tall, fair-skinned Scandinavians and Germans that she knew in Dakota. How could she tell if she were in safe hands? "Can you take me to this address?" She showed him the slip of paper she'd been clutching since she talked to the man in the information booth.

"Certainly, Miss." He moved toward a cab lined up in front of the station, opened the back door for her, and slid her bag in on the floor. Sarah had often been in Ed's car, but never in a taxi. If there was a protocol, a usual exchange between driver and passenger, she was ignorant of it. Needing reassurance, hoping she hadn't acted rashly, she asked, "Is it far to Wabash?"

"No, Miss. We'll be there soon."

She sighed. Seconds later, they were on a bridge. "Is that Lake Michigan?" she asked, looking down at the water that reflected the city lights.

"No, Miss. That's the Chicago River. We're blocks from the lake."

Darkened stores and brightly lit hotels decreased in number as they entered a residential area. After several blocks the driver pulled up in front of a three story house. She hoped the light over the door meant she was expected. Her heart began to pound and her anxiety shot up as she looked at the nondescript door, the door that opened on to her new life, her future.

A heavy-set, bosomy woman answered the door bell in seconds. "You must be Sarah. Welcome. I'm Mrs. Barkley. Your friend, John, called here to apologize for not meeting you. He'll be by tomorrow morning to explain. Would you like tea and a bite to eat before you go up to your room?"

Knowing John had left a message calmed her. She breathed more easily, knowing she'd see him soon. "No, thank you. I'm more tired than hungry. I'd like to see my room."

"Let's go up then. I'll give you a quick tour now and tell you more tomorrow. I like to serve breakfast to my girls between 6:30 and 7:30, but if you want to sleep late, that's fine."

As they walked up the stairs, Sarah said, "My trunk should be delivered in the morning."

132

"John can bring the trunk up to your room, but I do not usually allow men above the first floor, so please don't let him dally. And I really hope you won't dally here," she added as they looked into the communal bathroom on the second floor. "Five women live on this floor. Another has the room across from yours on the third floor."

Sarah's room was small but inviting. The narrow bed faced a mirrored dresser and was adjacent to a small table between the bed and a makeshift closet, a curtained off area. Near the window a Morris chair upholstered in green tapestry looked comfortable and reminded Sarah of a chair in Mrs. Hall's study. Exhausted, she thanked Mrs. Barkley and said good night.

She slipped out of her dress and collapsed on the bed. Everything is working out, she thought, as sleep invaded her consciousness: Mrs. Barkley, the room, and John will be here soon.

When she awoke, the sun was streaming through the window opposite her bed. An east window, she surmised—growing up on the prairie had at least taught her how to use the sun as a compass. Hungry and eager to see John, she put on the dress she'd tossed on the Morris chair, and left her room in a hurry. She noted the door across the hall and fancied she and the boarder who lived there would become friends.

After a quick stop in the bathroom, she flew down the steps inhaling the aroma of coffee that evoked memories of the dark brew Minnie made to please Peder. John was sitting at the dining room table across from Mrs. Barkley. He got up to pull out the chair next to him. He smiled and said, "I know I have some explaining to do."

"Just a minute, John." Mrs. Barkley interrupted. "Good morning, Sarah, What would you like for breakfast? I've made oatmeal, but I can scramble or boil an egg for you."

"Coffee and oatmeal are fine." Though happy and relieved to see John, Sarah needed answers. "I waited a long time last night.

133

Why didn't you leave a message at the information booth? " She wanted him to know how angry she was, but not how scared she'd been. If she was going to be a reporter, she had to face danger, to be fearless.

"A colleague asked me to cover for him. His wife went into labor unexpectedly and he wanted to be with her. How could I refuse? He'll cover for me later so I can be with you."

"Couldn't you leave a message?"

"I planned to, but the phone on the city desk was ringing off the hook. When I finally got a break, it made more sense to call Mrs. Barkley. I didn't expect you to hang around the station very long. Anyway, I knew you could handle the situation. You had the address."

She liked his flattery and accepted his excuse as reasonable. She hugged him, but resisted kissing him, not knowing when Mrs. Barkley would return. "What's next? After I eat and you lug my trunk up to my room?"

"I want to show you the Loop and introduce you to my boss. I've given him your best essays. He was impressed, but still only interested in assigning you to the Society page."

"Because I'm a woman?"

"Exactly. No editor sends a woman into Chicago's rough neighborhoods or even City Hall. It's not safe. A man has a much better chance of defending himself against a hoodlum. And we're less likely to be threatened in the first place."

"You weren't so negative about my prospects before."

"I guess living in Chicago has opened my eyes to a world I never imagined in Hughitt."

An image of the girl she'd seen in the station flashed through Sarah's head. "So I'll be stuck with reporting on social events." *There must be an editor somewhere who will give me a chance.*

"Probably, Sarah...sorry." As Mrs. Barkley entered with Sarah's breakfast, he continued. "But make the rounds. See what you're offered."

Sarah drank her coffee, pondered his words, and wondered why she'd asked for oatmeal, the soft mushy cereal she'd spit out when Minnie tried to feed it to her when she was little. She still didn't like it, even with maple syrup.

After she'd finished eating, she followed John up to her room. As soon as he'd put her trunk in the closet, he took her in his arms. "I can hardly believe you're really here. Is the room acceptable? I took it because this location is great and Mrs. Barkley seemed friendly and easy going." He kissed her twice before he gave her a chance to say anything.

"John, I need air." She smiled as she pulled back. "I'm excited to be here. The room is fine. I doubt I'll spend much time here except to sleep, maybe write. How are things with you?"

"Great, now that you're here. My job is good, though I've had no foreign assignment since the Panama Canal. I did get a raise, so I've decided to look for an apartment. I'm tired of boarding houses. I hope you'll help me find a place that we can share…after we're married."

"We'd better go downstairs. There's a rule about men above the first floor. I'd hate to be kicked out before I've even had a chance to settle in. We're not supposed to dally!"

"All right. Let's go. I want to show you part of the Loop before I take you to meet my boss, the city editor."

"Who won't consider hiring me. Right?" Nevertheless she tried to be optimistic.

They took a street car into the Loop and window-shopped briefly at Marshall Fields and Carson Pirie Scott. She loved the big stores, the Louis Sullivan architecture, and was beginning to feel more comfortable, even thrilled at being in a big city. Her entrance into the *Daily News* building and the city room barely modified that. After her experience in Hughitt, she expected catcalls and whistles, though she'd hoped for more than a flat rejection from John's boss.

In the days that followed she met with one rejection after another until her anger and frustration, expanding like Minnie's yeast bread, could no longer be contained. "Why are you so narrow minded?" she yelled at the tenth editor. "I want you to know I grew up on a farm and can take care of myself." An exaggeration, maybe, she thought, and added, "Anyway, there are plenty of neighborhoods where news happens. I am not fragile, but I'm a damned good writer. Give me a chance."

"Sorry, I can't use you, unless you're willing to report births and marriages."

She was shaking as she left his office and walked through the city room. She stiffened her back and looked straight ahead. In that moment she hated men.

Two weeks later, after more than fifteen rejections, she had to admit she'd not found her niche. No editor wanted her as a reporter, except for social events—debutante balls, weddings, and births on the North Side and even deaths, unless the deceased was an important person. One asked if she could write a personal advice column like the one Dorothy Dix wrote for the *New York Evening Journal*. Another suggested she go to New York where Jane Croly had founded the Women's Press Club. Only one editor said he might publish an occasional essay on suffrage; however, he guaranteed nothing.

When she reported everything to John, he said, "Sarah sweetheart, why don't you take a Society page job? It's a job and maybe it will lead to something better."

"Because I don't want to get stuck doing something insignificant. A non-writer can record vital statistics. I might as well have stayed at the newspaper in South Dakota. At least there my work with Mrs. Hall was important."

When she described her frustration to the boarders and Mrs. Barkley at dinner one night, the responses were mixed. "What did you expect? Reporting is a man's job," and "Take the Society page. What's wrong with that? You're too fussy."

Only Susan Storey, the woman across the hall, presented an alternative. "Come with me to Hull House. With your education Jane Addams will hire you as a teacher. She might also want you to write for her. She gives speeches and writes about education, labor laws, and programs at Hull House. I don't know how she manages it all."

Sarah's doubts almost trumped her curiosity. Writing speeches did not appeal right now and teaching she knew about only as a student. But what else did she have to do? "I'd love to visit Hull House, if only to see what a settlement house is like."

Later she talked to John. "Definitely," he said, "Meet Jane Addams. She's fantastic.

She created Hull House to help immigrants by offering all kinds of programs. She's active in education and labor reform, especially for women and children—anything that improves their lives. She's even a board member of a new organization, the National Association for the Advancement of Colored People. Being associated with her can't hurt you."

The next morning Sarah and Susan walked four blocks to take the Halsted Street trolley to Hull House, an 1850 mansion built in a part of Chicago fashionable before the fire. Now the noisy neighborhood was teeming with pushcarts and people who looked foreign to Sarah.

"They're mostly Italian and the smell is garlic. They sell really tasty food, different from Mrs. Barkley's meat and potatoes," Susan explained. "But not everyone here is Italian. Many Greeks and Jews, Irish and French Canadians, and others from near-by neighborhoods participate in Hull House programs." Sarah had never seen so many people in one place in her whole life, not even at the Chicago train station.

The refurbished Hull House, a haven for hundreds, was an elegant contrast to the neighborhood. With Susan leading the way, Sarah looked into classrooms—one where Susan taught—a nursery for infants and young children, a clinic, and more. But what intrigued her most was a group working on a play by Sophocles.

"*Electra* is not the first," Susan said. "The immigrants have produced several Greek and Shakespearean dramas. Miss Addams always attends. Let's go meet her."

Jane Addams was seated behind a large desk in an eight sided room, the Octagon, built by the original owner. Behind the desk, maps of the neighborhood—blocked off in red, blue, green or other colors to denote ethnicity—dominated one wall. Miss Addams' blue-gray eyes, pale skin, and medium brown hair almost matched Mrs. Hall's, but her size and demeanor conveyed even more self confidence and authority. She stood to greet Sarah.

"Come in. Have a seat. Susan has told me you're a suffragist. Also a writer with a college degree. I always need teachers and I'd also like a writer who'd help with my articles and speeches. Could I see what you've written on feminism?"

"Oh yes. I'd appreciate your comments." Thrilled, Sarah took the three essays she had brought at Susan's suggestion out of her bag and gave them to Miss Addams. At that moment she was so impressed with all she had seen around her, she knew she would like any job in this setting. But bad luck with editors had taught her to be cautious and not too hopeful.

"I've never taught, but it would be an interesting challenge. The writing appeals to me especially. I've been reading and appreciating your *Newer Ideals of Peace*."

Later when she met John, her enthusiasm bubbled over. "I don't have a formal offer, but I think I'll have a job soon. I may actually be writing for newspapers." She smiled. "Not a single editor I've met has impressed me half as much as Jane Addams."

He took her in his arms. "I told you she was a phenomenon. I'm glad you liked each other. I was afraid you might return to Hughitt—or worse, move on to New York City."

"John, sweetheart, I'll never leave you." Still in his arms, she kissed him.

After he kissed her again, he said, "I hope you really mean that."

Two days later, Sarah met with Ellen Starr, Addams' partner, to discuss how best to use her skills. "Helping Jane with her writing takes priority," Miss Starr said. "She's become progressively busy since we opened in 1889. But to write convincingly about Hull House, you need to be familiar with our programs. Teaching English to a class of Italian immigrants is a good place to start."

Within a week Sarah had started teaching English and was also preparing to gather data on the class sizes of grammar schools around the city. Miss Addams, a member of the city school board, intended to make a case for increasing the number of schools in the poorest Chicago neighborhoods. She asked Sarah to collect relevant data.

Sarah spent her free time with John. They walked in Grant Park, visited the Art Institute, and rode the Illinois Central to the South Side to visit the Museum of Science and Industry and the site of the 1893 Columbian Exposition. As they walked along the green stretch of Midway, John pointed to the Gothic structures to their right. "If you decide you want to continue your education, I'd recommend the University of Chicago. I took a few courses here."

"Maybe someday I'll want a master's degree. Right now I want to spend my free time with you. And I have a lot to learn at Hull House."

When warm weather arrived, they began exploring the beaches. In July Lake Michigan was still cold, but John occasionally braved it. Sarah admired his powerful stroke and had a large towel waiting for his shivering frame when he emerged. They'd often picnic and lie on the beach, or walk barefoot in the sand along the water's edge. On one of these days John proposed on bended knee.

"Sarah, darling, I've loved you since high school. We've been separated for long periods of time, but I've never stopped loving you. The last couple of months have been the best of my life, because I've been with you. I want to be with you all the time. Please, say you'll marry me."

"Maybe we shouldn't upset the apple cart. Life seems close to perfection now." She took his hand and kneeled beside him. "John, I love you too, but I'm not sure I'm ready to marry."

"When will you be sure? We've known each other for a long time."

He's right. Putting him off doesn't seem fair. "You've been so good to me. I'll give you an answer soon."

During the next few days, she spent hours pondering her resistance to marriage. She loved John and had declared herself ready to marry when the time was right. Was her mother's discontent a factor? Minnie quarreled with Peder, but Sarah was convinced her mother always loved him and never regretted her marriage, despite that disastrous trip to St. Paul.

Sarah had never met a man she liked better than John. In fact, only Robert Hall had seriously entered her consciousness. Though a spur to her intellectual development, he'd grated on her sensibility with his superior attitude. And he'd never written to her despite his promise on that one magical evening together.

Then what was it? She had no desire to sacrifice her life to good causes like Miss Addams, but she did want to do something significant with her life. She enjoyed her free time with John: the walks in the park, visits to museums, concerts, and picnics. What made her hesitate? If she couldn't identify it, how important could it be?

As she continued to rummage in the recesses of her mind, she knew she wanted to be with John, to be his wife and partner. But there was a catch. She also wanted to have a career—not babies, not yet. She didn't feel old at twenty-four, but at what age does one become an old maid? She knew Kari was already concerned for her, alarmed at her treatment of John, afraid she'd missed her chance to lead a conventional life. *But I want more than a conventional life.* Thank God John approved of her working, unlike many men who felt a working wife reflected badly on them. And if they had a baby—God forbid it be soon—she couldn't imagine a more dedicated father than John.

The following night she told him, "I've always loved you. I want to be your wife and the mother of your children." A second later she added, "But I'd like to put that last off for a bit." He gave her a hug and kissed her several times. She was elated, glad she'd finally made the decision. Eventually, between kisses, she asked, "How would you feel about a wedding in South Dakota?"

"Whatever you want, Love." John kissed her again, picked her up and swung her around. "I don't care where we get married so long as we do."

The wedding was a simple affair before family and a few friends, including Mrs. Hall who apologized for Robert's absence, at the Presbyterian Church in Hughitt. Kari made all arrangements, even preparing for Sarah and John's wedding night in the cottage that she and Ed had once occupied.

Minnie congratulated the couple, but later when they were alone, she said to Sarah, "Don't give up your dreams. You're blessed with intelligence and an education. Don't let them wither on the vine."

As Sarah thanked Kari later for her efforts, she asked, "Were you surprised that John didn't drop me after I treated him so badly?"

"Yes," she answered. "But, Sarah, don't push your luck."

"What do you mean?"

"Don't be offended at what I'm about to say. I've realized that you and John are both self-centered, more concerned about your personal goals than striving for a mutual or common end."

"Why must you be such a pessimist? John and I love each other and we'll support each other. You'll see."

CHAPTER 12
Parenthood and More

The newly-married couple returned to Chicago, promising each other a honeymoon the following summer. Sarah envisioned them as love birds, sufficient unto themselves, even after she became pregnant, feigning happiness at first to match John's enthusiasm. She'd hoped for a childless period, but she accepted her condition enthusiastically once she felt life. For the time being nothing seemed more important.

They named the baby John, but called him Jack to avoid confusion. They were anxious parents and Jack was a colicky, cranky baby at first. John spent more and more time at work, leaving Sarah with most of the child care. If her bonding with the baby had not been so powerful, she might have felt abandoned, resentful of his excessive and untimely, so it seemed to her, commitment to work. One morning after a hectic night, she pleaded with him to help. He took her in his arms to comfort her, while saying authoritatively, "It's your responsibility to take care of the baby. I'll pay more attention when he gets older."

Sarah returned to work two months after Jack's birth, leaving him in the Hull House nursery, where she could drop in to nurse and cuddle him when she wasn't teaching or gathering data for the latest project. The nursery made life easier, but her relationship with John was strained. He helped her get to Hull House in the morning, but he kept long hours at work and was frequently out of town with assignments in New York or Washington. Susan, her colleague and friend, or one of her students often filled in, helping her to or from Hull House with the baby.

In mid-July Sarah almost begged, "John, let's spend part of a weekend day at the beach like we used to. We hardly ever do anything together."

"I'll try to get the day off," John responded. But when Saturday came, he reneged. "I'm needed at the city desk." She tried again, unsuccessfully, the following week, but he said, "Jack is too young for the beach. Let's wait until next summer."

"If I can find a baby sitter will you go with me?"

"We'll see." But he never found the time.

During the winter, Sarah relied more and more on Susan and her students for help with Jack. He had become an easy baby who babbled happily when fussed over. Sarah knew how lucky she was to be supported by Hull House staff and students when John was not there for her.

The following summer John, though still too busy for the beach, was paying more attention to Jack, declaring him a genius because he walked at twelve months. In his place Sarah invited Susan whose interest in Jack had solidified their friendship. She lived nearby, was available for babysitting whenever Sarah needed help, and was a supportive colleague.

Jack was almost two when John announced he had a European assignment.

"Where and for how long?" Sarah asked.

"London and Wales. Probably two months. Possibly longer."

"Two months! Can't you arrange for an unmarried reporter to take over?" *The last two years have been hard enough. Now it gets even worse.*

"I *want* to go. I'm better qualified than any of my colleagues to investigate the coal strike in England, since I covered the miner's strike in Pennsylvania not long ago. Remember?"

His tone told her there was no point in arguing. She turned away—angry, jealous of his chance to travel in England and hurt by his eagerness to depart. During the next few days, she tried to feel happy for him, but it was hard and she was often curt when they talked about his preparing for the trip. On departure day, he grabbed her as she turned away from him. "Sarah, I'd like to leave on good terms. It may be months before I return."

"I know. I shouldn't be upset. You're never here anyway." Their last kiss was passionless. When she heard the door close, some part of her wanted to pursue him, but she stood immobile, angry, and missing him already. *Why can't I be like Minnie? I'm sure she never expected Peder to care for their babies. But at least my father was home every night.*

With John gone, Sarah spent more time at Hull House. She admired Jane Addams' endless energy, intellect, warm heart and generosity—a gentle lioness in a silk dress. When she declared her support of Teddy Roosevelt's Progressive Bull Moose party in 1912 and overcame TR's resistance to a women's suffrage plank in the party platform, Sarah's mood lifted for the first time since John's departure. But she declined an invitation to join a campaign trip. "I'd love to. I'm a Progressive through and through," she said. "But I can't leave Jack. He's only two." She was afraid she'd be gone too long; they'd miss each other too much.

When John wrote in February that he'd be returning soon, her negative feelings evaporated like a puff of smoke. She had missed him more than she liked to admit. Her joyous response to the good news was to smother a surprised Jack with kisses. A week later it was John. Soon after their happy reunion, he was busy at work writing articles about the coming election and Sarah was working long hours for the Bull Moose Party. She had been disappointed when Woodrow Wilson defeated Roosevelt, but she was proud and delighted when John, one of a hundred reporters, was invited to meet Wilson at the first formal presidential press conference. On his return, however, he refused to care for Jack so she could march with the suffragists in Washington on the day before the inaugural. She had wanted to attend with Miss Adams, Susan and others from Hull House, expecting to be among the ten thousand marchers in this biggest demonstration ever for women's rights.

"John, I supported you. Why can't you support me?"

"My job is more important than your participation with that mob in Washington, and I get paid. Anyway, you've given enough of your time and energy to woman's suffrage."

"I'll take Jack with me if you can't care for him for a couple of days."

"Don't be ridiculous. It's apt to be a violent scene. Remember what happened in London. Who knows what will happen here. You might end up in the hospital or jail. Sarah, for your own sake, stay home."

"No. I'm going, but you're right. I shouldn't take Jack."

She finally left Jack with one of his nursery school teachers who volunteered to keep him until she returned.

John was not happy, but she refused to give in.

"Who organized this parade?" Susan asked after the Hull House group had found seats together on the train.

"Alice Paul." Miss Addams responded. "She's been a tremendous force trying to revitalize the suffrage movement in this country. She became an advocate in England where the suffragests were confrontational. She actually spent time in jail. And was force-fed when she refused to eat because of abusive treatment."

A combined surge of patriotism and determination flooded Sarah as they drove within sight of government buildings and monuments that she'd only seen in pictures.

They joined the parade on Pennsylvania Avenue. They made good progress at first, until a group of hecklers, mostly drunk, blocked their movement. More hecklers yelled obscene language or spit on them. Finally, some began throwing rocks, while most of the police stood idly by.

Sarah staggered when a rock hit the side of her head. Dizzy, she dropped to the street. Before the women could help her up, a young policeman grabbed her, pulled her out of the parade. Her senses recovered, she tried to break away from him. He ignored her protests as he dragged her off.

A few minutes later, she was locked into a jail cell with four angry women, who were complaining bitterly about their treatment. They had no idea what was going to happen to them. A nurse came to attend to Sarah's injury. She cleaned the minor wound and agreed with Sarah that nothing more needed to be done. She had no answers to questions about the women's release.

What now? Will John come to get me out of here?

Two days later, she and only one of her cellmates had not been rescued.

CHAPTER 13
Friends, Old and New

She thought she heard a commotion. Someone was yelling. But "Release my wife immediately," came across clearly, no mistaking John's voice.

She was glad to see him, even though he was angry. "I'm missing important days at work...for what? I hope you've learned something, Sarah."

Her second day back at Hull House, she was called to Jane Addams' office.

"Are you okay? I want you to know that we tried to get you out of jail, but they refused. They did say they'd release you and the others the following day. I'm sorry I can't give you more time to recover from that misfortune, but I have a major request.

"I'd like you to represent me in New York at the Lenox Hill Neighborhood House. Ellen cannot go this time. I know this creates a babysitting problem for you. And you've just had a horrendous time. Can you manage to get away for three days? I would be ever so appreciative."

"I'll see what I can arrange for Jack. When do I go and what do I do?"

"Next week. They're adding programs and hope to learn from our successes...and failures."

Sarah knew John would not take charge of Jack for three days, but she had to ask him, so he couldn't claim later that she hadn't.

"Why do you ask? You know I work at night. Not very thoughtful of your boss to ask a mother of a young child. Especially after what you just went through. I think you should beg off."

"Like you beg off from work? My boss said she trusts me to handle this well and I consider it important, so I'm going to New York with or without your blessing. I'll ask Susan. She will be available this time…and willing, I think."

"Sorry, I'm just too busy to look after him now."

An Illinois suffragist, a participant in the Washington parade, sat next to Sarah on the 20th Century Limited, the train that would take her into Grand Central Station.

Talking about their common experience, the Illinois suffragist said, "Most of the crowd was supportive, but I did hear verbal abuse. I know rocks were thrown. What was your experience?"

"I was hit in the head with a rock, nothing serious. But a policeman pulled me out of the parade and put me in a jail cell with four other women. Before they let me out, this policeman told me that he was protecting me from more stone-throwers. I asked him why he didn't put the stone throwers in jail instead of the victims. No answer."

She fell asleep minutes after finishing her tale, not to awaken until they arrived in Manhattan the following morning. Excited at first, Sarah decided New York was not so different from Chicago, though some places seemed fancier, like Grand Central Station and parts of Fifth Avenue. She took a taxi to her hotel where she dropped off her suitcase and called the settlement house. She took another taxi to Lenox Hill where she spent the day talking to the director as they visited programs much like those at Hull House.

The next day she returned to finish her work, making suggestions about day care and teaching English to immigrants. Afterwards the director invited her to lunch in the cafeteria.

"I can't tell you how much I appreciate your sharing your experiences with us. I know this is your first visit to New York. I'd hate for you to leave tomorrow without taking in a cultural event. Are you interested in art by any chance?"

"I do like art. Especially the Impressionists… Monet, Renoir."

"There's a modern art show at the Armory that has everyone talking. Some say the exhibit is scandalous. I haven't been yet, but I'm curious. If this doesn't appeal to you, there's always the Metropolitan."

Sarah, also curious, took another taxi to the Armory. Before she was even close to the paintings, she was dazzled by Van Gogh's sunflowers. *Oh, Ma, you should see these yellow flowers. Van Gogh must have been in South Dakota.* She was mildly shocked by Gauguin's half-naked natives, and tentative about Cezanne's mountain. Picasso's blue period appealed to her more than his later work. Eventually she approached Duchamp's *Nude Descending a Stair Case,* the shocking, most talked about star of the exhibit.

A man suddenly moved in beside her. "Sarah, is it really you?"

"Robert, what are you doing here?" Flustered, she was afraid she sounded critical, as if he shouldn't be there.

"I just came to see the exhibit. You stood out...without a hat. That's rare, you know. How are you? It's been years. Mother wrote that you and John had a baby. Congratulations."

"Jack is almost three now. What about you?" She'd regained her composure. "Still in New York, I presume. Did you ever marry?"

"To a beautiful debutante. I'd like you to meet her. I'll have to check with her first, but how about dinner with us tonight?"

"I'd love to, but I can't. I already have plans." *Why did I lie? Intimidated by Robert or his debutante?*

"Maybe next time. I didn't even ask why you are here...or if you ever go home. To South Dakota, I mean."

"I work for Jane Addams in Chicago and I'm here as a consultant to a settlement house. I rarely get home to South Dakota...not since we got married. John is too busy. Do you?"

"My wife went once and said 'never again.' She's a city girl." He looked at his watch. "I have an appointment at the office. But first, tell me what you think of this painting."

"It certainly is different. I think in time I might like the Duchamp. How about you?"

"I prefer Gauguin's semi-nudes. But I enjoyed seeing you."

She smiled. "I enjoyed it too."

Her trip to New York infused her with energy and a renewed commitment. Her work at Hull House was no longer enough. She needed new inspiration. Her increasing restlessness helped her sympathize with John, become more tolerant of his U.S. trips. She still disliked the lengthy foreign assignments and was grateful that he was home most of 1913 and the first half of 1914. When the Great War started in July, 1914, she knew he'd be wrangling to go overseas. She rarely complained now about the effect of his absences, at times fully appreciative that he was never going to change.

Shortly after John left for France, she had a dream peopled with distorted and shifting images of herself and professors at Hughitt College, a dream still with her when she awoke. Did the dream suggest that she could be a teacher? A professor? The idea excited her, rekindled her desire to do something significant with her life, a wish that had stuck with her over the years like a tumbleweed caught in a barbed-wire fence. Would the University of Chicago accept her as a graduate student? How long would it take to get a Master's Degree? Would Jane Addams support her?

She talked to admissions and faculty at the university and learned she could probably complete the MA in history in two years which would prepare her for teaching—if not in Chicago, maybe Hughitt College. Occasionally, during one of their bitter fights, she thought of escaping to Dakota where Jack could be with family and she could work at the college.

The Misses Starr and Addams supported her educational plan, and the latter even promised to arrange a tuition scholarship. They were less happy about her plan to leave Hull House in two or three years, but Miss Addams' concern about the war in Europe and her efforts to organize a women's peace party were taking precedence over all local and national issues which had been the focus of Sarah's research and writing.

Sarah enthusiastically became a student again, majoring in World and American History, browsing in the stacks, sitting in classes mesmerized by brilliant professors, or engaging in conversations with students after class. Just being on campus was a pleasure. She wandered through the quadrangles defined by the Gothic structures that housed classrooms, Harper Library, the law and business schools, and dormitories. The greenery, especially the ivy which she'd never seen in such abundance in South Dakota, and the quiet setting, hardly disturbed by the students and faculty walking to their next destinations, contrasted with the hustle and bustle of Halsted Street bootblacks, vendors, and hucksters with their pushcarts calling out their wares in broken English, and children playing tag or ball games on the stoops or in the street.

She usually ate her lunch, a sandwich from home, sitting in one of the quads, unless inclement weather drove her to the small coffee shop on the far side of campus for a cup of hot tea or coffee. Early in the autumn quarter a fellow student saw her searching for a table in the crowded C-shop and invited her to share his. She recognized Ben Thomas, a tall, muscular, argumentative man with a cleft chin, who often challenged the two professors they had in common. She gratefully accepted, looking forward to a discussion of the Indian wars, a topic in their last class.

Before she'd sat down, he asked, "Are you a teacher?"

"No. But that's what I'm striving for." Hoping to end personal questions, she added, "What did you think about the discussion on the Indian wars this morning?"

"If you don't teach now, what do you do?"

"Well…I do teach English…at Hull House, the settlement house on Halsted and Polk Streets."

"You hardly need a Master's degree in history to teach English to Italian immigrants."

"No, but I'm hoping to teach in a college eventually."

"In Chicago?"

"Yes, or possibly South Dakota." She was saying more than she wanted, egged on by his questions. "You haven't said why you're in graduate school."

"Same reason as you really, except for the Dakota part. Why South Dakota?"

"That's where I grew up and went to college."

"Really? Are you a Willa Cather fan? I know she's from Nebraska, but they are both prairie states. Anyway, the last place I'd want to go is the farm in Southern Illinois where I grew up."

"I felt that way once. No more, but I'm not interested in reading about it, so I'm not a Cather fan." She finished her coffee and stood up to leave.

"Is your husband a teacher?"

"No." She looked at the wedding band and realized she missed John less now than she used to. Still she often felt lonely and wondered how much he loved her. Ben's intense gaze, reminiscent of Robert Hall, made her uncomfortable. To prevent more questions, she said, "He's a foreign correspondent," and departed with, "Thanks for sharing your table."

Two days later Ben approached her after their Western Civilization class. "That's a threatening sky. If you're planning to head for the C-Shop, I'd like to join you." He added, "I apologize for being inquisitive the other day. I promise not to ask so many questions again."

"There is nothing left for you to ask."

"I can usually think of something." He looked up at the sky. "We're going to be caught in a downpour if we don't hurry."

Sarah watched him, fascinated. He wasn't asking her, he was telling her. But there was no reason to say no. He seemed sincerely apologetic and she liked conversing with a man who spoke English impeccably compared to her Italian students. "Lead the way," she said, and a moment later the darkening clouds let loose, forcing them to dash for cover in the cloister adjacent to Bond Chapel.

Once protected from the cloudburst, Sarah explained, "My brother Joe kept track of all the skirmishes in the Black Hills between the Indians and the army. Matthew, my older brother, was sympathetic to the Sioux. He pointed out all the treaties our government broke. That didn't impress Joe. He considered the Indians savages and remained loyal to the army. What I know mostly came from those arguments."

Ben nodded as he grabbed her arm. "Let's make a run for it. The rain is letting up."

Finding a place in the crowded shop looked impossible until Ben recognized two students and asked if he and Sarah could join them. While he went to order two grilled cheese sandwiches and two coffees, the three introduced themselves and talked about their majors, until one of the men asked Sarah, "Why would a woman—especially a married woman—go to graduate school?"

Ben, returning with the coffee and sandwich, overheard the question. "Let it go, Fellas," he responded, "No reason a woman shouldn't strive for a better position in life."

"It's all right, Ben. I have an answer. I'm in graduate school because I want to do something important, contribute to the world in a significant way. I don't know how or what yet, but a graduate education can't hurt."

When the two students left, he turned to her. "I liked what you said. Now it's your chance to give me the third degree."

"Have you picked a thesis topic?" she asked, avoiding his private life, hoping to set an example for him.

"No, have you?"

"Something on feminism. I haven't decided specifically." As she finished her coffee, she said, "I should be moving on."

"To Hull House?" He stood up, ready to leave.

"Yes." She put on her raincoat and headed for the door. He followed.

"This is never going to stop," he said, watching the torrential rain cascading down a window pane and flooding the walkways. "Can I give you a ride? You may drown if I don't."

"You have a car? Are you sure it's no bother?" How could she turn down a ride in this miserable weather? "Just to the trolley," she added.

"I have an old Model T. Dropping you off is no bother. I'm heading in your direction."

By the time they got to his car, they were drenched. Her coat was too short to protect the bottom half of her skirt. He laughed and she giggled at their soggy clothing and dripping hair. "How can misery be so funny?" she asked. "What I wouldn't give for a dry towel." When they got to her trolley stop, she accepted his offer to take her the rest of the way on the condition that he'd let her give him a tour of Hull House.

As they stood in one of the large beautifully-furnished rooms, he said, "JaneAddams must be wealthy. How else could she afford mahogany furniture and fresh bouquets?"

"Her family was wealthy…She wears beautiful silk dresses. She also has rich friends; I know some are donors." They peeked into several rooms, including the classroom she shared with Susan, and stopped to watch the drama group rehearsing *Alcestis*.

"Fascinating," Ben said. "I should read Euripides. I'm interested because I've been thinking I might write my thesis on some aspect of the golden years of Athens."

"Not American history?" She was surprised.

"I've been teaching American history for two years. I want to explore a different era, broaden my knowledge." His response made her feel lazy or guilty for planning to write about feminism, a topic familiar to her. But her wish to be more than just a student was what made her eager to finish quickly.

"Well, thanks for the tour. By the way, how do you get home from here?"

"I take another trolley." She did not mention the four block walk after that.

"Let me drive you. I'm sure it's still raining. I'm going in your direction anyway."

"How do you know where I live?"

"Actually, I looked you up in the student directory. Sorry if my curiosity offends you."

She shook her head in disbelief. "I didn't even know there was a student directory." She hesitated briefly. "How do you feel about taking a young child too? I have a son here in the nursery." She watched his face contort in surprise and recover quickly.

"I like kids. I have two nephews that are preschool age."

Minutes later, she was introducing them. Jack's curiosity erupted into excitement when he heard about the car. "Can we go right now?"

"Sure enough, pal," Ben responded.

When they got to the apartment house, Sarah felt some obligation to invite Ben in, but hesitated to invite a strange man into her apartment when John was not there. What would he think? Nothing good, she decided. Jack, however, had taken a liking to Ben, or his car, and spoke up. "I want Ben to see my train set."

"Maybe another day," Sarah responded, wondering what Ben's smile meant.

"We'll do it some other time. I'd love to see your trains."

For several days, Sarah avoided Ben. Since he sat up front in the classroom and she sat in the back, it was easy to skip out the door after class and head for the library or a remote quad before he could catch up with her. One day he arrived late and sat in the back next to her.

After class, he asked, "How's my foul weather friend?"

"I finally dried out."

"I notice you make a quick dash for the door after class. Are you avoiding me? Do I have to wait for the next earthquake, hurricane, tornado, or blizzard to have lunch with you again?" He paused. "Have I offended you in some way? Tell me. I'd like to be your friend."

"No, you haven't done anything, but I'm married. I can't...." She didn't know how to complete the sentence. Instead, she added reluctantly, "Jack has been asking about you. You're welcome to come see his trains."

"Are you sure it's all right with you?"

It's alright with me. But probably not with my husband. "Yes." The sooner, the better, she decided. "Maybe we could drive to Hull House on Wednesday after class and pick Jack up? He'll love showing off his trains. I warn you, though, his trains are nothing special. Except to him." She took a deep breath, "Please don't misinterpret the invitation."

"How would I misinterpret it?"

"What I mean is, I don't want to encourage this friendship."

"Why? We're both students interested in history." He sighed. "You know, you kind of remind me of a thistle, a gorgeous flower with prickly spines."

"I'm not talking about me. Jack has taken a liking to you. It would be fine if I were divorced or a widow. But John will be coming home one of these days. I don't want Jack to get hurt, to suffer when your friendship has to end." *He's had enough of being left or abandoned by his father.*

"How could a friendship hurt Jack? But...no point in arguing. See you Wednesday."

Jack ran up to Ben. "I knew you'd come back. Can we go in your car?"

Sarah watched Ben pick Jack up and carry him on his shoulders. That should be John, she thought. I understand why Jack adores Ben. He's a really nice person. I'm attracted too, only partly because he responds so well to Jack. She was deep in thought when Ben pulled up in front of her apartment house.

"I hope you're not too unhappy about this," he said. She only knew she did not feel in control.

Once inside, Jack grabbed Ben's hand and pulled him to the toy box. Sarah retreated to the kitchen to read the latest letter from John. Typically, war news predominated with a few loving lines at the end. After preparing a casserole and putting the dish into the oven, she checked on Ben and Jack. They'd put the trains into the box and had settled on the sofa where Ben was reading *Jack and the Beanstalk*. Jack was leaning against Ben's shoulder as if he'd known him forever. In an instant Sarah's feelings were an unhappy mix— jealously of their closeness, fear and uncertainty about their future.

"Can Ben eat dinner with us?" Jack asked in a pleading voice

She couldn't resist Jack's appeal, "If he likes ham and scalloped potatoes."

"I do," Ben said, "But I warn you. I have the appetite of a field hand during harvest."

Sarah marveled at Jack's proper table manners, obviously intended to impress Ben. After talk about the trains, Jack began to describe Ben's two dogs. Sarah's heart sank. Would he start asking for a puppy again? "Ben says they're mutts and I can walk with them sometime."

"Two dogs in the city? How do you manage that?"

"Two keep each other company. A woman in the building takes them out in the afternoon with her dog. I walk them in the morning and at night."

"Ma, can Ben be my second daddy?"

Sarah felt the blood drain from her face. "No. You have one. You can't have another."

"Why? Pa isn't here."

She was trying to gather her composure when Ben responded, "I can't be your father, Jack, but I can be a good friend. We can have lots of fun together."

In the days that followed Jack often asked about Ben: "When can I walk the dogs with him?" Ben also asked about Jack when he bumped into Sarah in the library. One day Sarah asked him, "How soon can you take Jack for that walk with the dogs? He's constantly asking me."

"How about this weekend? The weather is supposed to be decent for March."

"Wonderful. Saturday morning, say eleven."

Jack was even more excited returning from the walk than when Sarah relinquished him to Ben. "Mommy, you should come with us next time." He was a little fountain bubbling over. "Can we go again next week? Can we? I love running with the dogs. And throwing a ball for them."

"I guess it's all right, if Ben is willing."

Two weeks later, Sarah arrived at Hull House to find the place in an uproar. Miss Starr rushed up to her and gently guided her to a chair. "Oh Sarah," she said in a shaky voice, "Jack has disappeared."

"What? How?"

"He went to the park with a group of five-year olds. They were walking back when the teacher discovered he was missing. None of the children have any idea what happened. We've notified the police. They're looking for him. Also several men…your students were eager to help. Some of them have children too. There should be no trouble spotting a blond, blue eyed child in this area."

Oh, God, please not kidnapped. "I need to search. Tell me exactly where they were walking."

"Sarah, best you not go. No one knows exactly where they were when he disappeared. Anyway you should be *here* when he's found. At least ten people are looking for him."

She knew Miss Starr was right, but her desperation ran high as she paced, trying to dispel the horrible images that invaded her mind's eye.

CHAPTER 14
New Friend; Jealous Husband

When a policeman walked in an hour later, she pounced. "Any luck?" She knew the answer. He was alone.

"Sorry, Ma'am. He wasn't on Polk Street. No word from any of the others?"

"No. And it's getting dark. What will you do now?" She felt as if she teetered on the edge of a precipice.

"When the captain reports in, we'll decide. He's in charge." O Captain, my Captain. No, no. That's a mourning poem. Sarah shook her head. Jack is not dead, he's lost.

Miss Starr put an arm around her. "Come sit, Sarah. Have a bite to eat. I know this is hard, but you need your strength."

"I can't. I don't want anything...only Jack."

The captain and two of Sarah's students returned from Halsted without Jack. Sarah felt nauseated; her heart was pounding as if it would explode. When the rest of the searchers straggled in empty handed, she announced, "I have to look for him." She grabbed the captain by the arm and asked for a policeman to accompany her. She wondered if a policeman might have frightened Jack into hiding, but doubted it. He'd never shown any fear of policemen and he was proud of being "brave."But could he have been enticed by a kidnapper who offered him a puppy, for example.

"Captain, we're wasting time. If he was kidnapped, they could be getting farther and farther away from here."

The captain conceded to her request, but wanted to check first with the others to see what territory had not been searched. They were about to leave, when Ben walked in carrying a limp child.

Visions of Jack being run over by a carriage or horse cart flashed through Sarah's head as she stared at the frightening scene. *Is he dead?* She was frozen in place until Jack turned toward her and smiled. Overcome with relief and joy, she embraced them both and smothered her son with kisses. "Where was he?" Not that it mattered now. He was safe and sound.

"He was shivering outside my door when I got home from school. I made cocoa to warm him up while he played with the dogs. I called your apartment but you didn't answer. I figured you must be here."

"How did he find your place? Isn't it blocks from Halsted?"

"He was there once after we walked the dogs. I guess he remembered."

Before she could ask any more questions, everyone surrounded them, cheering and slapping Ben on the back. Miss Starr broke out the sherry. "I think a celebration is in order."

Later, as Ben drove them home, Sarah's interrogation began. "Jack, why did you leave your teacher and the group? How did you find Ben's apartment?"

"I wanted to walk the dogs again. I saw the sign, Greenwood. Ben's street. So I turned when everybody else went straight."

"I'm very proud that you could read the street sign, but you must never, ever do that again. Do you understand? I was worried sick. Do you have any idea how many people were looking for you? We didn't know what had happened." She doubted her scolding, his only punishment, would have much effect, because Ben had arrived eventually with cocoa and a ride back to Hull House. Not to mention the dogs.

Jack hadn't responded to her last questions, but as they pulled up in front of the apartment building, he asked, "Can Ben come in?"

"No. We're having dinner and then you're going right to bed." *Punishment after all.*

As Jack climbed out of the car, he said to Ben, "Thanks for the cocoa. Can I walk the dogs with you again?"

Embarrassed, Sarah turned to Ben. "My son has better manners than I do. I can't thank you enough for what you did tonight. I was living a nightmare until you showed up. How can I thank you?"

"That hug was nice." He smiled. "And I wouldn't mind another of your home-cooked meals. But you don't owe me anything."

Winter quarter ended in late March. Sarah picked her way around patches of dirty snow, remnants of the last storm, as she headed toward Harper through the classics quadrangle. The lyrics of the *Alma Mater* came back to her as she admired the Gothic architecture—the "city gray" more enduring than the "city white," as the 1893 Columbian Exposition was called. Some remnants of that fair had endured: the Midway, the Museum of Science and Industry, the bridge and part of the park designed by Olmsted, and the charming workman's cottages which still served as artisan shops and studios.

Intrigued by the gargoyles, she vowed to research these medieval figures, believed to ward off evil spirits. But not yet. She'd started work on *Feminism in the Nineteenth Century,* her MA thesis. She was spending daytime hours doing research in Harper and writing at night. She often saw Ben in the library and on Saturdays when he and Jack walked the dogs, a routine she'd accepted to keep her son happy. And to have more time to write.

Since John's departure in August, 1914, he'd written to her almost weekly, mostly about the war: the battle of Lorraine, the Ardenne, the siege of Antwerp. She skimmed these lines and settled on the few at the end about his love for her and Jack and his eagerness to get home. Sarah saved every letter and read them over and over. Expressions of his wish to return home had intensified

161

with time. Eventually, he wrote that he was "war weary." In early May Sarah got the letter she'd been waiting for.

Paris, France April 30, 1915

Dear Sarah,

Great news. I'll be home in about two weeks, mid May. I can hardly wait to see you and Jack, to escape this bloody war. You're in my thoughts always. I hope you can break away from Hull House and the University for a few days. I have no idea if I'll return here, but I probably will if the U.S. joins the Allies. Let's make the best of whatever time we have. See you soon, sweetheart.

Love,
John

She read the letter three times before she jumped up and grabbed Jack. "Daddy's coming home." Was it really going to happen? She'd kissed her son before she realized he lacked her enthusiasm. How could she blame him? He hadn't seen John in seven, months, a long time for a child who had just turned four when his father left. "We'll have lots of fun together and daddy will be here for your fifth birthday. We'll go to the Indiana Dunes. You'll love the beach."

"Can I still walk the dogs with Ben?"

"Why not?" Anything to make him feel good about his father coming home.

The following Saturday morning, she invited herself to join them on their walk. "I need to get outside," she told Ben. "I've been inside for weeks, exercising my brain and my writing hand, but nothing else. I'm also celebrating good news"

"I'm glad you're coming with us. You need to lighten up. Enjoy life a little." A moment later, he added, "What's the good news?"

She heard the "lighten up" part of his response. "Have I been so grim?" She knew she was a drudge, but she had felt positive, thriving on reading and writing.

"Not grim, exactly. But you rarely laugh or smile. I must say, you do have more of a spring in your step today. Do you mind walking on the Midway? It's greening up fast. We could head toward Lake Michigan or west toward the Lorado Taft statue."

"I've been to the lake often, but I've never seen that statue. I really should find out more about Taft. I've heard he's been supportive of women sculptors."

"Good. We're off to see the *Fountain of Time*, if not the *Wizard of Oz*. Incidentally, did you know that the author of the Oz stories, Frank Baum, was a South Dakotan?"

"Yes. I read two of Baum's books to Jack. He liked them."

"Actually, I think many Chicagoans regard Taft as the *Wizard of Chicago*. But tell me how your thesis is coming along." As they strolled along 59th Street discussing their research, Jack and the dogs romped on the Midway. Ben's earlier characterization nagged at Sarah. *Maybe I'm trying too hard to finish by the end of summer. Especially now that John is coming home.*

As they approached Cottage Grove Avenue, Ben announced, "There's Father Time and the horde of humanity."

"It's so massive. That crowd of people. Ben, I'm hopeless. What does this mean?"

"Time remains while people move on—something like that." He turned to her abruptly, "Hey, you haven't told me the good news you mentioned earlier."

"John is coming home in two weeks." Had she mentioned his name before? "And I've had two papers accepted for publication in the *Journal of American History*."

"Congratulations! Is one of the articles part of your thesis on Feminism?"

"Yes, and the other is about the early Suffragist movement, a paper I wrote for Dr. Crane."

"No wonder you're in such a good mood." He hesitated. "Will you register for courses next quarter with John coming home?"

"Yes. He'll want me to stay in school." *I hope.*

Sarah waited for John's train in the same station she'd waited for him in 1909. Had it really been six years? Would history be repeated or would he arrive as expected? When his train was announced, she was nervous, but she was no longer a frightened, intimidated farm girl.

Still, when she first saw him, she momentarily felt faint. As they rushed toward each other, she saw the effects of a year of war. Though still handsome, he was thinner and the frown lines and the creases around his mouth were deeper. Jostled by the crowd as they embraced, he said, "Let's get out of here." As soon as they were clear of the hordes, "It's great to see you. You look absolutely wonderful. How is Jack?"

"He's good. Susan will bring him home from Hull House. Oh, John, I'm so happy you're back. I've missed you so much." She caressed his face. "You look good, but you've lost weight."

In the taxi they held hands, unable to take their eyes off of each other. In the apartment, John took her in his arms again. "When is Jack coming home?"

"We have about an hour. Susan said she'd drop Jack off around five."

"Then what are we waiting for?" They were in bed in minutes. She didn't bother with the negligee she'd bought for the occasion.

"Wow, Jack you've grown." John started to pick him up, but stopped abruptly. Sarah could feel his shyness, his tentativeness.

Jack was bolder. "Yeah, Mom says my pants are getting too short. Dad, my teacher says you were in the war. Did you shoot anyone?"

"No, Jack. I wasn't a soldier. I'm a reporter. My job is to write about the war. Anyway our country is not in the war yet. Maybe someday I'll be a soldier if I'm not too old."

At dinner Jack asked, "Dad, can I walk with Ben and his dogs tomorrow?"

"I guess so. Who's Ben?"

"He goes to school with Mommy. He has two dogs, Cinder and Spot. I have fun playing with them. Ben also has a car. We ride in it sometimes."

Sarah added, "Ben is a fellow student in history. He gave me a ride one day when there was a cloudburst. We picked up Jack at Hull House and he had his first ride in a car. When Jack learned that Ben had dogs, he asked if he could walk with them sometime. I was opposed at first, but I gave in to keep him happy."

"Will I meet this Ben tomorrow? I was hoping the three of us would do something together."

"If Jack goes with Ben in the morning, we'll still have all afternoon for the three of us. You and I can have some time alone while Jack is gone."

John awoke the next morning before Ben arrived and met him at the door. He faced a man approximately his age, with medium brown hair and regular features—except a cleft chin—a man, John decided, who might be considered good looking by many women. "Sarah tells me you're a history student at the University."

"Yes. Sarah and I've had a few classes together."

Just then Sarah and Jack joined them. "I see you two have met." She felt awkward. "Jack is ready and eager to go." The men shook hands before Ben took Jack's hand and they left.

"I need more coffee," John said as he put his arm around her waist. "How often do you see this guy?"

"On Saturdays when he and Jack have the dog-walking date. Occasionally, after class or in Harper Library. We've had lunch once or twice in the C-Shop."

"Doesn't it seem strange to you that this man is willing to pick up your son every week? Isn't he married? Doesn't he have kids of his own?"

"I've never asked about his private life. I don't think he's married, but I don't know for sure."

"Why did you encourage his friendship with Jack?"

"I didn't." *Why is he making me feel guilty?* "I tried to discourage it, but Jack was insistent about walking the dogs with him. Jack loves dogs." She moved toward the kitchen, his arm still around her waist. "C'mon, let's have coffee. Enjoy our privacy."

That night, after Jack was asleep, John asked, "Has Ben ever been in our apartment, beyond the front door?"

"Please, John, stop the questioning. Ben has been a good friend, that's all."

"I asked a question. I expect an answer."

"Ben had dinner here once after he'd driven me and Jack home in a rainstorm. Jack invited him in. I could hardly say no." His questions were beginning to upset her. She'd not been totally forthright, but it was the truth essentially. She'd left out the part about wanting a more constant male figure in Jack's life. *We'll have to talk about that if John accepts another overseas assignment.*

Although he asked no more questions that night, she sensed he'd ask more, that he didn't trust her completely. As she tried to fall asleep, she remembered her sister's accusation that she had mistreated John by dating Robert Hall. If John had known about the memorable kiss at the end of that evening, he would have had reason to be jealous of Robert. But he didn't know and he had been angry anyway.

She resented John's probing, but resolved to be gentle and supportive, and not take offence at his questions, knowing he'd been through terrible times, unimaginable to her. Having him home was what she'd longed for most. She would keep her distance from Ben and avoid anything that John could misinterpret. She'd admitted—only to herself and Susan—that Ben was attractive. If her love for John wasn't so strong, she might have succumbed to an affair when she was desperately lonely. And what about John? Of course she hoped he was faithful during his long stay overseas, but she would never question him. If she thought about it too long, she could feel her resentment building. No matter how often he questioned her fidelity, she would never ask him what he's up to on his long assignments.

During the next few months, she suppressed her negative feelings. To avoid potential conflict on Saturdays, she took Jack to museums, parks, and zoos to replace the walks with Ben. John was always invited and he occasionally joined them. Although Jack often asked if he could walk with Ben and the dogs, she remained firm to protect both of them from John's jealousy.

As in the past, John spent long hours at the *Daily News*. He also began writing a book about his war experiences. Although Sarah hoped the writing would be therapeutic, his restlessness persisted. She helped him by reading and editing, occasionally going to Harper Library to find a book he wanted or to do research for him.

One day she bumped into Ben as he was leaving the library. She tried to avoid him, to hurry past, but he saw her.

"Sarah, wait a minute. How are you…and Jack?"

"We're all fine. Ben, I don't have time to talk now."

"Just tell me if you finished your Master's thesis."

"No, I put it aside for the time being." She turned again to leave.

"I'm sorry. You were so close to finishing. I hope you don't put it aside for too long. I've decided to continue for a doctorate."

"Wonderful. Good luck with that." As she hurried away, she felt both jealousy and self pity. She'd like to be doing research for herself instead of investigating the diplomatic clashes in Europe immediately before the Great War. Later, as she sat on the trolley going home, she wondered if she should tell John about seeing Ben. *Not unless he asks*

Toward the end of November, she convinced John to take a week off and spend Christmas in South Dakota. He agreed when she impressed upon him the fact that his aging parents had never seen Jack. She was also eager to introduce their son to her family and to spend time with them. She especially looked forward to seeing her nephew Charlie, a Hughitt College student who had written her about law school as a prelude to a political career. She would also visit Mrs. Hall and hear about her latest suffrage efforts.

The reunion went well. Sarah was thrilled that Jack spent hours in the barn with Ed or Kari and played happily with his cousins and Champ, the puppy Ed and Kari had recently acquired. He helped his cousins decorate the large Christmas tree, visited his paternal grandparents, and joined in the singing as Minnie played carols on the piano.

Sarah, Kari, and the children accompanied Minnie to a Christmas Eve pageant at the church. Mrs. Hall spotted Sarah first. "Oh, my dear, it is so good to see you. I'm eager to meet your husband and tell you about our progress here. I want you to tell me about Jane Addams. Could you and John join us for dinner on New Year's Day?"

Sarah eagerly accepted, curious about the latest South Dakota suffrage news.

As Sarah turned to join her family, Mrs. Hall added, "One more thing. Robert and Elizabeth will be at dinner. They're eager to see you too."

Sarah wondered if Elizabeth was Mrs. Hall's older daughter who she'd known as a young adolescent. Or might this Elizabeth be the wife Robert had mentioned in New York?

CHAPTER 15
Peace and War

Sarah looked forward to seeing Robert again—despite their history of tense dinners—and finding out if the Elizabeth mentioned was his wife or his sister. She worried, though, that John, who knew Robert from their student days, might still harbor resentment toward him. Only recently she had begun to fully appreciate her husband's jealous streak.

The noisy chaos of New Year's greetings, introductions, and shedding of winter coats and scarves in the foyer faded as they moved into the sedate Victorian parlor. On the tea table in the center of the room, colorful punch filled a crystal bowl. Plates of nuts, cheese and crackers, and pastries surrounded it. In front of the bay window a brilliantly lit Christmas tree added to the festive air.

Robert, like John, was beginning to gray around the edges. His red hair looked better to Sarah now that it was diluted with a few strands of white. Otherwise, he'd aged less than John—no furrows in his forehead. He told Sarah she was "more beautiful than ever." *Really? After seven years?* Obviously, Elizabeth is the grown-up adolescent Sarah had known years before as Robert's sister. Why isn't his wife here, the one he mentioned when I saw him in New York?

Elizabeth, once described by Robert as "more talker than thinker" chatted with Sarah about her family. Her husband, a pharmacist, was home watching their two children so she could visit her friend in Hughitt. Flattered that Elizabeth remembered her, Sarah felt mildly guilty trying to break away, but excused herself to replenish her drink.

Although Mrs. Hall had never approved of alcohol, Robert had added liquor to her fruit punch. Sarah couldn't imagine how he'd achieved that concession, though she approved the result. Once the guests had drinks and were nibbling, Mrs. Hall retreated to the kitchen. When Elizabeth stood up to join her, Sarah offered to go in her place. "Your mother and I have a lot to talk about." The men were already discussing the war. She figured John could hold his own against Robert's formidable debating skills. After all, he'd been in the trenches, had seen the Great War first hand. What would they argue about? She guessed both were isolationists, though John had rarely talked to her about the war. Too bloody, too depressing.

"We are going to win the vote very soon," Mrs. Hall said, while removing a roast from the oven. "There is more support for us every time the legislature meets. Soon we'll be pressuring other states to join us in supporting a U.S. constitutional amendment. I believe all the women in this country will be able to vote in the next presidential election."

"Finally!" Sarah could not remember Mrs. Hall ever being so optimistic. She tested a carrot on a colorful tray of roasted vegetables. "These are ready."

"Tell me about Jane Addams." Mrs. Hall was sharpening a carving knife. "I should have Robert do this, but I want to talk to you alone."

"I hardly ever see her now. She's traveling and meeting with world leaders. Peace is her consuming passion. You may be sad to hear she worked hard for Roosevelt's election, until I tell you she convinced him to have a suffrage plank in the party platform. I still work for her, but I do less writing and research on local issues. I still teach English to immigrants and I'm finishing work on a master's degree. In her absence, her partner manages the settlement house."

"Wonderful. You just reminded me. When I speak around the state, I use material you wrote or information you dug up. I never thanked you adequately. So thank you, thank you for a major contribution to our success."

"My contribution was nothing compared to yours." She took a deep breath. "Mrs. Hall, I expected to meet Robert's wife today. I hope you can forgive me for asking, but I've wondered why she isn't here."

"I'm afraid you'll never meet her here. It's a sad story. Juliette was a beautiful New York debutante. Robert was to become a partner in a prestigious law firm, but he was never going to be as wealthy as her father or her other beaus who inherited their wealth. I think she divorced him when she realized that. This was the first divorce in our family, but Robert did not try to dissuade her. He knew it had been a mistake. Actually, it wasn't a divorce. She is Catholic and was able to obtain an annulment. I'm just grateful they didn't have any children." Without pausing, Mrs. Hall continued. "Now would you tell Robert to come in here and carve the meat, and ask John and Elizabeth to join us in the dining room?"

Sarah broke up John and Robert's heated discussion in the parlor, but after everyone had settled at the table and filled their plates, war talk resumed. "Robert, I don't see how we can humanely stay out of this War. The Germans are using gas. First in Poland and last April they gassed Canadians in Ypres. How can we watch our neighbors suffer this way without offering help? In May, shortly before I left Paris, a German submarine sank the *Lusitania*. Over a hundred American passengers died. We have to do something. German U-boats are wreaking havoc on the seas."

"Apparently they're trying to destroy the British Navy, not us. The Germans have made concession to Wilson about American ships," Robert responded. "Anyway, I don't see how our entry into the War will change things, except we'll lose American lives and capital. I hope the American public stays isolationist and Wilson continues to advocate neutrality."

"I'm sure the cost will be horrendous, but I don't think Wilson will keep us out. Public opinion is changing."

Convinced the men could go on for hours, Sarah interceded. "Can we put the war to rest for awhile? Robert, tell us about New York. I was only there once for a short stay." She was pleased that his intense gaze had not ruffled her today as it had so often in the past.

"Well, New York is not so different from Chicago where I do meet clients occasionally. New York has more cultural events, but we have crime and immigrants too. No settlement houses as famous as Hull House. To be honest, I'm less fascinated, enchanted—whatever it is—than I was once."

After dinner and cleanup, Sarah and John prepared to leave. Their departure was not easy for Mrs. Hall. As they hugged, both close to tears, Sarah said, "Maybe, I can visit when the legislature is about to pass the suffrage bill. I'd be able to sit in the legislative hall of the new Capitol and look up at the dome during this historic event." As Robert helped her with her coat, she considered asking him to call the next time he was in Chicago, but, on second thought, she doubted John would approve.

As the couple walked arm and arm out into the snowy white night, she said, "I'm proud of you. I would have let you continue on about the war, but you were never going to end. The ladies wanted something else. Anyway I heard all I needed to hear. I was an isolationist until you converted me. You clearly defeated my old debating nemesis. You're my hero and I want you to stay my *live* hero. I don't want you to go back to the Western Front, or the Eastern Front, whatever they call it." She stopped, looked up at him. "But I know you will go, even if it kills both of us."

"You've always known I wanted to be a foreign correspondent."

"I romanticized it. I had no idea how difficult the separations, the *long* separations, would be. The loneliness. Working at Hull House, taking courses at the U. of C. helped, but I missed you every day…at breakfast, at the end of the day, and every weekend."

As they brushed the fresh snow off the windshield of Ed's car, he said, "I missed you too, Sweetheart, but when you're in the middle of a bloody war…" He paused, "Knowing what you know now, would you still marry me?"

She reached out to touch him. "Of course, only I'd demand a concession or two."

"Like what?" He'd taken her in his arms.

"I'd make you promise you wouldn't go overseas for more than a month a year." She giggled. "I might as well dream big. How about not going overseas unless the U.S. declares war?"

"That's possible. You should know, though, I'm convinced we'll be fighting overseas before the year is over. I wish it weren't necessary, but the Allies can't stop the Central Powers without our help. And with the Germans continuing to sink our boats, Wilson will have to face the inevitable."

She reflected on John's last comment as they drove through the nearly deserted town. The colorful Christmas lights could not dispel her gloomy thoughts. Not only John, her brother Joe, and Kari's son, Charlie—likely "cannon fodder"—would all be in danger.

Charlie, who'd grown into a thoughtful, astute young man, was much on her mind as she and John planned their return to Chicago. Like John, he believed the U.S. could not avoid the conflict, the position held by his political science professors at Hughitt College. He planned to enlist immediately—to be a patriot, to serve his country. Sarah knew his interest in a political career stemmed from his wish to make life better for farmers like his father and grandfather. She also knew that a military background couldn't hurt a political career. Anyway, she doubted she could dissuade him from serving in the army if the country went to war.

She invited him to visit them in Chicago. She promised to take him to the University so he could taste what an education there might be like. She would show him around the city, trying to infuse realism into his idealism. She doubted he would change, but it

173

would be fun for her and Jack, as well as Charlie. John might even join them when he wasn't too busy.

During their stay in South Dakota, Sarah and John often left Jack playing happily with his girl cousins while they walked along country roads or into the meadow, one of Sarah's favorite places to experience the vast open prairie and endless view to the horizon. A thin layer of snow added a white coat to the fences, the windmill, the pump and well cover. Wind had whipped the snow into drifts along fences, leaving clear areas for strolling. She believed that escaping the city—the cacophony of street sounds, the pungent smells of foreign cultures, and the claustrophobia she often felt surrounded by buildings—was restorative. The cold, crisp air; the deep blue cloudless sky; the sweeping vistas; the orange, yellow, pink, blue sunsets on the broad horizon; the silence when they weren't talking helped her breathe easily and think more clearly.

Their heart to heart talks reaffirmed their love for each other and reinforced the scaffolding of their marriage. She promised not to nag as much about his frequent trips and he agreed to accept fewer overseas assignments. She acknowledged his desire to return to the Western Front if the U.S. entered the War. He encouraged her to continue working on her Master's and even beyond if she wanted.

After returning to Chicago in January, 1916, they settled into a routine. John's regular hours allowed time for lectures, movies, concerts on campus or downtown. On weekends they'd take Jack to a museum, the zoo, or walk with him along the Lake Michigan shoreline.

But as Sarah explored her course options for spring quarter, she realized John was increasingly restless, often grumpy, disagreeable, and short tempered. She confronted him one evening after Jack was asleep. "What's wrong, John? You seem unhappy most of the time."

"If you really want to know, I'm miserable." The anger in his voice frightened her. "I missed the first battle of Verdun in February and the third U.S. invasion of Cuba a couple of weeks ago. Now, General Pershing is chasing Pancho Villa into Mexico. But," his voice took on a sardonic tone, "I did get to interview Emma Goldman who was arrested for lecturing on birth control." He stopped. "Incidentally, that would have been a perfect assignment for you. And also my next interview with Margaret Sanger." He shook his head. "But next month I'll see the Chicago Cubs play their first game in the new ball park. That would be great if there weren't many more important things going on in the world." He sighed deeply. "I hate being stuck here. I'm sorry, Sarah, I can't keep our agreement any longer. I know you're disappointed in me. The truth is I'm disappointed too. What's happened to the independent girl I married? The girl with big dreams and the drive to achieve them? When did you become so needy?" He turned away and walked out the door.

Sarah felt she had no choice. To preserve her marriage, she had to let him go. Angry, sad, she cried herself to sleep before he returned. But he'd also pricked her pride. No more worrying about him. She was riled and ready to focus on her own interests.

Within days, John was in Mexico and Sarah was registering for courses. She'd selected one on recent European history, partly to acquire more understanding of the pre-war tensions on the continent she had researched for John's book. She was searching for reading material in the University bookstore and checking out recommended texts when Ben tapped her on the shoulder.

"That's a good course, or it was two years ago. How are you? I'm glad to see you're back."

They walked out of the store together. "I'm taking a full course load this quarter," she said. "Jumping into being a full time student again. It's been a year. I did some research for John last fall, but that's not the same."

"Is John in Europe again?"

"No. Mexico with General Pershing." She smiled. "His restlessness doesn't improve with age. But tell me about your work. How's your doctorate coming?"

"Slowly. I'm back to teaching—at Shimer College now—which doesn't leave much time for research."

Later, at Hull House she talked to Ellen Starr about taking on new projects before she picked up Jack. He knew she'd been at the University. "Mommy, did you see Ben?"

"Yes, I ran into him at the bookstore."

"Do you think I could walk with him and his dogs again?"

"I don't know. We didn't talk about the dogs. I don't even know if Ben still has Cinder and Spot."

"He loved them. Why wouldn't he still have them?"

Jack wasn't going to be put off easily. "You're right. We'll see, Sweetie."

As Sarah made dinner, thoughts about allowing Jack to see Ben again kept bumping up against more serious considerations about this latest chapter in her life. She looked forward to being a student again, maybe going for the doctorate; she believed she could manage a heavy academic load and her commitment to Hull House. The journal editor who had published two of her papers asked her to review a recently-published book on feminism. This seemed like an important step to an academic future.

Since John had declared his need and preference to be where the action is, she assumed he'd be home only for short periods between assignments. By creating a fuss, she could probably convince him to stay home for longer periods, but that would only create tension and misery for both of them. She decided to count her blessings, be grateful for the freedom to pursue her interests made easier by his absence.

She decided to talk to Susan about Jack and Ben. Unloading her problems on a good friend felt uncharacteristic, but Susan had distance and objectivity and they had shared a lot. The next day at lunch in Hull House, Sarah presented her problem.

"John was unhappy about Jack spending time with Ben. Or maybe he was really jealous of the time I spent with Ben. Should Jack be deprived of walking with Ben and his dogs because his father doesn't trust me?"

"Probably not." Susan looked intently at Sarah. "Unless John has reason to be jealous. How much time do you spend with Ben? And how do you feel about him?"

"I think that is less important than Jack having a man in his life—especially since John is rarely available to him. Even when he's not overseas, he spends long hours at work."

"You haven't answered my questions."

"Maybe more relevant: Why should Jack be deprived because I find Ben interesting and attractive? I admit it. Ben is someone who could fill the void John's absence creates. I've discovered during almost seven years of marriage that I want someone to love and love me…or, minimally, to be a companion…ideally more than one or two months a year. But I'm married to John and I do love him. I don't want to hurt him, but I have a son who—I believe—has the right to have a man in his life."

"You used to talk about going to Dakota so Jack would have male relatives around daily. Did you ever discuss that with John?"

"During one of our walks on the homestead, I thought we'd settled it. John seemed willing to give up long overseas assignments. But we never really quit fighting about my going to Dakota. John continues to get angry if I even mention it."

"Why were you so interested?"

"Charlie, my nephew, was in high school then. He could have taught Jack how to play baseball and basketball, things like that. But now he's starting college and he'll join the army as soon as he can if the U.S. goes to war. His father, Ed, is a wonderful man, someone Jack could look up to, so Dakota is still an option, if I don't find a teaching position here. But it's not as appealing now."

"I think Jack's walking the dogs with Ben is not a good idea. Listen to yourself, Sarah. You've said Ben is attractive to you and you get lonely. What happens if John is still overseas six months from now or longer and you're terribly lonely?"

"You don't think I can cool my sexual urges?" She laughed. "Maybe I have a problem. I know I would never have made a good nun. I do like sex and I get so little of it."

"Seriously, Sarah, you might lose John, even if the time you spend with Ben is innocent. Try to find other entertainment for Jack."

"It's hard for me to believe that John is that narrow minded? I have no idea how long he will be in Mexico with General Pershing or how soon after he returns he'll be off to Europe again. And Jack will hound me until I give in out of desperation."

"You're right. John will not be around long, given the drift of the war news. And Jack will not stop pestering you as long as those dogs exist. But be careful. Don't let yourself get drawn into something you'll regret later."

"Thanks for discussing it, Susan, but I still don't know what to do."

"Sorry. I wish I could help. Good luck with whatever you decide."

CHAPTER 16
Rejection and Rejuvenation

With John in Mexico, Sarah threw herself into a whirlwind of academic work. By late spring she had completed the course work, put the final touches on her thesis, and passed the Master's final exam. Her mentor, Dr. Crawford, accepted the third draft of her thesis and recommended it to the University of Chicago Press for publication. She could hardly believe her luck.

"When will I know if it's accepted for publication?"

"They'll send you a letter, but it will probably take three or four months or more."

She decided to take a vacation from academic work when John wrote that he'd be home soon. She longed for a few relaxing, loving summer days with him before his restlessness set in again and she'd lose out to Europe. Nothing would keep him home for long with the war raging.

A second letter advised her that he'd been delayed. With heavy heart she waited for him, thinking about her next research effort and wondering what was happening with her Master's thesis. Would it really get published? She spent the hot, steamy days of July at the 57th Street beach or the "Point"—the tiny green peninsula that jutted into Lake Michigan. Here she and Jack picnicked and admired the Chicago skyline, often with Susan. Jack played with a hodgepodge of children at the water's edge, while the women mostly discussed Susan's wedding plans.

"I want it to be simple. I'm glad you can be there and I hope John will be home by then. I'm eager for John and Stanley to get acquainted and be friends, like us."

"I look forward to knowing Stanley better. I've only met him two or three times. I hope John stays around long enough. I worry that he will be off to war in a month or two.

"Sarah, have you ever considered the possibility that the long breaks keep the romance more intense? For both of you. If John were home all the time, wouldn't he be less interesting?"

"I don't think I'd love him less or find him less interesting if he were only gone for a week or even a month at a time."

"Maybe I'm just an oddball. I like time by myself. Anyway, I've learned to be alone without being lonely."

"I'm sure couples can benefit from occasional breaks. But months on end? I don't think you understand. Stanley hasn't left you for even short periods."

"True. But I was alone for a long time before I met Stanley." She hesitated. "Sarah, we've become such good friends. I hope you won't be offended..." She adjusted the picnic blanket they sat on and tugged at the floppy, straw hat that shaded her open face and covered most of her dark, curly hair.

"What are you trying to say?" Sarah asked.

"You've changed. You were a free spirit, enthusiastic when I first knew you. You didn't seem as dependent on John as you are now."

"You saw my brave facade. I hate to admit it, but I've felt dependent on John since high school. He was the person who encouraged me to write, to become a reporter. Since then, I've leaned on him more then I like. But I'm determined now to stay focused on my goals. I've registered for courses next quarter and I'll stay in school no matter what he does."

John returned to Chicago in late September, long after Susan's wedding and after Jack began first grade in a public school. His stories about Pancho Villa's escape from the Americans interested Sarah less than his encounters with her brother Joe, who was serving in the Fifth Cavalry under General Pershing. Joe told John

180

that he'd never regretted joining the military or leaving the homestead when he did. As Sarah reflected on Joe's being the first of Peder and Minnie's children to leave home, she had a bad moment realizing that only Kari, the oldest of her parents' five children, had stayed in Dakota and embraced their farm life. Sarah wrote her mother that night. She reported on John's return, but her belief he'd leave again soon if the U.S. got into the war. She didn't mention the publication of her thesis, because she had not heard anything in four months and she was beginning to fear that it had been rejected.

John followed the Great War closely, believing U.S entry was imminent. The frenetic pace of Sarah's life did not change. She defined and redefined the central theme for her dissertation and the relevant topics she would research during winter and spring quarters. With no professor with more knowledge in this area than she, she was mostly on her own.

John announced his intentions to leave by May 1, though the U.S. had not yet declared war. She played with the idea of going to South Dakota for the duration of his overseas commitment—or for the summer at least. She was not eager to leave Chicago with Dr. Crawford urging her to settle on a dissertation topic, but she did not want to capitulate to John's demands either. And going to South Dakota should impress upon him how his absences affect her, Jack and their marriage.

"Why?" he asked. "You love Chicago. You have a rewarding job and a spectacular boss at Hull House. We have a comfortable apartment in a good neighborhood. And you have a professor at a great University who's encouraging you to get a doctorate."

"I wouldn't feel so alone if I were surrounded by family. And Jack will have Ed to teach him lots of things. Charlie too. He may be in the army, but he'll be there in spirit."

"You'd disrupt Jack's education? Exchange his school here for the country school?"

She glowered at him. "It was good enough for me. Anyway, I'll rent an apartment in Hughitt, so he can go to school in town. As for the farm, he loved it when we were there for Christmas. Remember his fascination with the animals, his excitement at being on a horse for the first time? Maybe he's destined to be an equestrian like Kari or Joe."

"Sarah, don't be an idiot. He loved the farm for two weeks. He was the center of attention. After two months, he'll hate it. I wanted to escape when I was young. And so did you."

"We'd go to the farm mostly on weekends and holidays... whenever Jack wanted to."

"Doesn't that defeat your purpose? Ed, only on weekends? *Think!* Sarah. What will *you* do there? Working with Mrs. Hall won't sustain you, emotionally or financially. You can't expect Kari and Ed to support you for long."

"I'll teach at Hughitt College. I have a Masters thesis that's going to be published." *Why haven't I heard?*

"How do you know Hughitt College will hire a woman without a doctorate? That's two strikes against you."

"I think I'd look pretty good with a Masters from Chicago."

"You're an idiot to drop out now before you have a doctorate. And don't forget the old adage about counting your chickens. Hughitt College can't afford more than two or three historians." He walked away, to return seconds later. "One more thing and then I'll shut up. If we're both gone, we'll have to give up this apartment. We'll never find another as good."

"We could move to Hyde Park near the U. That would be perfect."

"Don't kid yourself. Perfect, but impossible, even if we could afford it."

I'm not giving in yet.

On April 6, 1917 President Wilson declared war. Before John's departure, they quarreled again.

"I expect you to stay here, Sarah, keep this apartment, and finish a dissertation. Work at Hull House until you can find a college job, if that's what you want. *In Chicago.* There are lots of good small colleges here."

"Why can you come and go as you wish? But I have to bend to your wishes," she yelled. "I don't think you love me or Jack," The words gushed from her mouth. "Poor Jack. He has a father, and then he doesn't. You think you're important. I think you're irresponsible. What if you get killed," she screamed, then regretted even thinking anything so horrible.

"You think Ed will solve all your problems?"

"Well, he's better than nothing which is all we have here. And Charlie may be around."

"Don't be silly. If I know Charlie, he will enlist and be overseas before you know it."

That made her angrier. "You'll say anything to convince me to stay here. Why do you care? You're always somewhere else. I think all you really care about is having a place to stay when you return to Chicago."

"Sarah, drop this ridiculous idea. I'm telling you right now—if you're not here when I return, I'm not coming after you. I'm not going out there to convince you to come back here."

"You don't care how I feel." She began to cry, but suddenly embarrassed by her display of emotion, she ran out of the room.

He pursued her. "Stop it Sarah. You won't feel any better living in the country. You won't last long out there. Get a hold of yourself. Resurrect that vibrant suffragist I married…the writer, the feminist, the woman who doesn't need me every second of every day."

After John's departure, Sarah contacted administrators at Hughitt College to see about a possible job in the fall. Waves of resentment ebbed and flowed. There were days when defying John dominated her thoughts. Other days when she knew she wouldn't go to Dakota even if they hired her. Her stormy mental state came to an abrupt end when she received a mixed response. The college did not need a history instructor for another year, until the fall of 1918; they'd seriously consider her for a position then.

The shock of rejection was the shot Sarah needed to reinvigorate her enthusiasm for managing a complex schedule of studying, working, and mothering—especially reading to and overseeing Jack's school work. When occasionally reminded of John and Susan's accusations of her loss of independent spirit, she would question again what *she* really wanted to achieve. Though John was no part of this, he still occupied much of her thought, reinforced by a recurring nightmare in which he was engulfed by a mist that became mustard gas. When he would collapse, she would wake up shaking.

She was thinking about her dependence on John when she decided to revisit the Chicago newspaper editors who'd rejected her eight years earlier. Since then, she'd learned about immigrant cultures and city neighborhoods and written extensively about them as part of her work at Hull House.

As she considered which editor to tackle first, she began rereading a biography of Margaret Fuller, a feminist who figured in her Master's thesis. This woman's editorship of the *Dial,* a literary magazine in the 1840s, intrigued her more now than it had originally. She wondered what it took to edit a literary journal or any journal for that matter. Fuller was obviously brilliant and well educated with the backing of Emerson, Alcott, and other Transcendentalists. Even Hawthorne and Thoreau supported her.

Curiosity drove Sarah to Harper Library to investigate the *Dial* and other journals, old and new. To her surprise two current journals had been founded by women: *Poetry* by Harriet Monroe, well known in Chicago, and *The Little Review* by Margaret Anderson, another Chicagoan. *The Seven Arts,* though, made the biggest impression on her with anti-war essays by Randolph Bourne, whose views hardly deviated from those of Jane Addams. She also skimmed editions of *Scribners* because the librarian identified it as the publication most in demand.

She left the library, her head spinning, a beehive of ideas and information. Her heightened sense of living in a transitional age excited her, but acknowledging the loss of old verities made her uneasy, as though the floor might drop out from under her. She remembered her first night in Chicago, the anxiety of leaving a secure, familiar world for the unknown—however intriguing.

No doubt the strictures of the Victorian and Edwardian Ages were collapsing, values and attitudes were changing. Art history courses had introduced her to dark nineteenth century paintings and the later works of the Impressionists, all so different from the twentieth century visions of Picasso and Matisse, for example. She was enthralled with the idea of changing mores and customs through publishing wide-ranging essays and generating lively, fruitful discussions about the future.

Random thoughts about the journals were still swirling in Sarah's head when she met Ben on the stairs to the main reading room in Harper a few days later."You're back in school!" She heard surprise and pleasure in his voice. "It must be close to a year since I've seen you."

"I've been taking courses. I guess our schedules haven't overlapped. Are you still working on your doctorate?"

"An endless chore. Nothing I do pleases all three members of my committee at the same time, but they'll want to get rid of me one of these days."

"Still teaching at Shimer?"

"No. I'm at Loyola now."

"I'm impressed."

"And you're at Hull House? I suppose John is in Europe reporting on the war and Jack is finishing first grade."

"All true." Just then, an attractive woman approached Ben.

"Clara, this is Sarah, a former classmate and friend." He turned to Sarah, "Clara is majoring in Classical Greek. She's been helping me with Pericles Funeral Oration to the Athenians." A twinge of jealousy crept up Sarah's spine.

After the woman with the impressive Greek credentials retreated, Sarah turned back to Ben. "Before you leave, there's something I'd like to discuss with you. I've been thinking about working, or volunteering, on a literary journal or magazine." She didn't tell him that she was hoping to found her own journal someday, a fantasy to be shared with no one until she believed it might be a possibility. "Am I crazy?"

Briefly, he looked puzzled—an index finger to his lips, squinting eyes. "Honestly, I don't know. What's your reason? Before you waste too much energy thinking about it, Sarah, figure out what you want to achieve. Are you going to work on the doctorate at the same time? I hope you aren't giving that up. In the long run I'm almost certain that would be more beneficial. I wouldn't sacrifice precious time if I were you."

He walked up one step and stopped. "I have to hurry now, catch Clara before she leaves for the day. Let's talk more about this later."

"Thanks, Ben." She felt good. His interest gave her hope.

Sarah wrote John about her working on a journal, not wanting him to applaud the idea if he were only trying to humor her, to encourage anything that kept her busy and not fretting about his coming home. He responded positively, but as usual his letters focused mostly on the war. He wrote that the United State was unprepared with only a small army and insufficient transport for men and equipment; Pershing awaited the First American Expeditionary forces to train for trench warfare before they'd be sent to the front. She was thrilled that John did not discourage her, though he pointed out it would probably be *pro bono* no matter how effective she was. Before he signed off, he reminded her that he disapproved of her and Jack's socializing with Ben. Until that comment, she felt as if she'd achieved a minor victory.

As Sarah discussed dissertation topics with Dr. Crawford, she interjected questions about her volunteering to work on a history or literary journal. She knew he basically approved of her; he'd always supported her and positively critiqued the papers she'd written for him.

"You'd do an excellent job and you'd learn much about editing and publishing a journal, but have you seriously considered how much you'd be taking on? Writing a dissertation is time consuming. I won't give you any trouble, but you never know about other members of your committee."

Frequently during the summer, Sarah found herself day dreaming in Harper, watching students come and go, wondering about the height of this structure and whether or not the ceiling ever got cleaned of cobwebs. This day, feeling especially listless and unfocused, she finally left the library, hoping a cup of iced coffee would perk her up. The sunny quadrangle and the light summer breeze that greeted her outside contrasted sharply with the dark stillness of the reading room. Nevertheless, she drifted through three quads in a mental fog until the clamor of student arguments in the C-Shop, the clanging of dishes and trays, and the aroma of coffee penetrated her disengagement and reconnected her to the reality of student life.

While paying for her coffee and a large sugar cookie, she saw Ben and Clara at a nearby table. She approached and overheard enough to know they were discussing Pericles oration to the Athenians. "I don't want to interrupt."

Ben stood and pulled out a chair for her. "We're covering old ground here, getting repetitive. Have you thought any more about working on a journal or magazine?"

"I talked to Professor Crawford. He'll write a recommendation for me."

"I mentioned your interest to Clara. We may have a solution for you. We've both met Harriet Monroe and talked to her about

Poetry, the magazine she founded in 1912. She's made quite a reputation for herself, publishing an amazing array of modern stuff."

"I know. I've read works by Carl Sandberg and Edna St. Vincent Millay among others. But how do I get an interview with her?"

"I'd be willing to talk to her, try to make an appointment for you. She was open and friendly when I met her at a poetry event on campus. I got the impression she welcomes interested students."

"I was impressed too." Clara's expressive eyes and mouth conveyed her enthusiasm. "Working with a feminist poet who publishes the newest and best should be interesting."

Sarah's appreciation of Clara's response gave way to surprise when she opened a large colorful bag of Mexican design and retrieved a pack of cigarettes and a cigarette lighter. Sarah was intrigued and impressed. Almost all men smoked something, but she'd seen very few women smoke. After Ben lit the cigarette, she watched the smoke curl around Clara's face and thick hair, braided in a coil at the back of her head. *She's a beautiful, modern woman. I wonder if Ben is in love with her. I'm a little jealous…of her beauty and her knowledge of Classical Greek.*

"I'll leave the two of you to your Athenians. Thanks so much, both of you. Ben, do you really think I could meet with Miss Monroe.?

"I can't be sure, but it's worth a try."

"Thanks again."

CHAPTER 17
From History to Poetry

Ben's phone call came two days later. "I have an appointment for you for next Wednesday. I'll take you to her office if you meet me shortly before two in front of Harper. I'd also like to invite you to a lecture on Friday night that accompanies a new exhibit at the Art Institute. I think you'd appreciate it. Mary Cassatt is the featured painter. As a feminist you shouldn't miss it."

"I'm sure it will be interesting."

"Will you go with me? I still have the old Ford."

"Thanks, but...I don't know." *John would disapprove.*

"Oh, come on. We won't tell John, if that's why you're hesitating."

"Hey, don't be a mind reader. Anyway, that was unnecessary. There are many reasons to hesitate. I have to find a sitter for Jack. Isn't your friend Clara interested in nineteenth century art? Actually, Cassatt is still painting."

"I haven't talked to Clara about it. Anyway you need the diversion. You've always worked harder than anyone else I know."

"Am I looking grim again?" she laughed.

"I haven't seen that much of you. Well, what do you say to this chance of a lifetime? Mary Cassatt may never have a show of her own again."

"You convinced me." *John has no right to disapprove.*

Jack was at the door when Ben arrived. "Do you still have the dogs?"

"Yes, I still have them, only they don't run as fast as they used to. Maybe we can get together sometime, but not for awhile. I'm really busy now working on an important paper, like your mother."

"She's always working on some paper. Where are you going tonight?"

"The Art Institute. Have you heard of it?"

"I think so. Isn't that where they have all those pictures? There is a big one with people in a park that I really like. We always go see it first."

"That's the famous *Le Grande Jatte* by Seurat. Lotsa dots, if you look close, right?"

As they made their way around the gallery, Sarah doubted that John had ever appreciated this soft impressionistic style and feminine content, mothers and young children mostly. He gravitated toward more masculine art, the Cubism of Picasso and Braque. She took Ben's arm when they walked out into a warm spring evening and descended toward the lions, large statuary that flanked the steps.

"How about a drink at the Palmer House? We can discuss Cassatt and her work. If you've never been in that hotel, you really shouldn't say no."

When she didn't answer right away, he added, "Seriously Sarah, it's a grand old place, more elegant than anything you've ever seen—or expect to see again—and it's only a short walk from here."

She took his arm again. "Which way?"

She loved the Victorian ambience: the chandeliers, the Turkish carpets, the plush velvet drapes, and the polished mahogany woodwork. Whatever tension she'd felt knowing John would disapprove of her being with Ben dissolved as she sipped on a fancy drink he'd ordered for her. She felt good, relaxed, and bold enough to ask the question she often wondered about.

"Ben, have you ever been married?"

190

He looked straight at her before he gazed into the distance, as if searching for something. "Yes. I was married for four years to my high school sweetheart before she died in childbirth."

Sarah gasped and reached for his hand. "Oh, Ben, I'm so sorry. I shouldn't have asked."

"It's okay. I can talk about it now." He was looking directly at her again and she could see the sadness in his eyes. She wanted to hold him and be held as the memory of the pain of Willie's death welled up within her. "That was almost ten years ago. I was distraught for months, probably years. Going back to college saved me, brought me back into the world, something to focus on besides my loss. Before that I had little interest in anything, certainly not other women, until you showed up in one of my classes."

"Ben, stop."

"Please let me finish. I saw your wedding ring so I thought there'd be no danger of emotional entanglements. I *never* wanted to suffer another loss so painful, to ever fall in love again."

Stunned, Sarah didn't know what to say. She'd never expected anything so tragic. Both had finished their drink and Ben offered to order seconds. She sighed, "No. We should be going. Thanks for bringing me here. It's definitely a place to be seen."

On the drive back to Sarah's, Ben repeated, "I planned to tell you sometime, so don't feel guilty. You gave me the opportunity tonight." Before tonight, she would have discouraged his walking up to her apartment, but now she hung on his arm in their silent ascent. As they reached her door, she grasped both his hands, unable to articulate the bond she felt.

"Well, good night," he said. "Don't forget two o'clock on Wednesday."

As the baby sitter prepared to leave, she said to Sarah, "Professor Crawford called tonight. He said it's important for you to call him tomorrow. Something about your thesis and the U. of C. Press."

191

Ben was waiting for her in front of Harper. Had his face and arms always been tanned, his hair sun bleached, his smile so warm—or was she seeing him in a different light? She did think of him differently since his revelation at the Palmer House.

"We're headed for Cass Street, number 543," he said as they climbed into the old Ford. On the way he described his meeting with Harriet Monroe and her "open door" policy, her unbiased approach to poetry, her willingness to consider all viewpoints. Ben emphasized his glowing description of Sarah as "a brilliant student and ardent feminist who had written a Master's Thesis that was going to be published by the University of Chicago Press."

"Oh Ben, you didn't. I talked to Professor Crawford this morning. He told me they will not publish it. 'It's *not* what they're looking for right now.' He thinks the real reason is that I'm a woman and only a student. I guess I knew it was too good to be true."

"I'm sorry, but I'm sure Miss Monroe will understand. Your professor recommended it. And you do have two articles published in a good journal."

Miss Monroe's office in the living room of another converted mansion was cluttered with stacks of papers—submissions, letters, and copies of *Poetry*—and miscellaneous desks and chairs. Ben introduced the two women and left. For Sarah the wavy gray hair and delicate facial features of this attractive woman matched her soothing, musical voice. Though physically smaller than Jane Addams, she seemed equally forceful and direct. "I congratulate you on having your Master's thesis published by the U. of C. Press. That's quite unusual," she said.

Sarah smiled. "It had been recommended, but I heard this morning that it was rejected?"

"Because you are a woman? Don't take it too hard. It reflects badly on their editor rather than on you. Are you willing to fill in however you might be needed here: running errands, meeting with the printer, and helping me sort through poems, critiques, and other correspondence. I have lots of helpful assistant editors, but there's always more than we can manage. Mostly we discard or reject. We don't have the time to edit or rewrite."

Sarah nodded and Miss Monroe continued. "You may not know that I started this magazine to help establish poetry as a serious American art. Other arts have been recognized in various ways, but poetry has been mostly unsung."

"I'm interested in learning about publishing a journal, so I'm eager to do any relevant task. But I'm no expert on poetry."

"Poetry is very personal, subjective. I don't know if there is such a thing as an expert." She took off her glasses, rubbed her eyes. "I have no particular biases, except that the poem is composed by a contemporary."

Sarah wondered if she should say something about the few poems she'd read in *Poetry*. Suddenly, she had an inspiration. "I read *The Love Song of J. Alfred Prufrock* in one of your editions. What wonderful images! *The sky spread out like a patient...yellow fog rubbing its back...measuring out my life in coffee spoons.*"

"Yes. That proves my point. As many so-called experts disliked it as liked it. I'm still receiving letters about it." She put her glasses back on and looked intently at Sarah. "How many hours would you be available?"

"Would six hours a week, three hours on two days be acceptable?"

"Good. Can you start next week?"

"Yes. I'll look forward to it."

During the next few months, Sarah learned about publishing a journal, but gained little confidence in her ability to evaluate poetry. She helped at every level, occasionally dealing with the printer and often taking stacks of submissions home to do an initial screening. She continued teaching a few hours at Hull House, but her dissertation got shoved in a drawer to be rescued briefly when *Poetry* went to press.

CHAPTER 18
Ben

When the snow began to fall, Sarah wrote John, asking if he'd be home for the holidays. He responded that he'd probably not return to the States until February. She didn't want the holidays to go by without some kind of celebration, so she decided to have a supper on Christmas Eve. She had invite Harriet Monroe, Susan and Stanley, and Jack's friend, Raymond, and his parents. She hesitated before asking Ben, who offered to come early and bring a tree that he would set up. At Jack's request, she asked him to bring his dogs. He promised they would be well behaved.

Ben arrived with a balsam fir, a stand for setting it up, and the animals. The dogs and Jack entertained each other while Ben and Sarah worked on the tree. "I was surprised that you weren't going home for Christmas," she said.

"I went down on Thanksgiving. I won't be missed if my sister is there with her two kids."

Except for Miss Monroe, who declined because of a previous commitment, the rest of the invited arrived in time to help decorate the tree. Stanley, the director of a church choir, led them in singing carols as they drank fruit punch and hung bulbs, red and green cords, and strings of popcorn. Later they sat around the dining room table eating turkey breast, cranberry sauce, sweet potatoes, and green salad. Susan had brought a mince pie and Raymond's father, two bottles of Sauvignon Blanc.

The group prepared to leave when Jack fell asleep on the living room floor—everyone except Ben. Susan took Sarah aside and asked, "Are you all right about being left alone with Ben? If you're feeling vulnerable, I could stay longer."

"I'm fine, Susan." *I think I'm fine.*

Ben picked up while Sarah settled her son in bed with the dogs at his feet. By the time she had joined Ben, he had carried the dirty dishes and leftovers into the kitchen and straightened the living and dining rooms.

"Ben, you're a wonder. Thanks for the help." She wanted to ask him to leave, but she felt that would be rude after all he had done. She also admitted to herself that it felt good to have a man around.

"I'll wash dishes while you put the leftovers away." He began to roll up his shirtsleeves.

"Ben, it's not necessary. You've done enough."

"I don't mind. And I don't think removing the dogs before Jack is soundly asleep is a good idea." She could hardly disagree with that—anyway she didn't want to. She handed him a dishrag and began putting the leftovers away as the dishpan filled with water.

"I don't mind doing this alone. It might be better for both of us if you left now."

He laughed, "Don't worry about me."

When they had finished, she was adamant. "No more excuses. I'm sure Jack is sound asleep." She tried to sound casual, light hearted. She was not prepared for his response.

"It won't be easy. Tonight I feel as if I belong here with you and Jack."

I feel the same way. She turned away, walked into Jack's bedroom with Ben close behind. Rather than push the dogs off the bed as she had intended, she turned to face him. Without hesitating, he grabbed her shoulders and kissed her. Surprised, she took only a moment to respond to what felt like the most natural thing in the world. She stayed in his embrace and they kissed again. As her passion intensified and her resistance crumbled, she grabbed his hand and led him to her bedroom.

When she awoke, he was gone. Her first thought as she stumbled out of bed. *Oh my God, what have I done?* She found Jack, without the dogs, sleeping soundly. Guilt washed over her at the sight of him and engulfed her as she made a pot of coffee, totally nullifying the pleasure and satisfaction she'd enjoyed with Ben. She wondered how something so glorious could be wrong. But it was, and she couldn't rid herself of guilt even though she knew it was a useless emotion.

"I'm hungry, Mommy." Sarah was grateful that Jack appeared just as her thoughts had turned to John and the possible consequences of her behavior.

"I'll fix you some scrambled eggs and toast."

She refused a date with Ben for New Year's Eve and kept her distance during the rest of January. She missed a menstrual period mid-January, but this was not unusual, so she did not worry about it.

John arrived on the first Sunday in February. He had called from New York to say he didn't know yet which train he'd be taking, so she should wait for him at home. She was shocked at his physical appearance—his loss of weight and pallid complexion— and a hacking cough. "It's only a cold," he said "I'll be fine in a few days." For two weeks he resisted her ministrations, though he was eager to go to bed with her, and he rushed to the Daily News as if they wouldn't survive without him. She'd never seen him so frenetic. She thought he might be feverish, but he refused to take a day off or slow down.

He collapsed at work and was hospitalized at Billings. Sarah's feelings vacillated between relief that he was receiving medical attention and fear of a truly serious illness. Ever since his return with the barking cough, she'd been haunted by memories of Willie's death.

She rushed into the white, sterile setting that smelled faintly of carbolic acid or some other disinfectant, frantic to find John and talk to a doctor. A thin-lipped nurse directed her to John's room where a white coated resident bent over the patient, a stethoscope planted squarely on his chest. "Mrs. Anderson," the doctor stood, facing her. She nodded. "Your husband is gravely ill."

"Pneumonia?" *Is he going to die, like Willie?*

"He's a relatively young man. He has a good chance of beating this. Unfortunately, all we have to offer is good nursing care." For the next several days, Sarah spent most of her time sitting by his bedside. When she wasn't doing something for him, she read and wrote letters to her family and John's parents. She went home every night to sleep and see Jack, who was staying with Susan when he wasn't in school.

When incoherent, John ranted about the war, the dead, the wounded, and the trenches. When coherent, he appreciated her presence. He'd thank her for being there or tell her to go home and rest. He'd ask about Jack. She was watching over him the night the fever broke. The doctor reassured her that John was finally sleeping peacefully. Relieved, she went home to tell Jack and to write John's parents and Minnie that John was past the crisis.

One crisis was over, but she had a new worry. She'd missed her second menstrual period. Possibly the stress of the last few weeks was the cause, but she could not totally dismiss the possibility she was pregnant. She would put off seeing a doctor, hoping she was only late and everything would be all right soon. What would she do if she were pregnant? What could she do?

She decided she had to talk to someone, and Susan was her best friend ever, who knew her well, and was not judgmental. "I've missed two menstrual periods, Susan, so the possibility that I'm pregnant is high, but it is not certain. I've missed two periods before."

Susan said nothing for several seconds. "You're telling me because you're worried. And you're worried because the baby is not John's."

"Yes. No. I don't know for sure. I have slept with John more than once. I should have listened to you on Christmas night. What can I do? What should I do?"

"I don't know. I wouldn't tell John now, maybe never, given his feelings about Ben. I don't have any answers, but I will support you whatever you decide."

Two weeks later John was home, still weak, but enjoying a hearty appetite and entertaining Sarah and Jack with anecdotes about the hospital. He helped his son with homework and was soon making passionate love again to his wife. She was happy about this, but cringed at her deceitfulness, her thinking that John would naturally assume the baby was his. To make the most of his current domesticity, Sarah put her projects on hold until he announced he was returning to work.

"I promise to take it easy. Until I feel 100 percent. I'll follow doctor's orders. Believe it or not, sweetheart, I'm asking my editor for local assignments only. I'll let the editor's brother take care of the war in Europe."

Early in March, soon after Sarah had resumed her old routine, Ben met her outside of Hull House. "I passed my oral exam yesterday and I wanted you to be the first to know. I hope you've finally forgiven me for my behavior on Christmas. Come celebrate with me."

"There's really nothing to forgive." She shifted to a lighter, celebratory tone. "Congratulations, Ben. Will you be heading toward Harvard or Yale now that you have your doctorate or some other major university?"

"Of course, whichever makes the best offer. But you haven't answered my question."

"I'd love to celebrate with you, to invite you to dinner, but John is home now. So I can't do that."

"For your sake, I'm glad he's home. Forgive me. I'm just a little jealous of John. How about one glass of champagne at University Tavern...now?"

They sat in the quiet bar and raised a toast to Ben's future. "Now it's your turn," he raised his glass again. "Do you really want the Ph.D. or is journal editing a higher priority?"

"I don't know anymore. I'm more realistic now about the problems of editing a journal, but I've thoroughly enjoyed my work with Harriet Monroe. She and Jane Addams are so alike."

"They're both feminists."

"Yes, but there's more. They stay calm when they're berated, which is often. And they don't retaliate. Both have been unwavering in their hatred of war. Miss Addams has worked for peace for decades. Miss Monroe actually wrote an editorial that *blames* poets for glamorizing war."

"Interesting. Does Ezra Pound influence her selection of poems?"

"Absolutely. He brought Eliot to her attention. I've read several of Mr. Pound's letters. He's bossy and mercurial, tough to take at times, and he complains about his pay. But I think she handles him well. They're both really idealists with the same goals of supporting poetry and poets." Sarah finished her drink. "So far, I've done all the talking."

"Continue. It's fascinating."

"We receive tons of mail which I find at least as interesting as the poetry. Nothing dull like the letters I exchange with my mother. I can't believe how egotistical so many of the poets are. For example, Edna St. Vincent Millay, whose poetry I really like, almost begged for money, but complained about what she received." Sarah glanced at the clock over the bar. "I could probably go on all night, but I'd better go. Jack will be home from school soon."

With John back at work, Sarah returned to her dissertation. She reduced her hours at Hull House, but not at *Poetry*. Again, Harper Library became her second home. By late March she knew she was pregnant, but she wanted a doctor's confirmation before she told John.

As she sat in the waiting room, she tried to control her feelings. One moment she was excited to think Jack would have a brother or sister, but the next, she was miserable thinking how this had come about. She tried to be positive as she responded to the doctor's questions about her health and family life, more stressful than the discomfort of the physical exam.

Her heart was pounding as she got dressed and waited for the doctor to rejoin her. Her feelings were mixed and constantly changing. She didn't want this baby, but she did. If only she could be certain that it was John's, but how could she? John had only impregnated her once in almost nine years. She had only been with Ben once, but her first missed menstrual period had occurred in January. John didn't get home until February. Maybe she wasn't pregnant. Wouldn't the doctor have said something as he examined her, if she were not? She hadn't missed three menstrual periods since she was in high school. Well, she'd know soon if it had happened again.

CHAPTER 19
More Complications

She held her breath as the doctor, who seemed to hold her fate in his hands, smiled as he entered the room. She doubted he had any idea how mixed her feelings were.

"Mrs. Anderson, you are healthy and so is your pregnancy. If all continues well, you should deliver a healthy baby in late September."

"Or October?"

"Of course. Was your first child very late?"

I don't remember. I don't think so." *No. Jack came very close to his due date.*

As she left the doctor's office, her brutal thoughts were horrific, frightening. She tried to refocus on John's recovery and his new work attitudes. If only she knew what to tell him. She hated to lie or be deceitful, but his rage, if she told him what she thought was the truth, would destroy all of them.

She finally faced him in late April, "John, sit down. I have amazing news. I'm pregnant. I hope you're eager to have another child?"

He put his arms around her and kissed her cheek "That's wonderful, sweetheart. I didn't think that was going to happen to us again. Want a girl this time? It'd be perfect to have one of each, but another boy would be okay. Are you happy? You're the one who will have all the extra work. What does Jack think? Has he expressed preference for a brother or sister?"

"Slow down, John. Too many questions. I haven't told Jack. I'll tell him when the due date is closer, so the wait won't seem so long."

"And when is that, sweetheart?"

"Don't know exactly. October something." *That was stretching it. The first lie.* For one moment she wanted to tell him everything.

John complained to Sarah about his new assignments. "They're boring...the news, in general—except for the war. And the reports of several service men hospitalized with the Spanish Flu at Fort Riley, Kansas. It reminds me of the isolated reports of the flu when I was still in Europe."

Reports from Europe of Spanish flu continued to increase gradually until August 1918, when there were major outbreaks in Europe and at Fort Devens, Massachusetts. John, restless and eager for an interesting assignment, accepted his editor's request that he cover the story in the Boston area.

"John, don't accept that assignment. You know the disease is very infectious and you are barely recovered from a horrible bout of pneumonia."

"I'm in great shape." He told Sarah. "I just survived a major illness—proof I have a strong constitution."

"Maybe. But why take unnecessary chances? John, please."

"Sarah, sweetheart, I'm a reporter. It's my job to take risks."

Sarah hated to see him go, but she gave up arguing, knowing he had always done what he wanted anyway. She continued at *Poetry* and Hull House, hoping to work until the baby was born. On the rare day when she had spare time, she'd head to campus. One rainy afternoon, as she dashed for cover under the archway between the law school and Harper, she bumped into Ben.

"It's so good to see you. How are all the Andersons?" he asked.

"I'm fine. And very pregnant, as you can see. John is in Boston, writing about the flu epidemic. And Jack is doing well in school. How about you?"

"First, congratulations. Wish my news was good, but it's not. Two friends died of the flu last week. Both were stationed at Fort Devens. Aren't you worried about John?"

"I'm so sorry to hear about your friends. Of course I worry about John, but he does what he wants. I can hardly believe that you and I were celebrating the last time we were together. The flu wasn't a concern yet. By the way, why are you on campus? I thought you were through here."

"I came to pick up a cap and gown. I'm going to the graduation next week. I don't know why I changed my mind, but I think it has something to do with the flu—don't ask me what."

"I almost forgot. Congratulations again."

"Is John through with Europe now that the war is ending? Both of you must be thrilled about having another child. I'd think he'd want to be home now." Are you feeling good?"

"Yes, thanks. John came home from Europe in February. He was hospitalized with pneumonia about two weeks later, but during his recovery, he decided to stay in Chicago for local assignments. Until his boss asked him to go to Boston. I'd say everything was fine if only flu wasn't lurking in the background."

"I don't know if Susan told you, but I wanted to drive you to and from the hospital when John had pneumonia. She told me he was ill. She also told me to stay away. I guess John has reason not to like me. Are you still happy at *Poetry*, still reading fascinating mail? Still thinking about your own journal? And the dissertation?"

"Yes to all your questions, except I'm having trouble with the dissertation. Too much data to grapple with."

"When is the baby due? Is Jack excited?"

"Probably October. Jack wants a brother, but he says a sister would be okay."

Sarah first heard it the morning after he'd returned from his two week stay in Boston. John's cough had returned. As he dressed for work, he acknowledged that he did not feel well.

"Stay home today. I'll call Dr. Jackson."

"Be realistic. He's busy with a hospital full of flu patients."

"Well, I'll try." The woman who answered his office phone confirmed John's prediction. "The doctor is almost living at the hospital; he's too busy to make house calls."

John agreed to stay home. He crawled back into bed and was asleep within minutes. Sarah called Hull House and the *Poetry* office to cancel, telling them that John probably had the flu. His horror stories about crowded hospitals convinced her to keep him home. She could do what the nurses were too busy to do, be his private nurse. Her major concern about keeping him home was Jack. But he'd already been exposed at school and probably other places. She'd keep him out of the sickroom and away from John to the extent it was possible.

When John awoke, Sarah thought she should take his temperature. But did it really matter? She knew his flushed cheeks and hot forehead reflected a high temperature. He tried to get up but she held him down. "John, you need to stay in bed. You may have the flu. Please don't fight me. I'm your nurse. You're very warm, so I'm putting cold compresses on your forehead."

"Okay, boss." He gave her a feeble smile. "But can I go to the bathroom first?"

"If you must, but please come back." She laughed. *So like John, trying to be funny even if he's dying.*

"Where could I possibly go in this condition?"

He returned to bed, soon coughing up blood—a sure sign of the Spanish Flu—and shivering with chills. When blankets did not help, Sarah crawled in beside him. She curved around him, hoping to provide the body heat that would control his violent shaking. She stayed there until Jack arrived from school with his friend.

"Jack, your father is very sick. It's best if Raymond goes home."

After the boy left, Jack asked, "What's wrong with Dad?"

"I think it's the flu this time."

"Is going to die?"

"Oh sweetheart, I don't think so. I know we've heard such horrible things about the flu, but your father has survived pneumonia. He's a strong man." She hugged her son, holding him close in her arms for several seconds. *Oh, please God, don't let him die.*

Susan came as soon as she heard that John was ill again. "You look exhausted, Sarah. You need help. Let me take over for awhile."

"I can't leave John. Anyway, what would I do?"

"Take a nap or go for a walk. Get some fresh air. Visit Harriet Monroe."

As Sarah changed the cold compress on John's forehead, she said, "I'm going to Hull House. Susan is here if you need something before I get back. I won't be gone long."

At first being outdoors lifted her spirits: the bright mid-day sun, the fresh crisp air that replaced the stale atmosphere of the sick room, the green of trees and shrubs, the yellow primroses and chrysanthemums, red geraniums, and blue salvia that bordered walkways. Soon, however, the melancholy cry of the mourning dove dominated the birdsong and resonated more with her mood as the four block walk to the trolley sapped her strength and spirit.

She was grateful for not having to wait for a car. She collapsed on the first empty seat, but resisted the urge to curl up and sleep for fear she'd miss her stop. At Hull House the news of many colleagues down with the flu and Jane Addams ill with recurring kidney problems only added to her malaise. From there she dragged herself to the *Poetry* office.

"Sarah, you need to go home, to bed." Harriet Monroe looked concerned. "You're ill."

"I'm all right, just tired. I haven't slept much since John came down with the flu."

Miss Monroe shook her head. "I'm going to find someone to drive you home."

Sarah remembered nothing after that.

CHAPTER 20
Spanish Flu

She awoke, groggy and confused; Susan was standing over her. "Where am I?" she asked before the white walls and the metal hospital bed registered on her brain.

"Billings Hospital. You collapsed in the *Poetry* office two days ago. An ambulance brought you here."

Sarah struggled to sit up. "How's John? You left him alone? And Jack? My baby?"

Susan pulled a chair up close to the bed and took Sarah's hands. "John's doctor decided to hospitalize him. Pneumonia has weakened his lungs."

"Is he here, in this hospital?" Sarah rushed on. "And Jack? Where's he?"

"John is at Cook County. Jack is staying at Raymond's. He knows you and John are sick. He hasn't been crying, but he doesn't stop asking when you'll come home. I'll keep you informed about both of them.

"Sarah, I talked to a doctor about you and how this flu might affect your pregnancy. He couldn't give me definite answers. He said it depends on the person and the age of the fetus. Hopefully, it won't affect you or the baby seriously. Another thing. You got a letter from South Dakota. I didn't think you'd be up to reading today, but I'll bring it tomorrow if you wish."

"It's probably from my mother. She's been worried about us since John's first illness. I know she feels bad that she's not strong enough to come help out. Especially now that I'm pregnant. She'd like to do what you've been doing, my wonderful friend." She sighed. "Can you find another pillow? I'd like to sit up."

Susan found one and slipped it behind Sarah's back. As she helped her into a sitting position, a clump of Sarah's hair fell onto her shoulder. She gasped, "My God, what's happening to your beautiful hair?"

"What do you mean?" Sarah screeched as she saw a clump of auburn tresses in her friend's hand. She reached up and came away with another bunch of hair in her own hand. "Oh, Susan, my hair is falling out," she wailed. "Do you see bald spots? What's happening? Help me."

"Yes, I see bald spots. I don't know what to do. I'll call a nurse."

The nurse was sympathetic but told them hair loss was not uncommon among flu patients. "This flu is a demon. You never know what it's going to do. You might even go into labor before your due date. Luckily, you're far enough along that you don't have to worry about miscarriage or even prematurity."

"How will this hurt the baby? And will my hair grow back?"

"It's too soon to know. I think the baby will be okay. We've lost mothers but only very young fetuses. Time will tell about your hair."

Will John still love me when I'm bald?

Although the rest of her hair fell out in the next three days, Sarah was no longer feverish and she'd recovered her appetite. "Are you feeling well enough to come home?' Susan asked. "I'll take care of you, fix your meals and do your wash. Jack could come home too. Should we talk to someone about having you discharged?"

"Yes. I want to go home. I'm feeling much stronger and I'm sure someone needs this bed more than I do. I appreciate your offer, but I think I can manage on my own."

"We'll see. You may be weaker than you think."

"Well, one good thing. I won't waste energy brushing my hair." She tried to laugh.

Susan was unable to arrange for an ambulance, so she called Ben. Sarah squeezed into the Ford between her friends. As she jostled into the middle position, the scarf she'd tied around her head slipped off. Instead of rushing to retie it, she let Ben see her bald head.

"How do you like my new hair style?" she asked.

"Truthfully, it's not as attractive as the old one…but you're still beautiful."

"I know its grotesque. I shouldn't complain. If only John were doing as well as I am."

"I was sorry to hear he's in the hospital again."

"That's my real problem. Not my hair."

When Ben dropped the two women at Sarah's apartment, he offered to drive Sarah to Cook County whenever she wanted. She thanked him but hesitated to accept. John's feelings about Ben hadn't changed. She'd look into trolley schedules and see if she could get to the hospital without Ben.

Entering the apartment was a pleasure. The blues, reds, and yellows of the rugs, sofa pillows, and prints seemed intense after the white monotone of the hospital. By contrast, the muted sounds of street and apartment life were a relief after the bells and alarms, the rumble of orderlies pushing carts, and the moans and cries that echoed throughout her hospital ward.

Sadness, anxiety, and a touch of guilt replaced her joy of coming home when she saw the bed where she'd last seen John. Susan had removed all signs of a sick room, but she could not erase the images in her head. "I must see John. I should have let Ben drive me."

"No. You need to rest. You won't be able to help John if you get pneumonia or have a relapse. Leaving the hospital and coming home is enough for one day. I promise I'll go with you tomorrow. Besides, you should see Jack first. I'm going to Raymond's to fetch him right now."

Sarah saw Jack's shocked expression at the sight of her bald head, but she chose first to reassure him about her tears as she hugged him. "These are tears of joy. I'm so happy to be home with you. I wish you could come with me tomorrow when I see Daddy, but the hospital won't allow children under twelve."

Jack was still staring at her head. "Mommy, what happened to your hair? You looked better before."

"I know. My hair will probably grow back, but it will take time."

"Will Daddy come home soon? Will he be bald too?"

"I don't know when he'll be coming home. He's sicker than I was."

Susan helped Sarah maneuver through the hubbub of Cook County—its corridors overflowing with the bodies of moaning flu victims on cots and stretchers—to the over-crowded second floor ward where John's bed was separated from adjacent beds by curtains. Sarah had tried to be prepared mentally, but the sights, sounds, and smells had unnerved her even before she confronted John's pallor, his incoherent ranting, and his thrashing about. "John, I'm here darling. Can you hear me?" When his demeanor did not change, she turned to Susan. "When will I be able to talk to him? When will our nightmare end?"

Susan put an arm around her. "I'm sorry. They didn't tell me he was delirious."

When Dr. Jackson came by, Sarah asked, "How soon will he be...?" She choked up, trying to control her feelings. She had just seen a sheet covered body removed from the ward.

"There's no way to know, Mrs. Anderson. He's very ill. This flu is unpredictable. When the fever drops, we assume he's on the mend...otherwise." *Otherwise.* Fear clutched at her heart—as it her existence depended on his.

And so her vigil began.

The next day she asked, "What are his chances?"

"I don't know," Dr. Jackson responded. "But you should prepare yourself for the worst." The nurses were also evasive. *Don't they know anything, or are they just keeping the bad news from me?* Nothing seemed real as she sat at John's bedside. *How do you prepare yourself for the worst?* She remembered her father after his third heart attack, shuffling out to the back porch, his feeble attempt to enjoy the outdoors in his waning days. She remembered them all tiptoeing as if their footsteps would precipitate Peder's demise, a death they all knew was imminent. But Peder was old. *John is young.*

Willie's death had been harder. He was the brother she loved most, the one closest to her in age. Her eyes filled with tears now as she visualized again his coffin in the parlor car on the train trip back to Dakota. She had cried her eyes out sitting on Minnie's lap.

John's wracking cough and incoherent mumblings, though painful to hear, reassured her that he was still alive. She wanted a chance to tell him how good her life had been, how much she loved him despite the long absences she'd complained about so bitterly. She wanted to touch his face as she said these things, but when she tried, hoping her hand would calm and quiet him, he brushed her away as if she were an annoying insect. When she could not wait any longer for him to regain consciousness, she gave voice to her thoughts.

"John, I hope you can hear me. I want to apologize for nagging at you about your foreign assignments. It was just that I loved you so much and missed you terribly. And I didn't think you loved me as much as I loved you. I would never have left you, gone back to South Dakota without you. That was an idle threat. And I am so sorry."

She liked to imagine that he heard her and would respond if he could. "I understand, Sarah. You had reason to be angry with me. I did put reporting above most things, but not you and Jack. I've loved you ever since high school."

When she wasn't repeating her message or imagining his answer, she prayed—mostly the Lord's Prayer, remembered from Sunday school, and the Hail Mary that Minnie repeated under duress. *If God exists, will He listen or will He dismiss me as a hypocrite?*

She lost track of how many nights she sat there listening to his coughing and the labored breathing. Days felt like weeks that she searched the faces of nurses and doctors for a sign. They only shook their heads. They seemed so detached. Too many sick. John was just one of hundreds. More than one nurse told her to go home, take a long nap. Someone would call if any change occurred. Instead, she'd cat nap, her head resting on the edge of John's bed.

One day she did go home to see Jack. She fixed lunch, while he asked about Daddy. "When can he come home? He's been there a long time. Can't they make him better?"

"He's very sick, Jack. I don't think he'll be able to come home soon." Talking about it fueled her anxiety. She took Jack back to Raymond's and rushed to the hospital in a panic, afraid she'd left her post too long—as if her presence could ward off evil spirits.

A group of nurses and interns were milling around near John's bed, until they saw her and scurried away. She grabbed the arm of the nearest nurse. "What's happening?"

"You'd better talk to the doctor, Mrs. Anderson."

As she pulled aside the curtain, she saw a resident bending over John. He turned toward her. "I'm terribly sorry. We'll leave you alone now. Stay as long as you wish."

"John *can't* be gone. I haven't had a chance to talk to him."

"He died about fifteen minutes ago. He never regained consciousness."

She dropped into the chair where she'd been sitting for days. *What do I do now?* She felt like the little Sarah who would crawl up on Minnie's lap to be held and hugged when something bad happened. Only now there was no Minnie to hug and hold her. She sat staring at the now quiet figure on the bed. No more labored breathing, incoherent mumbling, or restless thrashing about, at peace at last. She moved closer, took his limp hand, kissed it, and repeated part of her earlier message. "I'm sorry for not being a better wife, for being so angry with you when you couldn't be with us. But I never stopped loving you."

She bent over him and kissed his unresponsive lips, dry and cracked from the fever. Only then did she really know he was gone. "Where are you now, dear heart?" she asked between sobs. *If only I believed in heaven, in God. But you will always live in my heart...*She kissed John's hand again and pressed his fingers against her cheek. *He's left us forever. Now he won't even send letters or see my bald head. What silly thoughts.* She stood up. "I should go home and be with Jack," she said as she stared at the lifeless form, suddenly desperate to escape the silence of death.

Susan brought Jack home as soon as Sarah called from the hospital. When she arrived, Jack rushed toward her. "I'm glad you're back, Mommy."

She began to cry as she clasped him to her bosom.

"Why are you crying? Where's Daddy?"

"Daddy is gone, Baby."

"Gone? What do you mean? Did he go back to Europe?"

"No, Sweetheart. Daddy died this afternoon." Still holding him close, she said, "We'll miss him terribly." Moments later, she added, "It will be hard, but we'll be okay."

Minnie had given Sarah their new phone number with a reminder that long distance calls were very expensive. Another small way our world is changing, Sarah thought. When Willie and Peder died, we sent telegrams. After talking with her family and John's elderly parents, she decided to have the funeral in South Dakota. Traveling would be difficult for her, but even more difficult for his parents, and they wanted their only son buried in the local cemetery in the family plot.

Before she left, she talked to Susan about an alternative to the scarves she wore in public to cover her head. Although her hair was beginning to grow in, she dreaded the months before it would be a decent length.

Susan—sensitive to Sarah's self-consciousness, and aware of her deep fatigue from years of overwork and stress—went shopping for her and bought a *cloche*, a stylish hat of French design she found at Marshall Field's. Sarah had always disliked wearing hats, but she was so delighted with one that completely covered her bare scalp that she went to Field's to buy more.

Two of John's colleagues at the *Daily News* took the train to South Dakota with Sarah and Jack. They helped her with luggage and entertained the boy on the long train trip with card games and anecdotes about his father. Sarah listened to their stories and occasionally added one of her own. But often she stared out a window mesmerized by the repetitive landscape into reveries of earlier trips. After her threats about returning to South Dakota, she actually was returning...with John. How ironic, she thought. She remembered a quote about searching the world to find what you need and coming home to find it there. *But where is home? Isn't Chicago my home now?*

Both families met the train. Sarah hugged and kissed Minnie. Then she embraced John's mother. This tiny, shriveled woman said in her unsteady voice, "Thank you for bringing him home." Sarah, struggling to keep from crying, gave her another hug and kissed her cheek. After shaking John's father's hand, she reminded Jack, surrounded by his girl cousins, to greet his grandparents. Finally, she turned to Kari and Ed. Both embraced her briefly. As Kari began telling her about the funeral arrangements, Sarah knew this was one time she was glad Kari had taken charge.

Two days later the Presbyterian minister's words at the funeral floated somewhere above Sarah's head, but the short service at the cemetery aroused intense feelings. Her breath quickened and her heart pounded as the coffin was lowered into the ground. She couldn't bear to see John leaving her permanently. As she stepped toward the open grave, Ed moved quickly forward to support her. She stood there for several minutes before she let him guide her to the hearse that would take the family back to the church for refreshments.

While she was greeting those who'd come back to the church to visit and offer condolences, Mrs. Hall, one of the mourners at the cemetery, approached and embraced her.

"I'm so sorry, Sarah. I met John only once, but he made a wonderful impression on me. How tragic that he and his second child will never know each other."

"Thank you. I think often about how much I learned working with you. I understand the suffrage work has progressed well here?"

"Exceptionally well, thank you. Come have tea with me. How long will you be staying?"

"I don't know yet. Maybe a week. I want to return to Chicago before the baby is born."

After they agreed on a time and date for tea, Mrs. Hall added, "Robert had a meeting to attend right after the service today. He asked me to tell you how sorry he is." She hesitated. "He also has exciting news, but I'll let him tell you about that."

CHAPTER 21
Robert's Plan

When Sarah arrived at the old Victorian for tea, Mrs. Hall lost no time reassuring her that women's suffrage would soon be a reality in South Dakota. "We have the votes this time, more than needed. I've begun to refocus my energies on the national campaign. I've already been to two conventions in Washington. I think we'll have a national suffrage amendment in time for women to vote in the 1920 presidential election."

"Wonderful," Sarah said. "And you've played an important role."

"Could you come to our celebration next winter? You worked very hard for this too,"

"I'd love to celebrate with you. And visit the new State Capitol. My second disappointment—after our suffrage bill failed to pass—was being in Pierre before the building, and, especially the dome, were finished. But it's a long trip from Chicago, and I'll have a baby."

Just then Robert walked into the parlor. "Sorry, ladies, I don't want to interrupt anything important."

"Come in, Robert. Tell Sarah about your plans."

He smiled, the smile that once had played havoc with Sarah's emotions. "Forgive my mother. Because *she's* interested, she thinks everybody else should be."

"Well, she's right about me. I'm certainly interested. I was surprised to see you at the funeral. I wondered why you were here and not in New York."

"First I want to say how sorry I am about John's death. He was so young. His death seems especially cruel at this time. This flu has taken a terrible toll."

"Thank you, Robert. Yes." She did not want to dwell on this subject. "Tell me about New York."

"I've left New York. I decided to come back here, take up my father's mantle. I've been State's Attorney now for a year."

"I'm surprised no one mentioned that in a letter. Do you live here or in Pierre?"

"Both. I move back and forth. But now I've decided to run for governor. If I win that election, I'll have to move full time to Pierre. If you hang around for a day or two, you may see *Hall for Governor* posters." He smiled at her. "What do you think?"

"You'll win. Did you ever lose a debate?"

"Yes. More than once to you or mother. And once to John."

"Your mother, maybe. I think running for governor is exactly what you should be doing. I'm sorry I can't vote for you."

"You could if you move back here. I'd love to have you working on my campaign. You'd be a terrific asset. And if I win— and how could I lose with you working for me—I'm sure there'd be a place for you in my administration."

"Robert, I will be a new mother very soon, as you can see. Not exactly the best time in my life to be working on a political campaign. But thanks for your thoughts. You certainly flatter me. Is this how you won all those debates?"

He smiled and threw up his hands. "I'd try anything that worked. Aren't you tired of Chicago? Hasn't city life worn you down yet?"

She could not suppress a smile. Robert could be charming. "Chicago has been my home for a long time now. My roots may be here, but I think a few have been transplanted. I like city life. If I start feeling claustrophobic, longing for the prairie and the big sky, I'll convince a friend to drive to the Indiana Dunes on the shore of Lake Michigan."

She fell asleep that night mulling over Robert's comments. Apparently, he preferred being a big fish in a small pond as opposed to being a little fish in New York City? Should she consider returning too? In her case it would have nothing to do with fish. Would it be better for Jack and the new baby? Could she take Kari's meddling? Would she die of boredom? She'd certainly miss the activities at Hull House and Poetry and even her classes and research at the U of C and Harper Library.

Seeing her first *Hall for Governor* sign prompted Sarah to ask Kari if she'd be voting for Robert.

"Of course. He's a home town boy, and he's a Republican. What more could one ask for? In fact, you should move back here and set your cap for him. You could be a governor's wife."

Sarah shook her head in disbelief. "Just like that, I'll be the governor's wife! Kari, he's never shown any interest in me and I've never been interested in anyone except John. Anyway, he has his campaign to worry about now, not getting married."

"I didn't mean right now. You're recently widowed and pregnant. You can't remarry for at least a year."

"What if he isn't elected?"

"He can't lose in this state. He's a Republican."

"What about the primary? He's certainly not the only Republican in South Dakota."

"Don't be silly. He's a Hall. That family carries weight here. They're pioneers with integrity and influence. And he's good looking and intelligent. And he's *single.*"

"Really! There was a time when you didn't like Robert."

"I know, but that is past. What are you going to do, Sarah? We're all worried about you."

"This conversation is ridiculous. What are you worried about? I'll miss John terribly, but I'll manage as I have in the past."

"You'll be a woman without a man to look after things."

"I've been taking care of myself for years. I don't need a man to survive, although it's nice to have one around sometimes to sleep with."

"Sarah!"

"You can't appreciate how hard, how lonely it was at times with John away from home. Ed is always here for you."

On the way into town the next morning in Ed's new model T, Sarah asked her brother-in-law about Charlie. "He writes when he can. Not much about battles, mostly about missing his family. So far, he's escaped the flu, though there've been victims in his unit. He is scheduled to come home because he's been wounded, though he insists it is not serious."

"Thank God, he'll be home soon. I've always been especially fond of my nephew. I hope this awful war will have a silver lining and reinforce his interest in politics and law."

Minutes later, Ed dropped her off on Dakota Avenue near Hughitt College. As a student she'd been indifferent to the size and style of the three buildings that comprised the campus. Now she wondered if she could be happy here or if Chicago's looming Gothic structures, spires, and gargoyles spoiled her for something as modest as Hughitt College? As she entered the main building, she bumped into one of her old history professors, who claimed she was one of his better students, and invited her for coffee in the small cafeteria. He wanted to hear about Chicago and she wanted to know if the history, English or Sociology departments needed another instructor.

"They may have hired someone already for a history position this fall. You should make an appointment with the vice president. He'll know if anything is available."

Sarah was half hoping there'd be no position, negating any question of her return, but curiosity drove her to the vice president's office. Was she lucky or not? He was on vacation and would not return until long after she'd departed for Chicago.

Sarah asked Minnie and Jack to walk with her in the meadow shortly after sunrise the next day. She wanted Jack to experience a bit of her childhood, part of what she loved most. She hoped they'd hear meadowlarks and see prairie chickens and gophers, and maybe a pheasant or two.

"Can I bring Champ?" Jack asked. His interest in the puppy, a descendant of old Sport, trumped all others.

"Of course," Minnie said. "He loves a good romp."

While mother and daughter picked wild flowers, Jack played with the dog. Sarah had been wondering if Minnie might expect her to make up for the loss of her sons. "Ma, how often do you hear from Joe and Matthew?"

"Matthew calls quite often now that we have a phone. Joe calls too, but less often. Are you thinking of moving back here?"

"Has Kari been putting ideas into your head?" Sarah asked with a smile.

"I know she'd like to marry you off...to Robert Hall. You were interested in him once, I believe. He is impressive, probably our next governor. But you've just lost your husband. You're more unsettled than you realize. You don't have to listen to Kari."

"Don't worry. I've become quite independent. As for Robert, I always felt challenged by him. He's less intimidating now. In fact, he's almost charming."

"I know you're doing well in Chicago. No need to come back here unless you want to. I never thought you cared much for it, except for the meadow and your suffrage work."

"Ma, if you had your life to live over, would you still come to Dakota?"

"Of course. I loved Peder. My mother thought I was young and foolish. She fantasized a musical career for me or marriage into a prominent family. She was disappointed that I gave it all up."

"But you *did* leave Peder once and returned to St. Paul."

"Yes. The worst mistake of my life."

"Sometimes I don't know what to do." Sarah sighed. "I love all of you and I'd love to have family around Jack and me and...the baby. And I could probably get a teaching job at Hughitt College."

"Is that what you want?"

"I don't know...no. Not really. I like my work at Hull House and *Poetry*. And I want to finish my dissertation before I look seriously for a college or university job."

"It sounds like you want to teach."

"And do research and write. I admire women like Jane Addams and Harriet Monroe who've made important contributions to society. And Mrs. Hall too. I'd like to feel someday that I've done something worthwhile."

"I'm sure you will, Sarah. You've already contributed to the Suffrage movement. As much as I'd like to have you stay here, I think you should return to Chicago. It takes time to recover from the loss you've just suffered and now is not a good time to make major changes in your life. One more thing. You're a lot younger than I was when Peder died. I know you believe you're independent. But none of us is really. Be open to meeting people. You're too young to spend the rest of your life alone. Life is better, fuller with a partner."

"I appreciate your wisdom, Ma. I've had a good life in Chicago and so has Jack. I'm going back, but I'll write and call you more often. And visit too. The trains are better now. If you come visit me, I'll take you to concerts and the Art Institute. We can walk in Grant Park and along the Midway." They were walking arm and arm now with Jack and the dog trailing behind.

"I want you to know I have wonderful friends in Chicago. I've written about Susan and Ben. They'd do almost anything for me. And I'll stay open to meeting people."

Minnie stopped walking. "Listen. I hear a meadowlark."

"Yes...over there on the fence post. I'll always have to come back here to walk with you in the meadow and listen for that special song."

CHAPTER 22
Decisions

Before Sarah left for Chicago, Robert called twice to repeat his request that she work with him on his campaign. "I realize this isn't the most opportune time in your life, but moving on to new adventures might help with the grieving process. And I'm sure your sister would be a big help with the baby."

"I don't understand why—even if I weren't a pregnant widow—you're interested in me," she asked, remembering how he'd tortured her in the old days, how he'd belittled or dismissed her.

"It's perfectly clear to me. You did spectacular suffrage work for my mother. You've worked with Jane Addams. You have a master's degree from Chicago and a start toward a Ph.D., so I know you have brains and persistence. You're also pretty and I like you."

"You used to think I was stupid." Though flattered, she wanted him to squirm a little, to pay for some of the misery he'd caused her.

"Never! I just had to be sure I was cock of the walk. I was afraid you'd turn out to be smarter than me. C'mon, Sarah, I was just a young, insecure wise-ass."

"Well, Jack and I are leaving tomorrow. I'll think about your campaign on that long train ride, but I'm pretty entrenched in Chicago. You certainly don't need me. You're a shoo-in."

Robert continued to call after she had returned to Chicago. Because Susan was present during one of the calls, Sarah filled her in on her present and past history with Robert and Mrs. Hall.

"How exciting! An amazing opportunity for you to have a greater influence than you'd ever have just teaching and writing." Susan's voice continued to rise. "Think of the great changes in education or health you could make in your home state. Maybe you'll marry the governor." She stopped short, took a deep breath. "Sarah, maybe you'll be the first woman governor in the U.S.—after Robert Hall moves on."

Sarah laughed as she shook her head. "You're really in fantasy land. Women don't even have the vote yet. Seriously, Susan, my mother—wisely, I think—advised me to take my time, not make any major changes in my life for awhile. It's more than enough that I'm about to have a baby, that I'm recently widowed. I haven't lost my enthusiasm for Hull House and *Poetry* and I'm eager to continue work on a doctorate. Besides, assuming Robert wins and he wants me in his administration, what do I know about administering anything? We haven't talked specifically about what happens after his victory. Whatever, I will feel like a fish out of water."

"Only briefly. Give yourself credit. Your mother's advice would be appropriate in most situations. But this is unique, special. You can't put this offer off for six months or a year. He needs you now."

Sarah was mulling over course offerings for the fall quarter when she ran into Ben at Harper Library the following week.

"I've wondered about you, how you're doing," he said. "I've been trying to decide when it would be appropriate for me to call. Grieving is tough and personal and I know how deeply you loved John even when you were angry with him. I wasn't sure you'd appreciate…"

"Ben, you're one of my best friends. A call any time is welcome. I could use a shoulder to lean on."

"How was it to be in South Dakota again?"

"Difficult at first. John's parents were so pathetic. Otherwise, it was the same. Except—did I ever tell you about Robert Hall?"

223

"A high school boyfriend?"

"More like a bullying big brother. I lived with his family when I was in high school. Now he's asked me to join his campaign for governor and be a part of his administration."

"Governor! That's big. What are his chances of being elected?"

"Good. Almost certain. He's a Republican from a pioneer Dakota family. He graduated from Yale law and is State's Attorney now."

"Why is he interested in you?"

"After high school, I worked for over a year with his mother, writing speeches and propaganda for women's suffrage. But our bill failed to pass in the legislature. I didn't have the heart to keep trying. Besides I desperately wanted to join John in Chicago, to be a reporter."

"I give the guy credit for wanting you on his team. You'll be good. When do you leave?"

"I'm *not* leaving. The baby is due any day." Surprise colored her response. She'd thought he'd try to convince her to stay in school, to stay within his orbit. "I hope you aren't trying to get rid of me?" Her mirthless laugh barely concealed her feelings. "Jack and I have a life here. I can't just abruptly depart Hull House and *Poetry*. Hull House will be a big help with the baby." *Your Baby, Ben.* For one second she considered telling him, but, instinctively, she said nothing.

"I understand that, but you can't turn down an opportunity like this. Misses Addams and Monroe will be so impressed with the possibility of your having political power, they'll push you out the door. And John—he'd expect you to jump at the opportunity. Think of the impact you could have—in contrast to teaching or editing a journal that only a few academics read."

Oblivious to Ben's positive message, Sarah was disappointed and hurt that he would send her off. She was also embarrassed and angry for thinking they had been on the same wave length, for imagining he was more in tune with her than he was. "You and

Susan seem to agree, but my mother advised against making changes. I guess I should give it more thought." She turned to leave, an injured animal needing to withdraw and lick her wounds.

Ben grabbed her arm as she turned. "Wait, Sarah. I have news too—not as earth-shaking as yours. Clara and I are engaged."

Not as earth-shaking? Sarah hadn't expected this either, though she had wondered about their relationship. *He won't have time for me now.* With those thoughts, wishing him well did not come easily. "Congratulations. That's wonderful, Ben. I'm happy for both of you." Now she really wanted to get away. "I have to go, get home before Jack does."

"One last thing, Sarah. Please don't refuse what may be the best offer you'll ever have. I care for you too much to want to see you throw away this chance of a lifetime."

Before she walked to the trolley, she sat in the Classics quadrangle watching the squirrels scampering about and trying to remember what she had finally said to Ben before she turned away and escaped down the familiar stairway. Still dazed, nothing seemed real to her until the pealing bells of the carillon penetrated her fog. She needed to hurry home if she were to beat Jack coming from school.

That evening, wanting to escape her thoughts, she devoted herself to Jack. They read together and played his favorite card games. She encouraged him to talk about Daddy. "Do you miss him a lot?"

"Yes. Sometimes I just pretend he's in Europe and he'll come home some day. I still don't understand why he had to die."

"I don't either, Sweetie. I know everyone has to die sometime, but Daddy was too young. It doesn't feel right." She ignored Jack's denial. "But we're strong. We'll be okay even though there will always be a hole in our hearts."

As she tried to fall asleep later, she could no longer suppress the turmoil aroused by the conflicting advice she'd received and the weighty decision she must make. Though Minnie had seemed so wise, Susan and Ben encouraged—more than encouraged—her to accept the new challenge. She had to figure out what was best for her and Jack.

She got out bed, hoping a glass of wine would help her relax. Sitting at the kitchen table reminded her of the party night Ben had kissed her. He is a special person—attractive and intelligent—and she knew she'd miss him. But she was not jealous of Clara. John was her true love, the one and only man she ever wanted to marry. Nevertheless, Ben's friendship had been important to her and to Jack, and she had to admit his engagement gave her second thoughts.

As she stood up to return to bed, a sharp pain pierced her abdomen and then another. She gasped for air, felt nauseous, and discovered she was bleeding. This was not like the labor she remembered. And the pains were one on top of the other. Frightened, she called Susan, "Something is wrong. I'm in terrible pain, having trouble getting my breath, and I'm bleeding"

"Sit down, take it easy. I'll be right over."

Sarah decided to wake Jack. She didn't want to scare him, but they would have to take him with them. If he woke up alone in the morning, he would be even more scared. She was helping the sleepy boy get dressed when Susan arrived and took charge.

"Jack, your mom is in pain because the baby is coming and that's why her breathing is different."

Once they were in the car, Sarah also tried to reassure Jack. "Having a baby is very painful, sweetheart, but I'll be fine as soon as it's over."

A nurse led Sarah away as soon as their reason for being in the hospital was obvious.

"How soon will the baby get here?" Jack asked Sarah.

"Probably very soon," Susan responded. She turned to face a doctor who said he wanted to talk to her.

"Are you a relative?" he asked.

"No. I'm her best friend. She's a widow with no family in Chicago. Is there a problem, doctor? What is wrong?"

"There is a possibility that the blood supply to the baby has been cut off. There are clear signs of fetal distress."

"How serious is the problem?"

"It could be very serious. I want to give her a shot to speed up delivery, to save the baby. But that can create problems too. I'd like the consent of a family member."

"Well, her husband died of the flu and the rest of her family live in South Dakota. I'm certain they'd want you to do whatever is best. Does Mrs. Anderson know?"

"Not yet. But I will tell her. She has a right to know."

"Why not let her make the decision?"

"I guess that's the way it has to be. We must hurry. We may be losing valuable time."

CHAPTER 23
In the Hospital

Frightening things went through Sarah's head as the doctor explained his reason for hastening the birth. But she was in so much pain, she welcomed anything that would end it. And he seemed to think it was the right thing to do.

The final tearing pain was the last. Everything seemed okay again. But she heard the doctor say to the other attendants, "I'm going to cut the cord here," without being able to make out what the others were saying.

But then someone asked "Isn't this an excessive amount of blood?"

"We may need to transfuse."

Then she heard the sweetest sound she could imagine, a newborn's lusty cry. And a nurses voice, "You've just delivered a beautiful six pound girl." The nurse held her up so she could see.

"Is everything all right? I know the doctor was concerned and I heard talk about blood."

"If we can stop the bleeding, everything will be okay. You may need a pint or two of blood. The baby is fine."

A few hours later Susan and Jack visited Sarah, but they had looked at the baby through the windows of the nursery first.

"Susan, that baby reminds me when Raymond's dog had puppies. They were all wrinkled and red just like her."

"She'll look good before too long. Just wait, Jack, all of us will think she's adorable in a few weeks."

Later, Sarah asked, "Who do you think she looks like?"

"Like all babies, she's red with a smashed face, and a big blob of black hair. Jack thinks she looks like one of Raymond's newborn pups. But I can almost see the beauty she is going to be. If I have to name someone, I'd say she looks more like you than anyone."

"I don't think she looks like anyone I know. That's good. She looks like herself. Now, what should Jack and I name her? I like old fashioned names, but I don't want to name her after anyone I know, so she'll feel identified with anyone other than herself."

"Mommy, I want to call her Jo."

"I like Jo. Reminds me of the heroine in *Little Women*. Her full name could be Josephine, but we'll call her Jo."

"Not worried about the connection to Napoleon's wife?" Susan asked.

"Probably any old fashioned name will have some questionable connection. If you can come up with a unique name, I'll consider it."

Two weeks in the hospital provided more than ample time for Sarah to think about her past and future. She revisited Minnie's advice not to make life changes too soon, to take time to adjust to John's death…and now Josephine's birth.

But Sarah's thoughts kept reverting to the political campaign. She did not reject living and working in South Dakota, only farm life for herself. But, with an infant, she was not sure she could be ready to join the campaign for the June Republican primary only nine months away. And this was an important election, because the winner was almost certain to defeat the Democrat in the general election in November. South Dakota almost always went Republican.

So, the timing was wrong for accepting the challenge. Maybe that was for the best. In the old days Robert, despite his intelligence and wit, could be arrogant, insufferable. Had he really been humbled, humanized by life's traumas, taken down a notch at Yale and by a debutante wife who divorced him? At least he had seemed wiser and kinder when she was last with him. Nevertheless, there was the possibility she would be under his thumb as part of his administration, working on projects dearer to his heart than hers.

And what would the future be like if he won? How soon would he move on to the U.S. House or Senate—as the current governor was planning to do? How would that affect her and Jack? And the baby? Would they return to Chicago in a few years? Was any of this relevant? Why not just forget the whole thing?

Eager to escape the confines of the hospital, Sarah argued with her doctor who finally released her in ten rather than the usual fourteen days. With Susan's help she had set up a crib in her bedroom and purchased all the necessities before her confinement. Because the first week home went well—the baby had no trouble nursing and she slept most of the night—she made an appointment with Dr. Crawford. She wanted him to know what she was turning down.

She called Ben before the appointment to get his perspective. "If I did leave, would I basically forfeit all the doctoral work I've done in the history department?" she asked.

"Depends. But let me congratulate you first. Susan told me you had a little girl. I'll bet Jack is excited. If you do leave the history department, a year or two probably doesn't matter, but I've known students who've had to start over because their major professor died or retired—or moved to another college. The longer you stay away, the more likely a problem."

"I'm probably not going anywhere, because of the baby. But just in case, thank God, Dr. Crawford is relatively young. I don't think he'll die on me, but I guess he could be lured to another school. You still think I should go the political route?"

"Yes. If I was in your shoes, I'd give it a try, depending on how I felt about the baby, and Robert too, how compatible his views are But talk to Crawford. He'll want to know what you are up to. You can't just walk out on him. He'll be very disappointed if you leave."

After a short stop to introduce and drop Jo off at Hull House, she took the streetcar to the University. She sat on a bench in the Classics quad waiting to see the professor, asking herself Minnie's question: *What do I really want to do? What is best for Jack and Jo?*

Was John right that pulling Jack out of a city school is a bad idea? Being around family might not work out as well as she hoped either. Pierre is over 100 miles from the homestead. Still, we could spend most weekends and holidays on the farm—if Jack wanted to.

Could she really be serious about going back to Dakota? Minnie regretted her return to St. Paul, blamed herself for Willie's death. But her situation was not like her mother's. This new venture could be rewarding, even negating regret about not completing the doctorate? Seeing her nephew again added another attraction. Charlie had been discharged from the army and was planning a campaign for a seat in the state legislature. If he were successful, he'd be living in Pierre—a possible big brother for Jack. She had wanted to share the exciting news about Charlie with someone, but John was gone and neither Susan nor Ben could be expected to have much interest.

She started to pace, propelled by her churning mind. When it dawned on her that Robert might be interested in the news about Charlie, she decided to call him that evening. All things considered, she would have to reject his offer, stick with her mother's advice. Her ambivalence and indecision reflected emotional instability, her not being ready for another major life change.

Minutes later she stood at the entrance to Cobb Hall. She climbed the marble steps to Dr. Crawford's office where his secretary told her to go right in. Sarah felt a little silly now, since she felt she had reached a decision.

"Dr. Crawford, I made this appointment for your help in making an important decision. I'd still like your opinion. I've been offered an unusual opportunity. If I accept, it would mean dropping out of school. But after deliberation, I don't think I will accept."

"Well, tell me. What is it?"

"To work on a political campaign and, assuming our candidate wins, be appointed to a position in the new governor's administration."

"What state?"

"South Dakota."

"Hmm....I'd be more excited if it were New York or California. But you say you're not going to accept it."

"I've been ambivalent, partly because I have a baby daughter now—I did send you an announcement. But I'd really like to finish a doctoral dissertation one day. Are there time limits? Could I return in a few years?"

"I don't have time limits, but the University or the department might. I don't know. My dear girl, I'd miss you terribly if you leave. You're the only woman in the department, the only one to keep me on my toes when it comes to women's issues. How confident are you that your candidate will win?"

"Pretty sure. But I've decided the timing is wrong for me."

Sarah called Robert that evening after Jack had gone to bed and the baby was sleeping. "I've given this much thought and I've decided I can't join you on the campaign trail. It's just too soon for me."

Several moments of silence preceded, "First, how are you and the baby. Mother is sending a gift from both of us. Not sure when." More moments of silence. "Woe is me. Is your decision final? I'm especially disappointed because Carl Wagner has declared his candidacy. He's one Democrat who'll be tough to beat."

"I'm sorry, Robert."

"Would you reconsider if you didn't have to join my team until early next summer after the primary in June? The baby will be nine or ten months by then. I've been reassured by the chairman of the state Republican party that I'm the only contender they are supporting in that race. They like me because they think I have the best chance of defeating Wagner in November." He added, "Would ten months give you enough time?"

It took a minute for Sarah to digest this new information. "Robert, I never told you when I was in South Dakota that I'd had the flu and lost all my hair. It was still too painful to talk about. I appreciated that you and your mother did not ask about my wearing a hat. Anyway, in ten months my hair will be grown out and Jo will be close to a year. Can I give you a tentative yes? Very tentative?"

"Of course. I'm sorry you can't be here for my first victory." He laughed. "I'm jesting, but it does seem pretty certain. You'll be needed more when I have to defend against the athletic and handsome Democrat. I'm almost sorry that women can vote. I'm sure they'll all fall for his charm."

"Be careful, Robert I could change my mind."

"It's obvious I need you around to help me keep my foot out of my mouth."

After she hung up, Sarah stared into space. Had she made the right decision, a move ahead, not regressive, even if it is back to Dakota? She'd have several months to discuss this new turn with Dr. Crawford and Jane Addams. But she wanted to know soon if Jack was upset.

She approached him the next day. He looked bewildered. "We won't live here? Will we live on the farm with my cousins? I won't be able to play with Raymond any more, will I?"

"We won't move until next summer, so you still have time. And maybe we can invite Raymond to come visit us next year." A twinge of guilt accompanied her doubt that Raymond's parents would approve. She added, "And if he can't visit us, maybe we'll come visit him and our other Chicago friends."

"I'd like to live on the farm if I could ride a horse again and play with Champ."

"I don't know if we'll live on the farm, but we'll spend time there. While you romp with the dog, I'll be looking and listening for meadowlarks with Minnie and Jo. And you and Jo can be there sometimes even when I can't be." Sarah was relieved that Jack could see the positive in the move. She hugged him and kissed the top of his head. "We'll miss our friends here, but we'll have fun and make new friends. Change will make us grow." Her doubts were evaporating. She visualized sitting in the legislative chamber of the new Capital and looking up to the magnificent dome. Not a tragic return like Minnie's. She'd have months to adjust to being a mother of two and also make progress on her dissertation before her return to South Dakota. By then she'd be eager for a challenging campaign and whatever followed.

My future looks as bright as a sunny day in the meadow with wild flowers in bloom and meadowlarks singing.

CHAPTER 24
Full Circle

As the train pulled out of Brookings, Jack leaned against Sarah's knee. "Mommy, will we ever get there?"

"I know it's been a long, long trip, but it won't be much longer." She sympathized with his restlessness. She wondered if by reading Willa Cather, she might have discovered something entertaining in this great wilderness that she has missed. If the November election went as hoped and she became part of the new administration—lot of ifs—she would need a sincere appreciation of this flat, open landscape as she travelled over it weekly.

A small contingent met them at the station in Hughitt. After greetings, Kari said, "Ed and I will take the children to the farm. Sarah, you can come with us or go with Robert to see the Republican headquarters, or whatever else you want to see in Hughitt.

"I'm exhausted, but I'd love a quick tour of Hughitt and a look into the Republican headquarters." If she had thought about it, she would not have been surprised to be revisiting the space where she'd come in 1909 with Mrs. Hall to find out what was happening at the Republican convention in Chicago, the convention that elected Taft as presidential candidate. That was the year she lived in Robert's room and read his copy of *War and Peace.*

This time only five people were present. They all had questions for Robert who introduced her to them. One was a student she knew at Hughitt College. Two were young women. One offered Sarah coffee and a muffin.

"Thanks, Grace." Robert turned to Sarah," Forgive me, you must be hungry. If you'd like something more substantial, there's a good restaurant down the street."

"No. The muffin is fine. I'm sure Kari will take care of the *substantial* tonight."Tell me about the large map of South Dakota that covers that wall. I see that the counties are marked off. What do the dots signify?"

"The red dots are where we've been and the blue are where we intend to go. We've been working mostly in pairs. Since this is the first time women can vote, I think it's important to remind them to register so they can vote. I've been blessed to have Grace and Claire on my team. And now you."

"I'm scheduled for the Black Hills this coming week—Rapid City, Sturgis, Custer, Belle Fouche, Deadwood and Lead. On the way, I'll spend a night in Pierre where a torchlight parade has been organized. I'd like you to accompany me on this, your virgin campaign trip.

"Sounds interesting. I've been in Pierre, but never farther west."

Grace interrupted, "Mrs. Anderson..."

"Please call me Sarah."

"Sarah, if you'd like to rest tomorrow—I'm sure you're tired after your trip from Chicago—I can go with Robert."

"Thank you, Grace. But I'm fine. I'll be ready after a good night's sleep."

"Grace, I want Sarah on this trip, because two lawyers in Rapid were classmates of hers. I'm counting on her to convince them to help us organize Pennington and nearby counties. This will be touchy, because it's Carl Wagner's territory. He grew up in Belle Fourche."

When Grace was out of earshot, Sarah asked, "Who usually accompanies you, Robert?"

"I've probably made the most trips with Grace, but, eventually, everyone gets to work with everyone else."

236

"Do you think she may feel I'm a usurper?"

"She shouldn't. We rotate as much as we can."

"But how does she feel about it?"

"I don't know. It's not something we talk about."

"Well, be careful." She hesitated briefly. "Does your mother ever go with you on these trips?"

"Only on short trips. Never overnight. She hates hotels. Likes her own bed."

"I thought she would be here. Will I get to see her today?"

"We're going to pick her up on the way to the farm. Your sister invited us to dinner tonight. We can go now, if you'd like, and drive by the high school and Hughitt College for old time's sake."

Over a cup of tea in the familiar old Victorian, Sarah and Mrs. Hall shared their experiences in Washington. "How many women do you think will vote now that they will be able to?" Mrs. Hall asked.

"Will you be terribly disappointed if the number is low?" Sarah responded.

"Disappointed, but not surprised. I suspect it will take time for them to fully appreciate what has happened, for many to realize voting is not only a privilege but also a responsibility."

The time required to get from Hughitt to the farm was much shorter than Sarah remembered. "It's amazing," she said. "Transportation is faster…roads are better. Progress kind of sneaks up on you. Do you always drive, Robert?"

"Yes. I don't like to deal with bus or train schedules. I come and go when it suits me. Our trip to the Hills would be more complicated if we had to worry about catching busses or trains. But we do need more and better roads in this state. That is a campaign issue. I'm one Republican who doesn't mind raising taxes if the money supports progress. Sadly, not all Republicans agree with me. And Wagner is very conservative for a Democrat."

As they approached the farm, Sarah's ambivalent feelings intensified. She was eager to see her mother, but not her sister. One minute she was glad Kari took charge, but the next, she resented her making decisions that were not hers to make. She wasn't really surprised when, during the middle of dinner, Kari announced, "I think you should live here with your children until after the election, four months from now."

"Sounds reasonable, except it means Jack would have to transfer in the middle of the school year. That's tough and not fair to Jack." *And John would never approve.*

"Well, think about it. No need to make a decision immediately."

After Robert and his mother left, Kari started in. "What a wonderful chance to renew your friendship with Robert. Four or five days travelling, eating, going to rallies and town meetings together. I hope you come back engaged."

"Please, Kari. We have a job to do. Robert wants to win an election, not get engaged or married. Besides, he has a young woman working with him who, I believe, is very fond of him. And she would make a better wife for him."

"Why?"

"She's young, single, and doesn't have children."

The next day Sarah was grateful to Robert for resisting Kari's effort to feed them a mid-day meal.

"Thanks, Kari, but I want to stop at the diner in Highmore. I'll do some politicking and get a sense of how things are going in Hand County while we have lunch."

He was describing the major issues in the campaign when signs for Highmore began to appear. "What do you want me to do here," Sarah asked.

"Just be friendly. Be a good listener. By the time we get to Rapid City, you should be well versed in all my opinions and arguments. But we've barely started, so keep it simple here and in Pierre."

The Republicans in Pierre had organized a torchlight parade that began at the Capital, proceeded toward the river, onto a road adjacent to the Missouri, and ended at the St Charles Hotel. The rally there attracted a large crowd who questioned Robert mostly about water rights, the Missouri, and damns.

The next morning they left for Rapid City. If the half of the state east of the Missouri River seemed empty, the land west was even more barren. A few large ranches, rather than farms, occupied this semi-arid area. "Not much population around here," Sarah noted. "I learned a lot last night about water, the Missouri River, and your views on hydroelectric power. What are the other most important issues to you?"

"Education is high on my list—especially funding for state colleges. Residents of Pennington county will be primarily interested in the Dakota School of Mines in Rapid City. The issue is always money. I'm for spending it if progress is served. Wagner is a very conservative Democrat who is more adverse to taxes than I am. I'm afraid he's won over many Republicans."

When they tired of talking politics, Sarah told him about her reading his copy of *War and Peace* and her long-ago wish to discuss it with him. They both agreed it was a favorite novel. He found Napoleon's retreat especially interesting. Sarah remembered the love story best. She did not tell Robert that the character, Pierre, had reminded her of him.

In the middle of this discussion, Sarah saw the flat earth dramatically transformed into magnificent geological formations that were beautiful, spectacular, and eerie. "This must be the badlands, right? I've never seen anything like it."

"Yes, it's amazing. Watch for bison prairie dogs, and other wildlife. We'll be in Rapid City soon."

Though forewarned, Sarah was surprised that Robert did not have the support in Rapid City that he had in Hughitt or Pierre. A group of progressive women asked her many questions and compared him unfavorably to Carl Wagner. She struggled to convince them that he had their best interests at heart and reminded them that it was his mother, Margaret Hall, who had worked harder than anyone for their suffrage. In the end, she felt that most remained committed to Wagner.

But the two lawyers who remembered Sarah agreed to organize Pennington County, and engage lawyers in Sturgis and Lead who they believed would work on Robert's behalf. One of them invited Robert and Sarah to a party at his home to meet several of his supporters. Food and drinks were abundant.

As they walked from the parking lot to their hotel, Robert said, "Sarah, any possibility you could fall in love with me? This is not the best time or place, but I'm falling in love with you. Believe it or not, I remember a kiss on a snowy night when we'd just left a Christmas program at the college. You probably don't remember."

"Yes. I do, but that was long ago. We were very young."

"I suppose it's foolish, but I've been wanting to repeat that kiss." He leaned toward her, but she pushed back.

"Robert, let's end this now, or you're going to hate yourself in the morning. We've both had too much to drink."

Sarah was discouraged when more negativity surfaced in Sturgis and Deadwood. "Robert, what can we do to improve your chances in this part of the state?"

"I don't know. Wagner is a native of Belle Fourche and I think these westerners have felt overlooked in the past. My name doesn't mean much to them, whereas Wagner is one of their own."

"Maybe you need to come back here again, several times, so that everyone becomes familiar with your name.'

"I will come back, Sarah."

As they were loading the car for the trip home, he said, "It will feel good to get back to Hughitt where we're appreciated by the majority. I forewarned you that this would not be an easy race."

"Yes, you did. I'm sorry I was not much help. I wonder if Grace would have been more successful."

"I doubt it. She has no connections to the Hills that I'm aware of. She's from Aberdeen. Sarah, there's something else I want to clear up. I was not drunk the other night and I do love you. Is it hopeless? Certainly, if I lose, you'll return to Chicago. I wish I weren't so pessimistic."

Sarah was glad but also disappointed that her children had managed so well without her. She planned a picnic with Minnie and all the children her first day back at the farm. She invited Kari, but she chose to take a break from the children and spend time with her horses.

The group sat on the edge of the meadow in the shade of the lone elm tree to eat their lunch. Josie with her two girl cousins sat on one blanket. Minnie, and Sarah sat on a second blanket. Jack was with them when he wasn't playing with Champ.

Josie suddenly stood up, babbling, "Nana, Nana, birdie, birdie," as she pointed to a meadow lark on the nearby fence.

"Yes, sweetheart, listen to his sweet song." Minnie looked at Sarah, "While you were gone, I brought her out here to pick flowers and listen to birds, like we used to do. And guess what, she won't keep a sunbonnet on either."

The campaign continued until the first Tuesday in November with trips to many towns, big and small. Many county chairmen had effective organization with designated poll watchers and rides to the polls for those who requested them. On election day Sarah was a poll watcher in Hughit and later helped count the votes. Spirits were high in the Republican camp because turnout was high and Robert got over seventy-five percent of the vote in Beadle county.

It was midnight when Richard and the county chairman came by to get the vote count and take Sarah, Mrs. Hall and others to the Republican Headquarters where data from all over the state was accumulating.

Numbers were recorded on a large blackboard and updated as information came in. At midnight, Robert Hall had a slight lead over Carl Wagner. Robert discouraged his supporters from celebrating. "It's not over. It depends on how I did against Wagner in his part of the state. We still have to hear from several western counties."

By one o'clock, most of the counties had reported. At two o'clock, someone shouted, "All the data is in. Unless recounts change things, Carl Wagner is our new governor."

Silence.

Until Sarah said, "Robert, ask for a recount in Pennington county."

"No, I did well where I expected to and lost only in his territory. A recount won't change anything. I lost fair and square. I apologize to all of you who've worked so hard. Especially, Sarah. You disrupted your life, moved your family here. I hope this hasn't been all bad."

"Robert, stop it. Aside from getting to know you better and spending time with your mother, I had my first trip to the Black Hills. Before I leave, I'd also like a tour of the Capital. It was under construction when I was last here. I especially want to look up at the dome.

Grace asked, "What do we do with the champagne? We were sure we'd be celebrating."

"Should we drink to another try in two years?" Robert asked. "Would anyone be willing to work for me again?"

"Why not?" Sarah asked, reflecting the response of the large crowd in the room. "The count is so close. A little more work in the west and you will be a shoo-in."

"I'm sorry you lost, son, but don't feel defeated. How often did I lose the suffrage fight in the legislature before we won?"

"I remember, Mother. I'm not sure I have your strength or perseverance. Enough data is in. Unless recounts change things, Carl Wagner is our new governor and Warren Harding is our new president."

EPILOGUE
1920

Sarah, with Jo in her arms, stood in the rotunda of the South Dakota state Capital. Mrs. Hall, Robert, Minnie and Jack were standing next to her. Charlie, a newly elected legislator, soon joined them.

"With three generations of my family here and two of the Halls, this feels like a celebration," Sarah said. "We lost Robert's campaign, but Charley won his, and I'm confident that Robert can win in two years. And finally, I get to look up at the dome whose beauty is only surpassed by the dome over the meadow."

She turned to Mrs. Hall., "After many failed women's suffrage bills, one finally passed under this magnificent dome. Do you think the dome softened the hearts of legislators?"

"As magnificent as the dome is, I believe your research and speech writing was more important. Anyway, our bill and those in other states prepared the way for the nineteenth amendment, a great victory for women in the United States."

"But don't stop now, ladies," Robert said, "Don't rest on your laurels. There's more work to be done."

"Charley, you're in a position now to sponsor education and other bills that will foster equality," Sarah said. "I hope Carl Wagner will be more progressive than he has seemed to be. But we'll take him on anyway if he decides to run for a second term. In the not too distant future, I hope Jack and Jo will join the ranks of those actively working for equal rights."

"Sarah, are you serious about coming back here in two years if I decided to try again?" Robert asked.

"Of course. Your loss actually works to my advantage. I'll have a chance to finish my doctorate before the campaign in '22. After two pressured years in Chicago, I will probably be eager to escape the big city."

"By then—if I'm lucky—you may also realize what a great catch I am," Robert said as he winked at Minnie. "I intend to stay in constant touch with you. Even visit the windy city. I won't leave you in peace until I hear when I can pick you up at the Hughitt train station."

AFTERWORD

A picture of my paternal grandmother, Minnie, hung in my bedroom in the house she occupied with her family during the 1890's and early 20th century. The original Victorian, now stripped of its gingerbread and wrap-a-round porch, had been divided into a duplex about the time of my birth to provide separate accommodations for her and my family. Growing up, I felt my grandmother's bright, piercing eyes, her steady gaze focused on me. I stared back at this attractive woman with her short-cropped, curly hair and firm mouth and wondered what she'd been like in her youth. Minnie, or my vision of her, would become a model for the Minnie in my novel.

My actual memories of my grandmother are primarily of an 80-year-old who spent her days bent over the flower-patterned rug she was currently hooking, a rug to be given eventually to a friend or relative. I inherited two. I also have a china dinner-ware set with blue and gold trim, hand-painted by her around the turn of the century, and a turquoise colored dress with pink rosebuds she crocheted for me when I was seven or eight.

From anecdotes told by my father, her second son, I knew she had traveled to Dakota Territory in 1882 with her father, a printer by trade, and her older brother. At the age of twenty, this tiny woman, less than five feet tall, lived alone for a year, including the winter, in a sod hut with only a dog for company. Six years later she lived through the Blizzard of '88 in a more weather-proof structure. Reading about this blizzard impressed upon me how difficult, even deadly, life on the prairie could be, especially in an era before modern communication and transportation. I'd always loved and respected my grandmother, but thinking about the hardships she'd endured, I admired her strength and courage even more.

Searching among family papers, I found an announcement of her marriage at Turtle Creek, Dakota, in 1884 to Charles A. Blake. Involved initially in real estate, he bought the Wessington Times which he published until President McKinley appointed him Registrar of the Land Office in Huron. In 1898 the couple and their four children moved from a rural setting to a booming county seat in South Dakota and the Victorian house mentioned above.

My grandfather died long before I was born, so my knowledge of him is second hand. My grandmother rarely mentioned him. When she did, she referred to him as Mr. Blake. I assumed that was the tradition in her era. Nevertheless, it piqued my curiosity about their relationship and how women fared in their marriages in those days.

Two other women, both from earlier generations than mine, inspired Sarah, the second major woman in this novel. The younger of the two grew up with my father and was active with him in Republican politics in South Dakota. She served in the South Dakota legislature in the 1920's, ran for governor in 1930 (unsuccessfully) and was South Dakota secretary of state from 1927 to 1931. In 1938 she was elected as a Republican to the United States Senate to fill out the term of a deceased senator until the full term nominee could take over.

Her mother, the inspiration for Mrs. Hall, had been instrumental in getting a woman's suffrage amendment passed in the S.D. legislature in 1918. Her efforts were also critical in the ratification by the South Dakota legislature of the nineteenth (suffrage) amendment to the United States constitution. In retrospect, I've wondered if she would have been so effective a Suffragist if she had not been widowed while in her thirties.

Judith Schaefer,
January, 2017